Polly Pepper's Book

THE FAMOUS PEPPER BOOKS

by Margaret Sidney

IN ORDER OF PUBLICATION

Five Little Peppers and How They Grew

Five Little Peppers Midway

Five Little Peppers Grown Up

Phronsie Pepper

Polly Pepper's Book

The Adventures of Joel Pepper

Five Little Peppers Abroad

Five Little Peppers at School

Five Little Peppers and Their Friends

Ben Pepper

Five Little Peppers in the Little Brown House

Our Davie Pepper

Polly Pepper's Book

ORIGINALLY PUBLISHED UNDER THE TITLE

The Stories Polly Pepper Told

By

MARGARET SIDNEY

———————

Grosset & Dunlap, Inc.

PUBLISHERS

NEW YORK

Prefatory Note

THE author has received from mothers and other persons interested in the Pepper Family, so many requests for the Stories told by Polly Pepper (to which frequent allusion has been made in the Series called the "Five Little Peppers" Books), that this initial volume of Polly's earlier stories has been prepared in obedience to these requests.

WAYSIDE, CONCORD, MASS.
March, 1899

Contents

I   THE LITTLE WHITE CHICKEN   1
II   THE PRINCESS ESMERALDA'S BALL . . .   12
III THE STORY OF THE CIRCUS   24
IV   THE LITTLE TIN SOLDIERS   35
V   CHRISTMAS AT THE BIG HOUSE   42
VI   MR. FATHER KANGAROO AND THE FAT
     LITTLE BIRD   51
VII THE MINCE-PIE BOY AND THE BEASTS . .   60
VIII THE CUNNING LITTLE DUCK   71
IX   THE OLD TEAKETTLE   80
X   THE PINK AND WHITE STICKS   91
XI   THE OLD STAGECOACH   100
XII MR. NUTCRACKER; THE STORY THAT
     WASN'T A STORY   110
XIII MR. NUTCRACKER   123
XIV THE RUNAWAY PUMPKIN   135
XV   THE ROBBERS AND THEIR BAGS   145
XVI POLLY PEPPER'S CHICKEN PIE   162
XVII PHRONSIE PEPPER'S NEW SHOES . . .   174
XVIII THE OLD GRAY GOOSE   189

XIX THE GREEN UMBRELLA 198
XX THE GREEN UMBRELLA AND THE QUEER
     LITTLE MAN 212
XXI THE LITTLE SNOWHOUSE 229
XXII LUCY ANN'S GARDEN 245
XXIII THE CHINA MUG 261
XXIV BROWN BETTY 271
XXV THE SILLY LITTLE BROOK 284
XXVI DOWN IN THE ORCHARD 293

Polly Pepper's Book

I

The Little White Chicken

"You see," said Polly, "the little white chicken was determined she *would* go into Susan's playhouse."

Phronsie sat in Mamsie's big calico-covered rocking chair. The last tear had trailed off the round cheek since Polly had come home and was by her side, holding her hand. The pounded toes were thrust out before her, tied up in an old cloth, and waiting for the wormwood which was steeping on the fire. Grandma Bascom, protesting that soon Phronsie wouldn't know that she had any toes, sank into a chair and beamed at her. "You pretty creeter, you," she cried, her cap border bobbing heartily.

"I wish she wouldn't talk," grunted Joel, burrowing on the floor, his head in Polly's lap, where her soft fingers could smooth his stubby black hair.

"Sh!" said Polly, with a warning pinch.

"Go on," begged Davie, hanging over her chair, intent as Phronsie on the fate of the white chicken. "Did she go in, Polly? Did she?"

1

Phronsie sat still, her eyes on Polly's face, her fat little hands clasped in her lap, while she held her breath for the answer.

"Dear me, yes," cried Polly quickly. "She stretched her neck like this," suiting the action to the word, for Polly always acted out, as much as she could, all her stories, particularly in emergencies like the present one, "and peered around the corner. Susan wasn't there, for she was up at the house sitting on a stool and sewing patchwork. But there was a black object over in the corner, and—"

"Oh, you pretty creeter, you!" exclaimed Grandma suddenly, at Phronsie, on whom she had gazed unceasingly, "so you did pound your toes—there—there—you pretty creeter!"

"Ugh—ugh! make her stop," howled Joel, twitching up his head from its soft nest. "Oh, dear, we can't hear anything. Stop her, Polly, do."

"Joel," said Polly, "hush this minute. Just think how good she's been, and the raisins. Oh, Joey!"

"They are dreadful hard," grumbled Joel, but he slipped his head back on Polly's lap, wishing her fingers would smooth his hair again. But they didn't, so he burrowed deeper and tried not to cry. Meanwhile Phronsie, with a troubled expression settling over her face at this condition of things, made as though she would slip from the old chair. "Take me, Polly," she begged, holding out her arms.

"Oh, no, you mustn't, you pretty creeter," declared Grandma, getting out of her chair to waddle over to the scene, her cap border trembling violently, "you'll hurt your toes. You must set where you be till you get the wormwood on." And Davie running over to put his arms around Phronsie and beg her to keep still, the little old kitchen soon became in great confusion till it seemed as if the white chicken must be left for all time, peering in at Susan's playhouse and the black object in the corner.

"Oh, dear me," cried Polly at her wit's end. "Now you see, Joey. Whatever shall I do?"

"Take me, Polly," implored Phronsie, leaning out of the big chair at the imminent danger of falling on her nose, and two tears raced over her round cheeks. At sight of these, Polly suddenly lifted her out and over to her lap, Joel deserting that post in a trice, and wishing he was Phronsie so that he could cry and be comforted.

"Dear, dear, dear!" exclaimed Grandma Bascom gustily, trotting off to the tin cup with the wormwood steeping on the stove. "She must have the wormwood on. Whatever'll become of her toes if she don't set still, I d'no. There, there, she's a pretty creeter."

"I don't want any on," said Phronsie from her nest in Polly's arms, and contentedly snuggling down. "Please don't let her put any on, Polly," she whispered up against her neck.

"I'll put it on," said Polly soothingly. "Well, now, Phronsie," patting the yellow head, and with an anxious look up at the old clock, "you know I can't bake Mamsie's birthday cake unless you have that wormwood on and sit in her chair like a good girl. And then think how very dreadful it would be to have Mamsie come home and it shouldn't be done. Oh, I can't think of such a thing!" Polly's hand dropped away from the yellow hair and fell to her lap, as she sat quite still.

Phronsie lifted her head and looked at her. "I'll have the wet stuff on, Polly, and sit in the chair," she said with a long sigh. "Lift me back, Polly, do; then you can bake Mamsie's cake."

So Phronsie was lifted back with great ado, Polly kissing her many times, and telling her how glad she would be on the morrow when Mamsie's birthday cake would be a beautiful success, and how happy Mamsie would be to know that Phronsie helped to bake it by being such a good girl. And the little toes were wet with the wormwood and tied up in an old cloth; and Grandma Bascom, dropping the tin cup which she was bearing back to the stove, with a clatter on the floor, created such a diversion as Polly and the boys ran to get cloths and spoons to save the precious wormwood and wipe the floor clean, that the little old kitchen rang with the noise and it was some time before Polly could get it quieted down again.

At last Polly drew a long breath. "Well, now, children, if you'll be very still I'll tell you the rest about the white chicken while I'm making Mamsie's cake. And I'll pull your chair, Phronsie, up to the table so you can see me."

"Let me, let me!" screamed Joel, hopping up to lay hasty hands on the old calico-covered rocker. "I want to, Polly; let me pull it up."

"I want to," begged David, just as nimble on the other side.

"So you shall; you can both help," cried Polly merrily, deep in thought over the intricacies of 'Mirandy's weddin'-cake receet.'

"Well," said Grandma, seeing Phronsie on such a high-road to recovery, "I'm dretful glad I found that receet. I put it in my Bible so's to have it handy to give John's folks when they come; they set great store by it to the weddin': and I must go home now, 'cause I left some meat a-boilin'." So off she waddled, Joel going to the door and gallantly assisting her down the steps and to the gate, glad to make amends. Then he rushed back.

"Now for the white chicken!" he cried, drawing a long breath and perching on the end of the baking table.

"Yes," said Polly, "but you've got to have on one of Mamsie's old slippers first, Phronsie."

"Oh, ho," Phronsie laughed gleefully, "how funny!"

So one of Mamsie's old cloth slippers was tied on to Phronsie's little foot with a bit of string through the middle, the children one and all protesting that it looked like an old black pudding bag; and Polly began again. "Now," she said absently, "I'll tell you about the little white chicken—just as soon as I have—oh, dear me! Let me see if I have all my things ready." She wrinkled her brows and thought a minute. Joel kicked his heels impatiently against the table side, while Davie clasped his hands tight so as not to say anything to worry Polly.

"Yes, I believe they're all here," said Polly, after what seemed an age to the children. "Well, there now, children, I'm ready to begin on the story. Oh, let me see, all but the big bowl," and she ran into the buttery and brought it out, and began to mix the cake with quite an important air. Phronsie drew a long breath of delight that ended in a happy little crow. "You must know that the white chicken made up her mind that she *would* go into Susan's playhouse, although—"

"You told that," interrupted Joel, filliping at the dish

where the raisins, with a plentiful sprinkling of flour, lay ready to lend their magnificence to Mamsie's birthday cake. "Go on where you left off, Polly."

"You said she saw a black object over in the corner," said Davie, with big eyes. "Tell about that."

"Oh, yes, so I did!" said Polly. "Now, Joe, you mustn't touch the raisins. Every single one must go into Mamsie's cake."

Joel drew away his hand, but it was impossible not to regard the plate on which he kept his gaze fastened.

"Well, in crept the little white chicken," said Polly tragically, and stirring briskly the cake mixture with the long wooden spoon, "hoping the black object wouldn't see her. She had to go in you see, because just outside the door, coming under the apple trees, was a noise, and it sounded very much like a boy; and the little white chicken had rather be scared by a black object in the corner inside than to let that boy spy her. So she crept in *very softly,* and was just beginning to tuck up her feet and sit down behind the door, when the black object stirred, and over went the little white chicken all in a heap."

Joel gave a grunt of great satisfaction and tore his eyes from the raisin plate.

"What was it?" gasped Davie fearfully, and getting nearer to Polly's side. Phronsie kept her wide eyes on Polly's face and sat quite still, her little hands folded in her lap.

"You wait and see," said Polly gaily, and stirring away for dear life. "Well, over went the little white chicken, and—"

"You said that," interrupted Joel. "Do hurry and tell the rest."

"Then she shut her eyes just like this," Polly stopped stirring, and turned to Phronsie, wrinkling up her face as much like a chicken in despair as was possible. "Oh, you can't think how she felt. She was *so* frightened! She tried to call her mother, but the 'peep—peep' that always used to be so loud and clear stuck way down in her throat; and then she knew she never in all this world could make her mother hear because she hadn't minded her. And outside she could hear old Mrs. Hen calling her brothers and sisters to come and get the worms she had just scratched up."

"And wouldn't the little white chicken ever get a worm?" broke out Phronsie in dreadful excitement. "Wouldn't she, Polly, ever?"

"No—oh, yes; she could when she was good," said Polly at sight of Phronsie's face.

"Make her good," begged Phronsie, unclasping her hands to pull Polly's gown. "Oh, do, Polly!"

"No, make her bad," cried Joel insistently, "as bad as can be. Do, Polly!"

"Oh, Joel!" reproved Polly, stirring away. "Whoever would want that little white chicken bad—any more than for a boy to be naughty."

"Well, make her bad enough to be scared, and have the awful black thing be a bear, and most bite her to death, and chew her head off," cried Joel, feeling delicious thrills at the dreadful possibilities that might happen to the chicken.

"Oh, dear me," cried Polly in horror. "The poor little white chicken!"

"Don't let it bite her *much*," said Davie. "But do make it a bear, Polly!"

"Well, I will," said Polly obligingly, "make it a bear, boys."

"And don't let it bite her any," begged Phronsie; and she put up her lip, while the brown eyes were imploringly fixed on Polly's face.

Joel squirmed all over the table end. "Just such a little bear," he remonstrated. "Hoh! He couldn't bite much. I'd just as lieve he'd bite me," baring his brown arm.

"No—no—no!" protested Phronsie, shaking her yellow head decidedly. "I don't want him to bite her any, poor little white chicken," and she looked so very near to crying, and Mamsie's old black slipper on the pounded toes began to flap so dismally, that Polly hastened to say, "Oh! I'll tell you, children, what I'll do; I'll have Tommy come out and shoot the bear right away."

"Oh, whickety!" whooped Joel. David clasped his hands ecstatically. This was much better—to have Tommy and the bear, than the bear and the little white chicken. Phronsie laughed delightedly. "Make him come quick, do, Polly!" she screamed.

"Hurry up!" called Joel. "Oh, Phron, don't talk. Do hurry, Polly!"

"Well, you see," went on Polly, stirring away for dear life, "that when Susan went into the house to sit on the stool and do patchwork, her brother Tommy thought he would take his gun and see if he could find anything to shoot, like rabbits, and—"

"No—no," cried Joel in alarm, twitching her sleeve, "bears, bears!"

"He didn't expect to see a bear," said Polly; "he went out

to shoot rabbits. But he found the bear instead, you know," catching sight of Joel's face, which immediately cleared up, and he settled back contentedly. "Well, Tommy went along by old Mother Hen clucking and scratching, and all the rest of the chickens, except the little white one; and just as he was going by Susan's playhouse he thought he would look in and scare the dolls with his big gun."

"Don't let him, Polly!" begged Phronsie in a worse fright than before. "Oh, don't let him; don't let him!"

"Ow, there ain't any fun. Phron keeps stopping us all the time," howled Joel. "Let him, Polly. Gee—whiz—bang! that's the way I'd do," bringing an imaginary gun to his shoulder and blazing away.

"Well, then he'd have scared the bear so he couldn't have shot him," said little Davie quietly.

"So he would, Davie," said Polly approvingly, and dropping the spoon to pet Phronsie. "If Joel had been there, the bear would have got away."

Joel, much discomfited at this, ducked suddenly and looked sheepish. "Well, go on," he said.

"And Tommy didn't scare the dolls, because you see he was scared himself. The first thing he saw was the little white chicken crouched down like this." Down went Polly on the old kitchen floor, and made herself so much like a little white chicken very much frightened that the children held their breath to see her.

"And then Tommy looked at what scared the little white chicken," went on Polly, hopping up and beginning to stir the cake mixture again. "And—he—*saw—the—bear!*"

It is impossible to describe the effect this statement had

on the old kitchen and its occupants; and Polly, well pleased, rushed on, dilating on how the bear looked, and how Tommy looked, and how the little white chicken looked, till, in a pause, the crackling in the old stove proclaimed all things ready for the baking of Mamsie's birthday cake, and she exclaimed, "Deary me, I must hurry. Oh, well! Tommy saw the bear getting ready to spring, just like this, and he put up his gun, like this, and it went bang—bang! And over went Mr. Bear quite, quite dead."

"Like this?" cried Joel, tumbling off from the table end to a heap in the middle of the old floor. "Just like this, Polly?" sticking up his stubby black head to look at her.

"No—no!" cried Davie, hurrying to make another heap of himself by Joel's side. "He stuck up his legs, didn't he, Polly?" and out went David's arms and legs as stiff as sticks, as he lay on his back staring at the ceiling.

"Hoh—hoh!" laughed Joel in derision. "Bears don't tumble down that way, Dave, when they're killed. Do they, Polly?"

"Yes, they do too," contradicted little David, not moving a muscle, "don't they, Polly?" while Phronsie tried to get out of her big chair to show, too, how she thought the bear would tumble over.

"Oh, no, Phronsie pet, you mustn't!" cried Polly in alarm. "You'll hurt your poor toes. Well, I think the bear looked something like both of you boys. He didn't stick his legs up stiff, but he was on his back like Davie."

"Well, I'm on my back," cried Joel whirling over, while David's stiff little wooden legs and arms fell down in a twinkling. "Well, now you boys must get me the cinnamon," said Polly with a brisk eye on the old clock. "Deary me, I ought to have this cake in the oven—it's in the Provision Room, you know."

"And then we'll get something to eat," cried the two bears, hopping up to race off.

II

The Princess Esmeralda's Ball

"It was a most beautiful place," cried Polly. "Oh, you can't think, children, how perfectly beautiful it all was," and she clasped her hands and sighed.

"Tell us," they all begged in one breath, crowding around her chair.

"Well, I can't till Ben gets back, because you know he wanted to hear this story"; and Polly flew out of her rapture, and picked up her needle again. "Dear me!" she exclaimed, and a wave of remorse sent the color flying over her cheek, "I didn't mean to stop even for a minute," and she glanced up at the old clock.

"Ben never'll come," grumbled Joel, racing to the window with Davie at his heels. "He's so awful slow."

"Well, it's slow work," said Polly, stitching away briskly, "to carry a great heavy molasses jug and a bag of Indian meal way up here from the store. Now, if you two boys wanted to go and meet him, you could help ever so much."

"I went last time down to that old store," said Joel, kicking his toes against the wall as he stared out of the window. "It's Dave's turn now, Polly."

"Oh, oh!" cried little Davie. "I've been ever and ever so many more times, Polly, truly I have."

"And we've just got through doing all our work," went on Joel, ignoring David's remarks, "and we had such a lot to do today Polly," he added in an injured tone.

"You needn't go if you don't want to," said Polly with a fine scorn. "I said if you *wanted* to go."

"Well, we don't want to," declared Joel loudly, and he kicked his toes triumphantly. Phronsie, curled up in a ball on the floor at Polly's feet while she nursed Seraphina, stared at them gravely.

"I'll go, Polly," she said at last, laying Seraphina, with a sigh, on the floor, and getting up to her feet.

"Oh, no, pet! You can't go," said Polly quickly. "You're too little. Why, you aren't bigger'n a mouse, Phronsie"; and she began to laugh, but she turned a cold shoulder to the boys.

"I'm very big, Polly," said Phronsie gravely, and standing up on her tiptoes. "See—oh, so big! And I must go down and help poor Bensie. Let me, Polly, do!" and she put up her lips, and the tears began to come into the brown eyes.

"Now you see, boys," began Polly, casting aside her work to take Phronsie on her lap.

"Oh, I'll go, Polly!" cried little Davie, springing forward, his face all in a flame. "I want to go. Truly I do."

"No, I will," howled Joel, dashing away from his window. "You've been ever so many times, Dave. I'm going."

"Joel," cried Polly, as he was rushing off, "come here a minute."

He came back slowly, with one eye on Davie. "What do you want, Polly?" he cried impatiently.

"David *wants* to go," said Polly slowly, and looking steadily into his flushed face. "Now, unless you really want to go to help Bensie, why you must stay at home."

"I—want—to go—to help Bensie," declared Joel insistently, with a very red face. "Oh, Polly, I do! Let me go." He was so near to crying that Polly said hastily, "I know, Joey, you do want to help Bensie. There, there," and she gave him an approving little pat.

"I want to help Bensie," cried Joel, his smiles all come again to the chubby face, and off he dashed.

"Now, Davie," said Polly in her briskest fashion, and setting to on the long seam, "I think if I were you, I'd play with Phronsie a bit," with a glance at the disappointed little face.

"Come on, Phronsie," said little David, gulping down his disappointment; for now that Joel was fairly on the way to meet Ben, nothing seemed better than to be of the party. But he sat down on the floor where Phronsie immediately crouched beside him, and in a minute the only sound in the old kitchen was the soft hum of their voices and Phronsie's delighted little gurgle as the play went on.

"I better be going over that story again in my mind," said Polly to herself. "I've a good chance now, it's so quiet and lovely," and she beamed at Davie when he looked up, in a way to make his little heart glad. And then Polly was lost in the depths of her story till the old kitchen and the Little Brown House and the children faded away, and she was reveling in the glories of the palace, with retinues of courtiers and servants at her beck and call, and all the paraphernalia of royalty around her. For was she not the Princess Esmeralda herself? And a smile played around Polly's lips as she stitched on, all unconscious of the task her fingers were performing.

"Hi-hi!" It was Joel shouting close to her chair, and there was Ben coming in the door with a pleased look on his face. "Now for the story," screamed Joey, setting down the bag of meal with a bang on the table; and down tumbled Polly's castle all around her ears. "Well, I'm glad I've got it fast in my mind so I can tell it good," she said with a sigh of relief. "Yes, I'm ready," and she smiled at Ben.

"That's good," said Ben heartily, "that you didn't tell that story until I got home, Polly."

"Did you suppose I would, Ben?" said Polly with an air of reproach.

"No, I didn't really," said Ben, wiping his hot face. "But it was good of you, Polly, to wait for me. And it was good of you Joe, too, to come to meet me, for I had to go around to Parson Henderson's with a letter."

"Oh, Ben!" exclaimed Polly. "Did you have to go all around there with those heavy things?"

"Yes," said Ben, "I did. But you wouldn't have had me not go, Polly, for Mr. Atkins said Parson Henderson had been for his letters very early, and this came afterward, and he wouldn't be there again today."

"Oh, no, no, of course not," said Polly hastily. "I mean I wouldn't have had you not go for anything in this world, Ben Pepper. You know I wouldn't," and she looked so distressed that Ben hastened to say most assuringly:

"I know you wouldn't, Polly; and don't you think, Mrs.

Henderson said it was a most important letter indeed, and if Mr. Henderson hadn't had it today it would have been very bad."

"Oh, I am so glad he got it today, Ben Pepper!" Polly flew out of her chair to run and throw her arms around him. "And you were the one to carry it to him."

"And then when I got to the Four Corners," went on Ben, "there was Joel running to meet me. You can't think how good it seemed to see him!"

"Oh, Joey! Did you get clear down to the Four Corners?" cried Polly, turning to him in a transport.

"Yes, I did," bobbed Joel, glad to think he had run every step of the way without stopping to think, and forgetting how his arms ached carrying the meal bag. "Now, Polly, tell us the story quick, do."

"So I will," cried Polly merrily, rushing back to her chair and the sewing. "Oh, it's so splendid that Ben's back! We've got a whole hour now before Mamsie's to be home. Now, then," as the group huddled up around her. "Once upon a time, long years ago, there was one of the richest kings and queens that the world has ever seen. Why, they had so much money that nobody had ever counted it; they hadn't time, you know. And it kept coming in until the bags of gold pieces filled up all one side of the courtyard, and they had to build great sheds to put the rest in."

"Where'd it come from?" broke in Joel abruptly, unable to keep still at thought of such a state of affairs.

"Oh, the things they sold in the whole kingdom were so many," said Polly. "There were millions—no, billions of bushels of corn, and wheat and rye and silks and ribbons and butter and cheese, and laces and artificial flowers and candy, and—"

"Oh, my!" cried Joel, smacking his lips.

"Like the pink sticks old Mrs. Beebe gave Phronsie the day she hurt her toe?" queried David, his mouth watering at the remembrance.

"Yes, the very same," said Polly.

"Now, you children mustn't interrupt every single minute," commanded Ben. "If you do, Polly and I will go off into a corner, and she will tell me the story. And Phronsie— we'll take her, because she hasn't said a word."

"Oh, we won't—we won't again, will we, Dave?" cried Joel, with a punch on that individual's back.

"No," said little David promptly. "Please go on, Polly."

"You see, everything that anybody wanted to buy—I mean the people in other countries—was all for sale in this kingdom; and big ships went sailing off ever so many times a day with the things piled in them; and when they came back the captain brought all the money he got for the things, tied up in big bags; and the ships kept coming back, ever so many a day, so that there was no hope that the gold pieces would ever be any less. And one day the king walked up and down his palace hall, wringing his hands. 'Oh! I wish there wasn't so much money in the world,' he cried, 'for pretty soon I shall be turned out of doors, with all the gold pieces crowding me out.' And he looked so very sad as his wife, the queen, put her head in the doorway, that she said, 'My dear, we will have the golden coach brought around to take us out to drive.'

" 'Don't say golden anything to me,' cried the king in a

passion, for he was almost beside himself. 'I'm sick of the sound of the word, my dear,' and he beckoned her to him and they went and sat together on the great throne at one end of the hall. It shone with diamonds and rubies and emeralds, and all manner of precious stones; and it had great curtains of twisted ropes of jewels looped up over their heads; and there they sat, and he held her hand. 'I'm really afraid,' and he looked in her face, 'that something must be done, for this is a dreadful state of things.'

" 'Now, if you are going to talk business,' said the queen tartly, 'I think it is time to call Esmeralda.' You see, whenever there was anything to decide in the kingdom, the king and queen never did the leastest little bit of a thing about it, without at first calling Esmeralda and laying the case before her. So now they rang five or six golden bells in turn, and the king blew a blast on a glass horn, oh, ever so many feet long, that hung by his side of the throne; and the queen whistled on a tremendous silver whistle that hung by her side of the throne; and pretty soon Esmeralda came running in all out of breath. She was dressed in sea-green satin, over a white lace petticoat pinned up with diamonds, and she had a bunch of flowers in her hand that were sweet with the morning dew. She had long floating yellow hair, just like Phronsie's," and Polly paused long enough to glance lovingly at the small head snuggled up against her knee.

" 'Good morning, father,' and 'Good morning, mother,' said the Princess Esmeralda, kneeling before her parents sitting on the throne; and she laid the flowers, with the morning dew on them, in their hands.

" 'We have summoned you, Esmeralda,' said the king in

a troubled way, 'because we are in dire extremity, and must have your advice.'

"Esmeralda wrinkled her pretty brow and looked very wise, but her heart beat dreadfully against her bodice and—"

"What's a bod—" began Joel.

"Ugh!" cried Ben with a warning finger held up, as Joel ducked instantly.

"It's a waist that princesses always wear," said Polly, "and Esmeralda's was all spangled with gold and silver. It shone so that no one could look at it more than a minute at a time. Well, so she said, 'Yes, father,' and 'Yes, mother.'

" 'We have too much gold,' said the king, smiting his hands together. 'Esmeralda, I tell you truly, if it keeps coming in we shall all have to move out from this palace and find another home. What shall we do, my child?'

"Esmeralda jumped up from her knees, and ran to the casement, and climbed up the golden seat beneath it, and peered out. There were the ships below her in the harbor, with the men taking out the bags and bags and bags of gold; and as far as her eye could reach, there were more ships and more ships and more ships all coming in, filled with bags to the very brim. She got down and ran back. 'It is certainly very dreadful, father and mother,' she said, clasping her hands.

" 'Indeed it is,' declared the king; and he began to tear his hair.

" 'Husband, don't feel so badly,' implored the poor queen at that sight, throwing her arms around him. 'Esmeralda, you must think quickly, because you see we are both going quite distracted.'

"So Esmeralda said the first thing that came into her head. 'You might tell the men to untie the bags, and pour the gold pieces into the sea at the mouth of the harbor.'

" 'The very thing!' exclaimed the king in delight, and his face was covered with smiles. 'Oh, what it is to have a clever child!' and the queen fell upon Esmeralda's neck, and kissed and kissed her.

"So then the king rang all his bells, and blew his long glass horn, and then he struck a big silver gong that was always the signal for the lord high chamberlain to appear. And when he popped in his with his robes of office all caught up in his hands, to let him run to obey the king's call, and his high peaked hat awry for the same reason, the king gave him the order just as Esmeralda said; and then the lord high chamberlain plunged out, after bowing himself before the throne five and twenty times to the marble floor; and the king said to the queen, in the greatest satisfaction, 'My dear, we must give Esmeralda a ball for being so clever.'

"And the queen said, 'Yes, a ball,' with the greatest alacrity. And Esmeralda hopped up and down in glee, she was so happy; and she danced and danced until off flew seventy-nine of the diamonds from her lace petticoat, and rolled away into as many cracks and crevices in the corners of the marble hall. But she didn't care, for there were bushels in her room, and a dozen or two women always sitting on their crickets, with their needles threaded with silver thread, ready to sew on more.

"So then the word went out from the palace all over the kingdom, that there was to be a ball for the Princess Esmeralda; and all the while the golden stream was pouring out every minute from the big bags into the mouth of the harbor. And Esmeralda fell asleep every night to dream of the beautiful music and flowers and lights, and the gay young princes to be sent for as company from every other kingdom; for you must know that never had there been such a ball in all this world before as this one was to be. And every morning Esmeralda waked up quite, quite happy, because the ball night was just so much nearer. And at last her dress was all ready, and laid out upon her little white bed. It was"— Polly paused most impressively to allow her hearers to take it all in properly, "it was made out of the very finest cobwebs that had all been spun in the sunshine of the palace courtyards. For this, millions of spiders had been caught by the command of the king, who had sent out an edict for that purpose; and they had been set spinning until they had made this beautiful dress of the princess. And it was trimmed around the bottom and the neck by a rainbow, and—"

"Oh, Polly!" exclaimed Ben.

"There, Ben's talking!" broke in Joel in huge delight. "Hoh! Hoh!"

"Yes, a rainbow," repeated Polly stoutly, "a beautiful red and green and blue and yellow rainbow. Oh, you can't begin to think, children, how perfectly lovely Esmeralda did look when she was all dressed ready for the ball. Well, and then the princes began to arrive. There were two hundred of them, and each one brought the princess a present. But the king had said that she should not accept anything of gold, so it had been some little trouble for them to get anything that was nice enough without having it golden. But they did, and there were two hundred presents set out in the palace hall. And Esmeralda was to walk up and down the whole length, and choose the present she liked the best out of the whole collection; and then she was to dance with the prince who had given her this present. Oh, dear me, she thought she would cry her eyes out when the king decided this must be done, for how was she to choose between so many perfectly beautiful things, and there would be one hundred and ninety-nine princes feeling very unhappy indeed. She was just going to say, 'Oh, my father! I cannot do it'; and then she knew the king would ring, and strike his big silver gong, and blow for the lord high chamberlain to take him off from the throne and put him to bed, and then the lights would be turned out, and everybody would go home, and there would be no ball at all. She couldn't do that, of course, as you see. So she stopped a minute to think, as she always did when she had hard questions to decide, until the king roared at her. 'Do as I say, daughter, or out go the lights'; and then she said the first thing that came in her head. 'I like all the presents best, and we'll all dance together at once.'

" 'Dear me!' exclaimed the king, 'how clever!' and he screamed joyfully to the musicians to begin; and the princess and the two hundred princes all began hopping and jumping about the hall, and presently it looked so nice, the king gave his hand to the queen, and she slid down from the throne, and began to hop about too; and the lord high chancellor picked up his flowing robes, and danced on the tips of his toes; and the court ladies skipped back and forth; and the servants came to look in the doorways, and so did the retinues of soldiers. And they couldn't help it, the music was so fine, and oh, dear me, it went just like this,"—and Polly broke off into a merry little tune as she sprang to her feet and held out her hands, "Come on, let us all dance!" and she seized Ben's arms, and danced him half across the old kitchen floor.

"Take me, Polly!" begged Joel, who had tumbled over himself in surprise, and now got to his feet to run after the two spinning off so finely.

"Can't," said Polly over her shoulder. "You take Phronsie," and then she began again on the gay tune—Ben whistling away for dear life as an accompaniment.

"Dave's got her," said Joel in great discomfiture, turning around to see little Davie and Phronsie's pink calico gown flying along at a merry rate. "I haven't got anybody," seeing which Polly stopped short. "Come with us," and she held out her hand, and Ben grasped Joel's arm, and away they went till the old kitchen rang with the fun.

III

The Story of the Circus

"You see," said Polly, "as it rains today, I think we ought to have the circus story."

"Oh, oh, oh!" cried all the Five Little Peppers together, Ben not being ashamed to add his shout of approval too.

"Do you think you really ought to, Polly?" he asked, coming out of it, and leaving the others in the babel of rejoicing. "Won't you want it more for some other time?"

Polly ran over and caught him by the jacket sleeve.

"I really think we ought to have it today, Bensie," she whispered. "You see, they've been awfully good, and it's rained for three days now, and you know there wasn't enough mush for breakfast, and Mamsie couldn't get any coats to do this week, 'cause Mr. Atkins didn't dare let her have any more to sew until he'd sold what he had, and trade's so poor." And Polly sighed and wiped away two tears. Ben turned away a moment and swallowed something hard that was in his throat. Polly, at sight of this, began to laugh; and she said gaily, "Yes, indeed, we'll have the circus story now. Get your chairs, and let's sit around in a ring, children."

With that the babel of rejoicing changed into a scuffle for chairs and crickets, Joel protesting that he should sit next to Polly, and Phronsie scuttling along to crowd into Polly's lap, till the little old kitchen fairly rang with the noise.

"Let's sit in a ring on the floor, Polly, that's best," begged little David. So they all got down, and Polly had Joel on one side and Phronsie on the other; though to be sure everybody was next to everybody else, as the ring was constantly moving up closer till it was a bunch of Five Little Peppers, and everybody looked as if there had been plenty of breakfast, and all sorts of good things in the Little Brown House—enough for all time to come.

"Now, you know, children," said Polly, folding her hands in her lap, and feeling quite elegant to be sitting down in the morning telling stories, and she looked at them impressively, "I've promised you the circus story for a lo-ong time."

"Yes, we know," said Joel, hitching impatiently. "Don't talk, but begin."

Polly shot him a reproving glance that made him duck behind Davie, who sat next, as she went on," "And now today I'm going to give it to you. I know Mamsie'd say 'twas best, everything's all clean spick span," and she glanced with pride around the little old kitchen that shone from top to toe.

"Mamsie'd like it," cooed Phronsie, and she patted her pink apron down and looked at Polly to begin.

"The circus story," said Polly, beginning with a great flourish, "is about so many best and splendid things that you must keep quite still and not interrupt me a single teenty wee bit."

They one and all protested that they wouldn't say a word. So she began, while each one sat as still as a mouse.

"Way far over the top of a high mountain," said Polly, "so far that no one had ever been entirely over it, at least to come back, lived a big man. He was so large that he couldn't have found any house in all Badgertown big enough to get into if he had tried ever and ever so much. He had arms and legs and eyes to match, you know, and feet and ears, so he could take perfectly dreadfully large steps, and he could lift as big rocks in his hands as the one hanging over Cherry Brook. Oh, and he could see with his big eyes that stood right out of his face just like cannon balls, so that nothing could hide from him, even if it tried ever so much."

Joel twisted uneasily and wriggled up nearer to Polly's side. "And one day the big man sat down on a spur of the mountain and dangled his feet down the side. This was his swing, you know, and he always sat there when he was thinking hard over anything, or making plans.

"Well, there he sat thinking—thinking away as hard as ever he could. And pretty soon he got up and slapped his knee, just as Mr. Tisbett does, you know, and he roared out, 'The very thing—the *very* thing!' And folks down in the valley all ran to their windows and said it thundered, and they drove into the barns and sheds and got ready for the storm. Well, after the big man stopped roaring 'the very thing,' and slapping his knee, he looked down the mountain, the side he lived on, you know, and the first thing he saw was a hippo—hippo—moppi—poppicus." Here Polly paused to take breath. She was very fond of long words, and it was her great delight to wrestle with them; so now she thought she had done very well indeed, and she ran on in the best of spirits—"Oh, he was so big—there isn't any-thing, children, that can tell you how big he was! Well, the big man no sooner saw him than he ran like lightning on his perfectly dreadfully large feet down his side of the moun-tain, and he said to the hippo—pippo—poppi—moppicus—'Here, you, sir, put your head in this,' and he twitched out of one of his side pockets a string. It was made of leather, and was just as strong—oh, you can't think. Well the 'hippo,' I'm going to call him that for short," said Polly sud-denly, quite tired out, "took a good look all around, but he saw no way of escape; and the big man kept growing more dreadfully cross every minute he waited, so the poor hippo at last said, 'As you please, sir,' and he put his head into the string and was tied fast to a big tree that was one hundred and sixty-seven feet around. Then the big man laughed a perfectly dreadful laugh, and he said, when he had finished, 'Now you are going to the circus, sir, and see the pennies taken in at the door.' Then he went off up to his mountain spur again.

"And presently he looked down his side of the mountain again, and he spied a gre-at big snake—oh, a beautiful one, all green and gold stripes, and great flashing green eyes to match. The big man watched Mr. Snake raise his head as he wriggled along, and he ran down his side of the mountain on his dreadfully large feet as quick as a flash, and stood in front of Mr. Snake, who looked this way and that for a chance to escape. But there was none, you see, for the dread-fully large feet of the big man took up all the room. So at last Mr. Snake said in a tired-out voice, just like this: 'If you please, sir, would you move just a *very* little?'

" 'Put your head in here, sir,' roared the big man at him,

so that the snake shook and shook just like a leaf on one of our maple trees in a storm. Well, and at last he had his head with the flashing green eyes fast in a big bag which, you must know, in a twinkling the big man had pulled out of his other side pocket, and then he was left to go flopping and flopping around on the ground most dismally. And then the big man scrambled up to his mountainside again.

"Well," said Polly with a long breath, "the next thing he saw was a gi-raffe, as much bigger than the others as you can imagine. And he got him fast, too, so he couldn't get away; and then he went up to spy out more animals. And by the time the sun went down behind the mountain, and he couldn't catch any more, he had two hundred creatures all tied fast to trees, or with their heads in bags. And then he sat down on a big stone to rest."

"I should think he'd have to," said Ben under his breath.

Polly shot him a reproving glance, and hurried on. "Well, after he was all rested nicely again, he jumped up from his stone and looked them all in the face. That is, he looked those who were tied to trees in the face, but those with their heads in bags, of course he couldn't, and he said, 'My friends,' for he thought he ought to treat them kindly, they'd been so good to him, 'I'm going to take you to see the world a little.' Then he untied those who were tied to the trees, and set them in a line, the hippo in front, because he had him the longest, so it was right to give him the first place, and the creatures with their heads in the bags he set in the middle, because they didn't need to see, but could just follow the noise of the animals stepping in front of them, and then a long line of more animals. Then the big man cut down one of the large trees and switched it at the heels of the last animal, which was a rhododendron."

"Oh, Polly!" gasped Ben.

"Yes 'twas," she declared positively, with red cheeks, "I'm quite sure of that word, for I saw it in the book Parson Henderson lent us. So there, Ben Pepper!"

"Well, never mind," said Ben faintly. "Go on with the story, Polly." So Polly made her rhododendron move as swiftly as all the others in the line; and presently the whole procession, with the big man at its rear switching the heels of the last animal, was at the top of the mountain; and then he called in a loud voice, "Come, Mr. Circus-Man, and get your menaj-menaj-arie." Polly got over this very well, and hurried on glibly. "And all the people who had opened their barn doors and houses, thinking there was to be no storm, clapped them to again in a fright. All except one man, and they screamed to him that he was risking his life; but he didn't care, and he wouldn't pay any attention to them. So he poked his head out of his doorway, and he screamed, 'I'm going up the mountain to see for myself if there's going to be a storm.' And they all bade him good-by, and said they were sure they should never see him again. And then they locked their doors, and padlocked them, and away he ran up the mountain.

"The big man was waiting for him, and he said to his animals, 'Now, my friends, when that man's head begins to show over that scrub oak there,' pointing to the tree, 'do you all say, "How do you do, and *how* do you do, and how do you do again." ' So the animals said they would; and as soon as the man's head was to be seen peeping over the treetop, as he ran pretty fast, they all said it. The hippo roared it, and Mr. Snake grumbled it clear down half his length, and the rhi-rhino-cerus squealed it, and the elephant howled it, and the—"

"What did the rhododendron do?" asked Ben.

"And the guinea pig—oh, I forgot to tell you there was a perfectly splendid guinea pig in the collection," said Polly, not taking any notice of Ben, "and he said it big and loud in his natural voice, and the monkey shrieked it, and—"

"Oh, is there a dear sweet little monkey?" cried Phronsie in a transport. "Oh, Polly! I want him to play with, I do."

"Oh, no, Phronsie, you can't," said Polly, hurrying on, "the Circus-Man has to have him, you know. Well, and oh, dear me! Every single one of those animals said, 'How do you do, and *how* do you do, and how do you do again.' And the man took one look at them and he said, "Pretty well, I thank you.'

"And the big man said, 'You're the man for me; and I give all these animals to you, for you are the only one who isn't afraid. Now, march, and good-by.' And the Circus-Man rubbed his eyes and looked again, and there wasn't any big man; all that was left was the long line of animals and crawling things. So down the mountainside the procession went. And at the foot there were sixteen red carts with yellow borders, and a cunning little carriage drawn by ever and ever so many dear sweet ponies no bigger than dogs, and then in a minute, out from behind the trees came rushing as many as a dozen, no, two dozen big horses with long tails. And they swept up to the Circus-Man to have him scratch their noses."

The Five Little Peppers now became dreadfully excited.

And Joel jumped up. "Whoop-la!" he screamed, as he pranced around and around the group on the floor, stepping high, and slapping himself as he raced along. "Come on, Dave. This is the way I'd make 'em go, all those horses."

"Polly, do you suppose we'll ever see a circus?" cried little Davie with shining eyes. "Ever in all this world?"

"Ever in all this world?" hummed Phronsie, while Ben set his teeth tight together and looked at her. "Yes, indeed," declared Polly confidently, with eyes only for Ben. "Don't look so, Ben," she cried. "We'll see one sometime."

"Polly always gets her flowers," said little Davie in a moment, in a reflective way.

"And if we don't ever get to see a really, truly circus," cried Polly impulsively, "we can hear all about it same's we have already from Mr. and Mrs. Beebe. So just think what those children must have to do who don't ever have anybody to tell them about it as we have." She folded her hands in her lap and was lost in thought.

"Whoop-la! Whoopity-la! G'lang!" cried Joel with an awful noise, making his steeds put forth all their best paces around the little old kitchen. "And I'm so glad," Polly was saying, "that Mr. and Mrs. Beebe did see a circus when they went down to Rockport. It's the greatest comfort. Now, if you don't stop, Joel, I can't tell the rest of the story."

"You make so much noise we can't hear anything," said Ben.

So Joel gave up slapping his imaginary beasts and bounded into the middle of the group again, and the little old kitchen quieting down, Polly took up the story once more.

"Well, but you ought to have seen the big white tent that was really the home of all the animals and crawling things, when they actually got home and stayed still," exclaimed Polly, starting off. "Oh! it was quite magnificent, I can tell you. It was as big as the church green, and it had a great flag on top that swung out in the breeze at every bit of wind, and there were rows and rows of seats all around it in a ring, and down in the middle was the place where the horses danced, and—"

"Like this?" whooped Joel, breaking away again from the bunch of Five Little Peppers on the floor. But Ben picked him by the jacket sleeve and made him sit down suddenly. "Hold on, there," he said. "You keep still, Joe, you're worse than a tornado. Go on, Polly, I'll hold him," as Polly laughed and hurried on.

"One day they were having a beautiful time. The band that always rode in the red wagon with the yellow wheels was playing away, oh, such lovely music," sighed Polly, "and the big tent was just crammed full of people, and the horses were dancing, and everybody was just as happy as could be, when a great big man, oh, his head was almost up to the top of the tent when he stood up straight, came up to the door and stooped down and peeked in.

" 'Go right away!' screamed the doorman at him, as cross as he could be.

" 'Where's the Circus-Man?' asked the great big man, and he kept peeking in. 'I shan't go till I've seen the Circus-Man.'

"So somebody had to run and get the Circus-Man, and they made him stop, although he was just in the midst of showing off the monkey who was having a waltz on the back of the biggest elephant. He was pretty cross, and he marched up to the great big man and he pretended not to know him, and he said very sharply, 'Go right off. You're making a perfectly dreadful noise, and you haven't paid, and you can't go in.'

" 'Don't you know me, Mr. Circus-Man?' cried the great big man, and he stood up quite straight, and his eyes, that stuck out like two cannon balls, stared at him.

" 'Go right away!" said the Circus-Man angrily. 'I never saw you before in all my life. I'll set the dogs on you,' and he snapped his whip.

" 'Oh, I'll go,' said the great big man. 'Good-by, Mr. Circus-Man. The next time you come up to my mountain you needn't stop to see me. Come every single one of you beasts and beastesses, and reptiles and reptilesses, and animals, it's time to go home,' he roared. And everybody inside the big tent screamed that it thundered, and that they'd all be killed, and the elephant knocked the monkey off from his back, and Mr. Snake slipped out, and the rhinoceros jumped over the heads of the children who were giving him peanuts, and the hippo ran, and—"

"And the rhododendron," said Ben—"what did he do? Don't forget him, Polly."

"And the gi-raffe," said Polly, with a cold shoulder for Ben, "and all of them, they just ran and jumped and skipped and hopped and wriggled out of that tent, and the great big man was going off on his perfectly dreadfully large feet, till he was miles away in a few minutes. Off they all hurried, every single one of them, after him; and although the Circus-Man chased and chased and *chased a*fter them, he never could catch them. And that's all," said Polly, leaning back quite exhausted.

"Well, well!" exclaimed Mother Pepper, coming in suddenly upon the absorbed little group. "Now, that looks comfortable," and her face lighted up and she beamed at Polly.

"Oh, Mamsie!" screamed every one of the bunch as they sprang to their feet and surrounded her.

"There was a sweet dear little monkey," cried Phronsie stumbling up, dreadfully excited, "and a gre-at big man. Take me, Mamsie," and she snuggled up to Mother Pepper's wet gown.

"Take care, child," cried Mrs. Pepper, hungry to get her baby to her heart. "Mother's all wet. There, there, Polly, Mr. Atkins let me take the umbrella, so I did very well. I've set it in the Provision Room. That's a good girl," she added, as Polly took off the big shawl and hung it up to dry.

"Now, Ben and you boys run and put some more wood in the stove, do," cried Polly. "Oh, I do so wish you had some tea, Mamsie," and her face clouded over, and the corners of her mouth drooped.

"It's better than tea to see all you children," cried Mamsie brightly. But nobody dared ask her if she had any coats and sacks to sew, for there wasn't any big bundle, and Polly sighed and looked at Ben.

IV

The Little Tin Soldiers

"You must know," said Polly, "that they had cakes every day, little cunning ones, and Sundays they had pink on top of 'em."

Nobody spoke. At last Joel managed to ask, sitting on the edge of his chair, "On every single one of the cakes, Polly Pepper?"

"Yes," said Polly decidedly, "every single one of 'em Joey."

"Not *every* Sunday?" asked Joel incredulously.

"Yes, every single Sunday, as surely as Sunday came around," declared Polly in her most decisive fashion. "They didn't miss once."

"Now, I know you aren't telling us true things," cried Joel in a loud, insistent tone, " 'cause no one ever has cake every day, and pink on top every Sunday. So there, Polly Pepper!"

"Of course I'm not telling you true, live things," retorted

35

Polly in her gayest tone. "I'm making 'em up out of my head as I go along. And a person could have cake every day with pink on top of 'em, if there was enough to go around."

"Oh," sighed little Davie, clasping his hands with a long sigh.

Phronsie never took her eyes from Polly's face, but she said not a word.

"If you keep interrupting all the while, Joe, Polly can't get on with her story," said Ben who was mending Mother Pepper's washboard over in the corner, with one ear out for the narration proceeding under such difficulties.

"Well, go on," said Joel ungraciously, his mouth watering for the cake with pink on top. "But I don't b'lieve Johnny ever had all that, every day and Sunday."

"Well, you must believe it," said Polly, shaking her brown head at him, "or I'm not going to sit here telling you stories. Joey Pepper, you must act as if you believed every single word I say, else you won't be polite."

"Oh, I'll believe it," exclaimed Joel in alarm at the thought of Polly's stories ceasing. "I wish I had some of the cake with the pink on top, now, I do. Tell on, Polly."

"And I," said Phronsie putting out a little hand. "I wish I had some too, Polly, I do."

"Well, we haven't any of us got any," said Polly. "But I'll tell you all about Johnny's. Sit still, pet. You joggle me so I can't sew straight, and these seams must be done before Mamsie gets home, else she'll sit up tonight to do 'em."

Polly was stitching away on one of the sacks that Mrs. Pepper had promised Mr. Atkins she would take down to the store on the morrow, her needle rushing in and out briskly. She glanced up at the old clock: "Oh, dear me! If I don't hurry, I sha'n't get to the time when Johnny's little tin soldiers ran."

"Oh—whoppity-la!" screamed Joel in a transport, forgetting how his mouth watered for the pink-topped cakes. "Tell about the soldiers, Polly. Tell about them."

"Well, I can't if you keep interrupting me all the time, Joel," said Polly. "I was just going to when you stopped me about the cakes."

"That's just it," said Ben over his shoulder. "I wouldn't tell him a single thing if he goes on like that. Take my advice, Polly, and don't promise him another story."

But Polly was already launched into her gayest and best narration, and Joel slipped off from his chair edge to the floor where he snuggled up against her feet, his head on her knees. Phronsie longed to do the same thing, but remembering what Polly had said about sewing Mamsie's seams, she sat up very straight in her chair and folded her hands in her lap.

"Did Johnny have tin soldiers too?" asked David in an awe-struck tone.

"Of course, child," said Polly, with a little laugh. "Why, he had a big house full of just *everything*."

"Make Dave stop talking," said Joel irritably. "We can't hear anything. Do go on about the soldiers, Polly. You said you would."

"Now, the first one of you children that says a word," said Polly merrily, "will have to go out into the Provision Room and stay till I finish this story. I never shall get through at this rate. Now remember!"

"Good for you, Polly." Ben bobbed his approval and set in two or three nails with smart little taps of his hammer.

"Well, Johnny made up his mind that his tin soldiers had too easy a time because there hadn't been anybody to fight, you know, for one thing, Johnny being off for three days fishing with the Mullen boy who lived next door, and too busy to get up a battle with anyone, and so things had got to be pretty easy. And the tin soldiers were just as lazy as could be, and some of them, don't you think, were lying on their backs on the closet shelf. One had even rolled off and was having a nap down in the corner where he thought nobody could see him."

" 'Wake up there!' hallooed Johnny, flinging wide the closet door very suddenly. 'There's going to be a big battle. Attention—Get ready—Form!' "

"Ugh—ugh!"—grunted Joel, starting up. Then he clapped his two brown hands over his mouth and sat down again.

Polly ran on, with an approving smile at him. "And then Johnny saw the poor little fellow fast asleep in the corner." Here she caught sight of Phronsie opening her mouth, and she hastened to add, "And he picked him up and set him straight. 'Now, fall into line, my men!' he shouted at them; and before anybody knew just how, there they were, every single little tin soldier out in the garden under the grapevine arbor and—"

"Ugh—ugh—*ee!*" cried Joel explosively. Then he ducked and came up red and shining, his lips tightly pressed together.

"You're such a good boy, Joey!" exclaimed Polly. "Now,

you see how perfectly elegant it is to tell stories without having to stop every minute to explain things. Well, and there were Jack Mullen's wooden soldiers all standing up to fight, with Jack as proud and stiff as he could be, back of them. They weren't as nice as Johnny's because, you see, Jack had left his out in the rain the night his mother gave a party— he forgot to take 'em in—and the paint was all washed off, and one soldier had his legs chipped off a bit where Jack's little cousin had tried his new knife on it, so he went lame; and another one had his gun smashed where it got stepped on by the hired man when Jack dropped it in the barn one day. But they were brave as they could be, and there they were all ranged up in battle array when Johnny brought out his soldiers.

" 'Hoh-hoh-hoh!' cried Johnny, prancing along, driving his soldiers down the path. Their swords and guns were clanking and they looked so smart in their scarlet coats and caps with the nodding plumes. 'My men can beat yours any day, Jack Mullen!'

" 'You'll see,' cried Jack, firing up. 'Let's get 'em to work, that's all I say,' and he stuck his hands in his pockets and laughed long and loud.

"Johnny went around among his men, and whispered something in each ear. It sounded like 'cakes'; and then every soldier nodded real pleased, and smacked his lips, and—"

Here there was tremendous excitement among the children, but Polly pretended not to see it and, only stopping to bite off her thread, she hurried on: "And suddenly Johnny screamed, 'Wait a minute,' and off he dashed and ran into the kitchen. 'Jane—Jane! I must have sixteen—no, seventeen cakes today. Make 'em big, Jane, and put pink on top, same as my Sunday ones.'"

"*Gee!*" screamed Joel. But Davie, in alarm lest Joe should be sent off to the Provision Room and just in the most splendid part of the story, jumped off from his chair and flung his arms around him in distress.

" 'Hurry up!' roared Jack after him; 'else I'll begin the battle and shoot every one of your men's heads off. Bang—Bang!' " Here Polly put down the big sack a minute and thrust up an imaginary gun to her shoulder to show exactly how Jack Mullen looked. Ben dropped the washboard and came out of his corner to look at her.

"And sure enough," said Polly, with kindling eyes, "he was at it when Johnny got back, red and breathless, from his run from the kitchen. So of course his tin soldiers had a perfectly awful time from the very beginning. Oh, you can't think, children, how they did have to fight! And don't you believe they were crowded off inch by inch down that perfectly beautiful garden path under the grapevine arbor, until there was only one little corner to stand on for a place of defense. And the guns banged, and the cannon roared, and the smoke was so thick you could cut it with a knife, and in and through it all were the scarlet coats and caps with the nodding plumes of the little tin soldiers. And every one of 'em was as brave as could be, and saying 'cakes' to himself. But there must come an end, and—"

Joel was just going to scream "No—no!—don't let it come to an end, Polly," when he remembered in time, and she ran on gaily, "And Johnny was hopping up and down, feeling dreadfully but trying to get up a last charge, and Jack was screaming, 'We've beaten you—hurrah for my men!' when a dozen boys jumped over the fence, and dashed right into the battlefield.

" 'The circus carts are coming down this street,' screamed every single one of 'em. 'Come on!'

"The tin soldiers, of course, supposed, in the din of battle and all that dreadful smoke, that a terrible charge from the wooden soldiers had come, set on by those perfectly dreadful boys, and the wooden soldiers thought that the boys were helping the tin soldiers. So each side started to run away from the other, and the tin soldiers ran the fastest because they were thinner and lighter, so they didn't find out their mistake until too late, and they all fell into the fishpond at the bottom of the garden. Meanwhile, after Johnny and Jack had climbed the fence and were off at the corner of the street with the twelve boys, Jane came out with seventeen little cakes with pink on top, and not finding anyone, she placed the tray on the seat under the grapevine. And the black cat, the largest one at Johnny's house, you know, the one with the green eyes, came stepping softly up, and smelled them all over. Then she yowed for the neighbor's gray cat, with whom she was quite sociable, and they ate them all up, every crumb."

V

Christmas at the Big House

"You must know, children," said Polly, most impressively, "that there was to be a Christmas at the Big House."

"Christmas!" Each of the three younger Peppers, "the children," as Polly and Ben called them, set up a shout at the magic word. Ben set his teeth together hard, and listened. No one of them had ever seen a Christmas, or knew in the least what it was like, only from what Jasper had told them. And now Polly was to draw from her imagination, and give them a story Christmas. No wonder at the babel that ensued.

"The Big House," began Polly, "had ever and ever so many windows and doors to it, and it set back from the street; and there was a road up for the carriages, and another for folks to walk up—oh, and there were lots of children that belonged to the house—as many as we are," and Polly glanced around on the bunch of little Peppers. "Well, you know the Big House had always had a Christmas every year whenever it came around. They had hung up their stockings and had trees, just like what Jasper told us of, and all sorts of nice things they'd tried time and again, so what to do this Christmas, why, none of them could think. At last Jenny, she was the biggest girl, proposed that each child should write out what he or she wanted to do most of all, and not let any one else see what was written, but fold the paper and tuck it into Grandpapa's white hat in the hall. Grandpapa always wore a tall white hat whenever he went out, and when he was at home the hat stood on its head on the hall table. And no one was ever allowed to touch that hat. So the children knew it would be a perfectly safe place to drop the papers in, and then when all were in, even the baby's, because Jenny would write hers for Mehitable, that was the baby's name, why Grandpapa would take the hat and turn out all the papers and read them and decide what they better do in order to keep Christmas. Well, every single child in the Big House had written on his paper and put it carefully into Grandpapa's big white hat, and Grandpapa had taken out all the papers. The children had seen him as they peeked out of the door into the hall, and then he went away into another room and shut himself in.

" 'Children,' he said, as at last, after what seemed to them a perfect age, he opened his door and came out, 'we will have a tree this Christmas.' Then he laughed, and held up seven papers—for you must know that besides the five children who always and every day lived at the Big House, there were two cousins, a girl and a boy, who were visiting there. 'Every single paper,' declared Grandpapa, as soon as he could speak, 'had "Tree" written across it.'

"Well, you see by that, the children were not tired of Christmas trees, and as soon as Grandpapa told them that they were to have one, they were quite satisfied, although Jenny did say that if she had known everyone else had chosen it, she would have written some other thing on her paper. But that didn't make any difference now, and what they all had to do was to get ready. The next day found the whole Big House in—oh, such a bustle! You would think they never had gotten a tree ready for Christmas in all their lives, there was such a fuss made. In the first place, Grandpapa had to go out and speak to a man to send up into the country and get him a big spruce tree of good shape, not long and spindling, but stout and with a pointed tip, for the Big House was in the city, and of course no city trees could be cut down without folks being put into jail for it. And then everybody had to sit down and count up the money they had to spend, and if that wasn't enough they had to go to the bank and draw out some more; that is, the big folks did. And as the children were emptying their banks to see how much they had, Grandpapa came up behind them and dropped a gold dollar into each one's pile."

It was impossible for the Five Little Peppers to keep still at that, but after they were quiet once more, Polly occasioned a fresh outburst by saying, "And then Grandmamma came up behind them, and she dropped a gold dollar on each pile too."

"Polly," cried little Davie, quite overcome, "did they have the tree too?"

"Yes, child," said Polly, "and dear me, lots of other things too—a big Christmas dinner for one thing."

"Oh, Polly!" cried Joel. "Turkey and pudding?"

"Oh, my, yes—and candy and raisins and everything," declared Polly, "with flowers in the middle of the table."

"And roast beef and fixings?" Ben for the life of him could not help asking this.

"Yes—yes," answered Polly. "You can't think of anything that those children didn't have at that Christmas dinner. But I must tell you about the tree. Well, you must see it took a great while to get everything ready. Besides the things that Jenny and her cousin Mary, and Jenny's brother Tom, and his cousin Edward were making, there were ever so many presents to buy. And to get these, all the children had to go to the shops with Grandmamma and Grandpapa and with each other, and then they had to hide them in all the out-of-the-way places they could so that no one would find them until they were hanging on the Christmas tree. Oh, there was just everything to do, and the day before Christmas they all went to the shops for the last things that had been forgotten till then. It had snowed the night before but it was sunny and cheery on this afternoon, and the walks had a little bit of snow, too hard to clear off nicely and just enough to slide on, when the procession came out of the Big House and turned down the street where the shops were. Everybody was out buying things. They had little bags of money dangling by their sides, only some held their purses in their hands, and kept looking at them to be sure they were there—but oh, the shops!"

"Tell about them," begged all the other Peppers together. "Tell every single thing that was in them," said Joel.

"Oh, I can't begin to tell half that was in those shops,"

laughed Polly merrily. "Mercy me, Joey, there was just
everything there—drums and tin soldiers, and little boxes
that had music shut up in 'em, and dolls and jew's-harps,
and mittens and comforters, and trains of cars, and candy
and flowers, and birds in cages, and, oh, boots and shoes and
books and, oh—just *everything!*" Polly brought up suddenly with a gasp, being quite tired out.

"Go on," urged Joel breathlessly.

"She can't—there's too many things," said Ben. "Never
mind going over them. Just tell what the folks did, Polly."

"Well, you see the children each wanted Grandmamma
and Grandpapa to help them choose things that all the
others were not to see," said Polly, "and Grandmamma and
Grandpapa couldn't go in seven places at once, so at last
one of them—it was Tom—thought of a plan. It was to
rush off himself and choose something, and then come
running back down the shop length. When the others all
saw him coming they were to hurry away from Grandmamma and Grandpapa and let him whisper what it was
into their ears so nobody else heard, and 'Would you?' and
then if Grandmamma and Grandpapa said 'Yes,' away Tom
would rush and buy it, whatever it was. So all the other
children tried the very same plan; and don't you believe
when they asked 'Would you?' Grandmamma and Grandpapa always said 'Yes, my dear.' They did every single time.

"Well, and finally they came out of the last shop, and
the lamps in the street were being lighted, and the snow
under their feet shone and creaked as they stepped, and
every one of the children would have slidden if their arms
had not been full of bundles clear up to their chins. And

Grandpapa laughed and said they ought to have brought an express wagon; and Grandmamma said, oh, no, she wouldn't have them sent home if she could, it was so nice to carry bundles. And everybody they met had big and little white paper parcels, and people knocked into each other, the streets were so crowded and the bundles stuck out so. And so finally they got home and all the bundles were put in one big room where the tree was, and the door was locked and Grandmamma put the key in her black silk pocket.

"Well, in the middle of the night when the Big House was still as could be and all the children were asleep in their beds, something came softly over the roof and stopped right by the chimney. There was just a little tinkle-tinkle, like the noise Mrs. Henderson's cow makes when she shakes her bell, and then a paw-paw, just like one of Mr. Tisbett's horses when he puts his foot down quietly—the gray one, I mean—and somebody said, 'Hush, there, you'll wake up the folks.' And before anybody could think, up springs something, with a big pack on his back, and down he goes right through the chimney."

"I know, I know!" screamed Joel and David together. "It's Santy Claus!"

"It's Santy," hummed Phronsie, dreadfully excited. "Oh, I want to see him, Polly, I do!"

"Perhaps you will sometime, Phronsie, if you are a good girl," Polly made haste to answer. "But never mind now, pet. I must go on with the story."

"Well, it was Santa Claus who hopped down the chimney with his pack on his back, and Mrs. Santa Claus sat in the sleigh and held the reins. And he went into every room, and looked at each sleeping child, and he could tell by its face whether he had been good or bad."

"And had they?" cried Joel eagerly. "Say, Polly, oh, make them be good! And did Santa Claus give them a lot of presents?"

"Most of the children had been good," said Polly, "but there was one, and he had been bad, very bad indeed. He had eaten up his brother's piece of cake, and then he had cried and screamed for more, and made everybody unhappy. And Santa Claus stood over his bed and said, 'Poor child.' "

"And didn't he get any presents from Santa Claus?" cried Joel. "Do let him have a little bit of a present, Polly," and he stuck his fingers in his eyes, trying not to cry.

"Why, how could he?" cried Polly, "when he had been bad, Joey?"

"P'raps he—he won't—won't eat up his brother's cake any more?" mumbled Joel in great distress. Then he broke down and laid his head in Polly's lap and burst out crying.

"Joel—Joel!" cried Polly, shaking his arm. "It's only a story. Stop, Joey, you'll make Phronsie cry."

"But I want—want that boy to get a present from Santa Claus," sobbed Joel, unable to be comforted.

"Do fix it some way," whispered Ben over Polly's shoulder. "Phronsie is beginning now." And so she was. She had gravely insisted on getting into Polly's lap, and now she hid her face on Polly's arm, while soft little sobs shook her figure.

"Dear me!" cried Polly aghast. "Was there ever such a time! Children, now stop, both of you. I'll tell you what Santa Claus did. He looked at Teddy sleeping there and he said to himself, 'Now, I'll give this boy something to make him good, even if he is bad now. And then, if he keeps on being bad, why he must give it back to me next Christmas. And besides, I'll have a rod for him.' So he slipped a toy in Teddy's stocking and—"

"And was he good?" cried Joel, thrusting his head up quickly and wiping his wet face on Polly's gown.

"Yes. Oh, you can't think how good Teddy was all through that year!" said Polly happily. "His mother called him 'Little Comfort,' and his father said he was a little man."

"That's nice," said Joel, smiling through his tears.

Phronsie, when she saw that Joel was all right and that no one else was crying, lifted up her head from Polly's arm and laughed gleefully. So on Polly ran with the story.

"Well, and after Santa Claus had gone, for you know he had so many other children to go to see, and it was pink all over the sky, and the children were out of bed, why, it was the hardest thing to keep them out of that room where the tree was. And that day, oh, it was the very longest in all the days of the year! But at last it was night, and then the candles on the tree were all lighted. Oh, I guess there were two hundred of them, and they gleamed out such a sparkling brightness, just like little stars, and—"

"Two hundred candles, Polly!" cried everyone.

"Yes," said Polly. "I surely believe there were two hundred candles, all lighted and winking away on that beautiful tree. And somebody, the children's mother I believe, played on the piano and everybody marched in line, and the big door was thrown open, and there, with its tip almost to the top of the room, was the most beautiful tree. Every branch was crowded with presents and everybody got what was most wanted, and there were flowers everywhere. Oh, and a little bird sang—they'd put the cage at the bottom of the tree because it was too heavy for the branches, and there sat Dicky-bird, his black eyes as big as could be, and he was stretching his throat and singing at the top of his voice. And then everybody took hold of hands and danced around and around that most beautiful tree a whole hour I guess, and Santa Claus all the while was peeking in at the window. You see, he goes around the next night as soon as it gets dark, to see how the children like his presents. Oh, children," and Polly glanced out of the window, "if here doesn't come Mrs. Beebe!"

VI

Mr. Father Kangaroo and the Fat Little Bird

PHRONSIE was wailing dismally, sitting up in the middle of the old bed. Her face pricked, she said, and she was rubbing it vigorously with both fat little hands and then crying worse than ever.

"Oh, me, oh, my," cried Polly. "How you look, Phronsie!"

"I want my Mamsie!" cried poor Phronsie.

But Mamsie couldn't come. She was sewing away for dear life, to keep the wolf from the door. So Polly curled up on the bed beside Phronsie and fed her mouthfuls of the toast, with its unwonted richness—the sweet butter that Mrs. Henderson, the parson's wife, sent over—while she told the doings of all the chickens in the Hendersons' hencoop, then gaily launched off into other stories. And this is one of the stories she told:

"You must know," began Polly briskly, as Phronsie leaned

51

back against the pillow, the last morsel of toast dispatched, "that the children had never seen a kangaroo, and—keep your toes in bed, Phronsie," and Polly jumped off the bed, and gave a quick pull at the bedclothes, "Oh, dear me, or the dreadful old measles will catch 'em."

Phronsie pulled in her fat little toes where she had stuck them out from the edge of the patched bedquilt, and huddled them under her in terror. "They're so hot, Polly," she wailed. "Oh, dear! Will the dreadful things catch 'em? Will they, Polly?" hugging Polly around the neck.

"Not if you keep 'em in bed, child," said Polly, patting the little bunch under the bedquilt reassuringly. "There, stretch 'em out, Phronsie. There won't anything hurt 'em if you keep 'em in bed."

"Won't they, Polly?" asked Phronsie fearfully, still huddling up in a heap.

"No, no! Come on, Mister Toes," sang Polly gaily, pulling at them. "Doctor said you mustn't get cold, or the measles would run in. There, that's all right," as Phronsie's toes came down again. "Now everything's just splendid, and I'll go on about my lovely kangaroo. He—"

"They're so hot," sighed Phronsie, wriggling all her toes, "and they prick, Polly—they do—"

"Well, we can't help that," said Polly. "You see that's the measles. And I suppose the kangaroo had prickly toes too, sometimes, Phronsie. Now I'm going to get up on the bed again and hold your hand, and then we'll hear all about him." So Polly hopped up beside Phronsie and took her hot little hand in both of her bigger ones, and began again. "You see he—"

"Please don't let him have the—the—" broke in Phronsie,

turning her flushed face eagerly toward Polly's on the pillow. "Don't Polly," she begged.

"Have the what?" cried Polly, racking her brains to think what she could do with her kangaroo. She must tell Phronsie a good story about him. "Well, I've seen the picture of him in the minister's book, and I guess I can make up something about him that she'll like. What is it that you want me not to do to him, Phronsie?" she asked.

"Don't let him have—th—these—things—like mine?" pleaded Phronsie, the tears coming into the brown eyes. And despite all her efforts, she wriggled her toes and cried, "Oh, it pricks so, Polly," burrowing down deep in the old bed, and rubbing her chubby face.

"Oh, he shan't have the measles!" cried Polly, "and you mustn't do so, Phronsie," all in one breath. And pulling Phronsie up against the pillow again, Polly seized both of the little fat hands and held them close. "There, there, just hear all about my lovely kangaroo, Phronsie. Why, he ran into the forest, and he carried all the little bits of kangarooses in a bag with him."

"Did he have a bag?" asked Phronsie. And she let her hands stay quite still in Polly's clasp, and the two tears on her round cheeks ran down on the old quilt unheeded.

"Yes, indeed, a big bag that hung down in front of him, and whenever he called, all his little children kangarooses would run and hop, and jump into that bag."

"Oh!" screamed Phronsie delightedly.

"Yes, and then the old father kangaroo would peek over the edge of the bag and say, 'Lie still, my children, and don't kick each other,' and then he—"

"Did he tie it?" asked Phronsie anxiously, poking up her

head to peer into Polly's face. "Please don't let him tie it tight, Polly,"

"No, he couldn't tie it," said Polly, "because you see there were no strings to his bag."

"Oh," said Phronsie, sinking back very much relieved.

"He gripped the edges together fast, and—but the little kangarooses had cunning little places they could stick their noses out," she hastened to add, as she caught sight of Phronsie's face. "Oh, they liked it ever so much. And then the old father kangaroo would run—oh, such dreadful big steps he would take, Phronsie, you can't think, as big as all across this bed in one hop!"

Phronsie's eyes widened delightedly, and she gave a long sigh of content.

"Tell me some more," she begged.

"Well, one day Mr. Father Kangaroo was out in the forest getting dinner. He had short little wee feet in front, and he couldn't walk very fast you see. And—"

"Where was the mother kan—what was it, Polly?" interrupted Phronsie. "Tell me, Polly, do."

"Kangaroo? Oh, she was in the house, working away. You see, with so many children kangarooses, Phronsie, there was lots and lots to do," said Polly, growing quite desperate at the thought of Mother Pepper sewing out there in the old kitchen, and all the dishes not yet washed, and everything else at a standstill. "Now, you lie still, and perhaps you'll go to sleep while I tell the rest."

"I can't go to sleep," said Phronsie, putting up her lip sorrowfully.

"Never mind," said Polly merrily, "don't try.—Oh, where was I?"

"You said Father Kangaroo went off to get some dinner," said Phronsie, concluding not to cry.

"Oh, yes—well, you see, they hadn't any of them had any breakfast. Just think of that, Phronsie, and you've had toast and elegant butter," and Polly's mouth watered, for she hadn't tasted any of the little pat that Mrs. Henderson sent.

"Hadn't they?" asked Phronsie sadly.

"No, not a single bite. Well, Father Kangaroo just stalked off, that is, he hopped with great big hops, for he knew he had to get some dinner else the little bits of kangarooses would starve to death. And pretty soon he came right into the very middle of the forest, and there under the trees, in the midst of a bramblebush, lay a little bird—Oh, such a cunning little bird, you can't think, Phronsie, so fat and juicy!"

"Oh, don't let Mr. Father Kangaroo catch the little bird, Polly!" screamed Phronsie in terror, and springing up she seized Polly's neck with both hands and burst into tears.

"Oh, dear me, what shall I do?" cried Polly in despair, and cuddling her up. "No, he shan't eat the bird, Phronsie. Now, stop crying this minute. The kangaroo shan't eat him, I say. I'll make the little bird go home with him, and sing to the children kangarooses—there—there—now, says I, we'll lie down again."

So she patted and tucked Phronsie in again under the clothes, and wiped her face dry with the old soft handkerchief Mamsie had left under the pillow, and then she began once more.

"Deary me, where was I? Oh, I know, I was going to

have the little bird go home with Mr. Father Kangaroo."

"Yes," said Phronsie happily, "you were going to, Polly."

"So Mr. Father Kangaroo looked sharply at the fat little bird lying there in the middle of the bramblebush, and he asked, 'What's the matter down there, little bird?'

"And the little bird cocked up one eye at him just like this," said Polly, suiting the action to the word.

Phronsie poked up her yellow head to see, and smiled gleefully.

"And the little bird piped out, 'Oh, Mr. big Kangaroo-Man, I can't get out.'"

"Oh, make him help him, Polly," cried Phronsie, very much excited and pulling her hands out of Polly's to clasp them together tightly. "Do, Polly, quick!"

"Yes, indeed I will, pet. So Mr. Father Kangaroo leaned over the bramblebush and roared in a big voice, 'Here, I'll hold the brambles away with my paws, and you can jump into my bag.'"

"Oh, oh!" screamed Phronsie in delight. "And he did, and up jumped the little fat bird," said Polly, tossing her hands out with a whir, "and in he came flopping oh, so quickly, into the big bag of Mr. Father Kangaroo. 'Twas just as nice, Phronsie, oh, you can't think!"

"'Twas just as nice," cooed Phronsie happily. "The little bird in the big bag. Tell some more, Polly, do."

"Well then, you see, the big Mr. Father Kangaroo didn't know what to do with the little fat bird so he said, 'Now, my dear, don't you want to fly out of my bag and go home?' And the little fat bird huddled down into the darkest corner of the bag and he piped out, 'Oh, I haven't any home, Mr.

Kangaroo. A great cross old squirrel came up to my nest this morning, and ate up all my brothers and sisters, and I flew away and tumbled into the bramblebush.'"

"Oh, dear!" cried Phronsie in dismay.

"But wasn't it good that Mr. Father Kangaroo found the fat little bird?" cried Polly in her cheeriest fashion.

"Yes," said Phronsie, "it was good, Polly."

"Well, so Mr. Father Kangaroo said, 'I'll take you to my home.' He didn't know what in all the world he should do, for he had six—no, seven hungry little kangarooses, and not a bit to give them for dinner. But he couldn't leave the poor little fat bird to starve, you know."

"He was a good Mr. Father Kan—what is it, Polly?" declared Phronsie, clasping her hands.

"Kangaroo. Yes, wasn't he, Phronsie? So he looked down into the bag, and he said, 'Now don't you cry, little bird, and you shall go home with me where the cross old squirrels cannot catch you,' for he thought he heard the little fat bird sobbing down in the dark corner."

"And was he?" cried Phronsie.

"Perhaps so—a little wee bit. But he didn't cry any more, for as soon as he heard Mr. Father Kangaroo say that he chirped out, 'Thank you, Mr. Kangaroo-Man, and I'll sing for you all the day long.'"

"That was nice in the little bird, wasn't it, Polly?" cried Phronsie, wiggling her toes in a satisfied way.

"Yes, indeed. Well, so away they trudged—I mean Mr. Father Kangaroo trudged, and hopped, and skipped, with great long steps, and pretty soon he came to his home. And the little kangarooses saw him coming and they all ran and hopped out to meet him, screaming, 'Oh, pappy! Have you brought us our dinner?'"

"Oh, dear," said Phronsie, very much troubled, "he hadn't any dinner."

"But just think what a dear sweet little fat bird he had brought them, who was going to sing all day long, Phronsie!"

"Yes," said Phronsie, but she sighed. "Tell me some more, Polly, do."

"Well, so Mr. Father Kangaroo didn't say anything about dinner for he thought if they saw the little bird first, and heard him sing, they would forget all about that they were hungry."

"And did they?" asked Phronsie.

"Yes, indeed. They never thought of it again. And they hopped and danced all around the fat little bird, and he told them of good Father Kangaroo who had saved him when he got caught in the bramblebush, where he fell when he flew away from the cruel squirrel. And then he sang—oh, it was just lovely to hear him sing, Phronsie." Polly lay back upon the pillow and folded her hands, lost in thought.

"Tell me some more, Polly," cried Phronsie, pulling her sleeve.

"Oh, yes—well, then, you see, all that noise brought Mother Kangaroo in and she just held up her paws in astonishment. And she didn't like it very well, and she said, 'What! Bring another hungry mouth to feed, and you haven't any dinner for us?' and Father Kangaroo sat down in the corner, and his big head went down on his breast, and he sat still to think."

"Don't let Mother Kangaroo send the poor little bird

away, Polly. Don't let her do it!" protested Phronsie in distress.

"No, I won't," promised Polly. "Well, when Mother Kangaroo saw Father Kangaroo sitting so sad and still over in the corner, she hopped over to him and put both her paws around his neck, and she kissed his furry cheek. 'The little bird shall stay,' she said, 'and I'll go out and get some dinner.' And all the little children Kangarooses took hold of paws, and danced around the fat little bird in delight."

"Oh—oh!" cried Phronsie in delight.

"Mercy me!" exclaimed Mrs. Pepper, putting her head in the doorway, "I thought Phronsie was worse. Now, that's cosy," and she beamed at Polly in a way that made the little sunbeams sink right down into Polly's heart.

VII

The Mince-Pie Boy and the Beasts

" 'TISN'T time to go to bed," grumbled Joel; "and you and Ben are going to whisper and wink your eyes as soon as I go."

"We shan't have to whisper when you are out of the way, Joe," said Ben. "Come, hurry up and start." "Now, Joey, you promised," said Polly reproachfully. She was aching to talk over all the splendid plans with Ben; and there were the bright bits of paper left after they had covered the nuts; and just this very night she was to set about making Phronsie's paper doll, and Ben was to begin on a windmill for Davie, and Mamsie was to sit down at the big table drawn out from against the wall, and make Seraphina's bonnet. And Christmas was getting *so* near!

"Oh, Joe!" exclaimed Polly suddenly, in such a tone of despair that Ben said sharply, "Go along or she'll stop telling you stories. You won't get another one tomorrow—sir!"

"I'll go—I'll go," cried Joel, clattering over the stairs in a trice. "I'm going, Polly—you'll tell me another tomorrow, won't you—won't you, Polly?" he screamed at the top.

"Yes, indeed," cried Polly merrily, running along to the foot of the stairs leading to the loft. "That's a good boy, Joey. I'll tell you a good one tomorrow."

"It's got to be a long one," said Joel, "not such a little squinchy one as 'twas today. Hoh! That was no good."

"Hush up there," shouted Ben at him from the kitchen, "or you'll wake Dave up. Come on, now, Polly."

So Polly ran back again and the two pulled out the kitchen table; and Mamsie brought her big basket, and Seraphina's bonnet was snipped out of the piece of ribbon so long waiting for it; and Polly whisked out the bits of bright paper from the bureau drawer in the bedroom; and Ben got out his big jackknife, and commenced to whittle bravely; and everything was as brisk as a bee and as cheery —and the tongues flew just as fast as the fingers till the little old kitchen was alive with the work of getting ready for Christmas.

But on the next morning, all the signs of the coming festivity tucked carefully away and the everyday work done up, then didn't Polly just have to spin off a story when in marched Joel with a, "Come on, Dave, Polly's sewing. Now for the story!" he whooped, and threw himself on the floor at her feet.

"Oh, Joel"—Polly was just ready to cry out, "I can't think of a thing." And then she remembered that she had promised. "Dear me, Joe, what do you want?" she asked, making her needle fly faster than ever.

"Oh, something nice—about having mince pie"—Joel

smacked his lips, "and bears and wolves and crocodiles. Tell a good one, Polly. And it's got to be long"—he waved his arms as far as he could—"long as that. Now begin."

"I'll tell about a mince pie," said Polly, wrinkling her brows. "That's the first thing you asked for, and—"

"And bears and wolves and crocodiles," said Joel hastily. "I want all those. You've got to, Polly, 'cause I go to bed every night, and you said you would."

"I can't get all those things into one story," said Polly.

"Hoh! Yes you can," contradicted Joel. "That's just as easy. Now begin, Polly."

"Well, once there was a boy," said Polly, with a flourish of her needle as she put in a new thread, "and his mother had to hide the mince pies whenever she baked any, 'cause she was afraid to leave 'em around, and—"

"Don't tell such a story," howled Joel in disgust. "Tell something nice, Polly." He winked his black eyes fast, and Polly thought she saw something shine in them; and then he dug his fists in them, and hid his stubby head on her lap in among her sewing.

"So I will, Joey," she cried, dropping her work to lean over and drop a kiss on his black hair. And then it all came to her what to say, and before she knew it, she had begun again on The Wonderful Mince-Pie Boy and the Beasts.

"You see, it was long, long ago," ran on Polly in her gayest fashion, "and almost anything could have happened then— why, Adolphus lived ages before this time when we are living in Badgertown, so he had all sorts of funny people as his neighbors and they did all kinds of queer things. And the animals all talked just like boys and girls, and everybody understood them. And it was just the strangest world, you can't think! And that's the reason that the story is just as it is."

"Go on," said Joel quite himself again, and his mouth opened in an expansive smile. "Come on, Dave. Gee-whickety! Polly's going to tell an elegant buster of a story."

"Joel, I shan't tell a single thing if you say such dreadful words," declared Polly sternly, as little David came in and sat down on the floor by Joel's side.

"I won't," cried Joel in alarm, "say it again ever, Polly."

"Think how badly Mamsie would feel to hear it," said Polly reprovingly. "Oh, Joe! How can you?" Down went Joel's head on her lap—

"I—won't again—Polly," he burst out, trying not to cry. "Oh, Polly! I won't—I don't—want—Mamsie to feel bad" —and he burrowed deep in her lap.

"He won't, Polly," said little David anxiously, patting Joel's stubby head with one hand, and with the other pulling Polly's gown—"I most know he won't say any more dreadful words."

"See that you don't then, Joe," said Polly, "and both of you boys must remember that it would make Mamsie sick to hear you say any such things. Well, now for the story— The Wonderful Mince-Pie Boy and the Beasts."

"Oh, oh!" cried Davie in a transport, and clasping his hands. Joel sat up quite straight, and held his breath.

"The mince-pie boy lived in an old stone house," began Polly, "all overgrown with vines. There were big trees that sent their arms clear across the top of his house, and the vines ran all over them so that it looked for all the world as if it was a great arbor. Well, and just a little ways off, about as far as from here to Grandma Bascom's, was a gre-at big cave. And that was all grown over with vines too, and funny dangling trees that looked as if they were upside down.

"Oh!" laughed Joel. "How funny!" And, "How funny!" said little David.

"Yes, but it wasn't half so funny as it was inside of the house and the cave," said Polly, sewing away busily, "because you see the man who was Adolphus's father owned all the wild beasts that were in the cave. And as he had them all brought out of the cave and up to the big house sometimes, when he had company and he wanted to amuse them, why, you know everything was made so they might show off, and the people could have a good time."

"Tell about it," cried Joel, crowding up to Polly's work so closely that she couldn't see where to set her stitches. "Take care, Joe," she warned, "I sewed that crooked. Mr. Atkins won't give Mamsie any more sacks to do if they're done badly. And I want to learn to sew them all for her." And Polly's face was very sad as she picked out the poor work.

Joel huddled out of the way in dismay. "There, that's all right now," announced Polly in a minute. "You didn't do any mischief, Joe. Let me see, where was I?"

"You said Adolphus's father had all the wild beasts brought out of the cave and into the house when he had company," cried Joel. "Oh, make him bring 'em all in now, Polly, do!"

"So he shall," nodded Polly. "You see, boys, Adolphus's

father had lots and lots of animals in his cave, but he liked the wolves and the bears and the crocodiles the best."

"Oh, dear me!" said Davie quite overcome.

"Now Adolphus liked the best thing in the world—yes, the very best thing in all the world—mince pie. And he had it for breakfast, dinner, and supper."

"Whick—oh, dear me!" exploded Joel.

"Yes, all the beasts liked mince pie too, every single one of all those sixteen hundred beasts."

"Were there sixteen hundred of 'em?" cried little David with flaming cheeks, and pushing up close to her work.

"Yes," said Polly recklessly. "Adolphus's father had sixteen hundred wild beasts in his cave, and—"

"Make it some more," cried Joel. "Make him have eighteen hundred, Polly, do."

"No," said Polly firmly, "he hadn't a single one more than sixteen hundred, not a single one, Joe."

"Well, go on," said Joel.

"But the beasts couldn't get any mince pie, ever," said Polly, hurrying on.

"Why?" broke in both of the boys.

"Because Adolphus's mother said that she couldn't spend the time to bake mince pies for so many beasts and beastesses, because you see, all the animals would have to have a pie apiece. And Adolphus used to go out into the front yard, and eat his pie; and all the creatures would come out of their cave, and stand in their yard, and lick their chops, and wish they had some."

"And so do I wish I had some, Polly," declared Joel, licking his mouth. "Did it have plums in, Polly?"

"Gre-at big ones," declared Polly. "Oh, so rich and juicy! My! There never was such a pie as those that Adolphus got every day—one for breakfast, and one for dinner, and one for supper."

"Oh, dear me!" exclaimed both boys again, unable to find other words.

"Well, one day there was a great stir in the big house under the vines, and everybody far and near knew that Adolphus's folks were going to have company. And that very same night the beasts and beastesses got together and held a meeting. And when everybody in the big house was sound asleep and nothing was stirring but the mice scampering up and down in the walls, all the creatures in the cave were wide awake and talking all together.

" 'I'll tell you what,' said a big white polar bear—"

"What's a polar bear?" interrupted Joel, with a shout.

"You mustn't interrupt," said Polly. "It's a bear that lives at the Poles."

"What poles? Are they clothes poles?" asked Joel persistently. "Say, Polly, and did the bear help to hang out the clothes to dry?"

"No, no—don't ask so many questions, Joe. I never shall get through if you do. This bear came from the North Pole, where it is dreadfully cold. And he loved mince pie, oh, terribly! And he began, 'Now, fellow bears and bearesses, and wolves, and—and—wolveresses.' "

"And crocodiles," said Joel; "don't forget them."

"No, I won't. 'And crocodiles and croco—crocodilesses and all the rest of you,' because, you see, he couldn't mention them all by name, for he wouldn't have had time for his speech if he had, 'we must get some of that boy's mince pie. It isn't fair for him to have so much and we to have none. Now, I have a plan, and if you will all do just as I say I will get you some mince pie.' So they all—the different beasts and beastesses—crowded around the white polar bear and he spoke out his plan.

" 'You know the company is coming to the big man's house'—the beasts always called Adolphus's house by that name—'and we shall be sent for as usual. Now, when we get there, let us march into the hall as if we were going to perform. But instead of that I shall go right straight up in front of the big man and that dreadful mince-pie boy, and shall roar at them: "I will eat off your head and scrunch your bones, unless you give me some mince pie this minute!" ' "

Polly roared it out so loud and looked so very dreadful that Phronsie came running in from the bedroom where she had been putting on her red-topped shoes which Mamsie let her do sometimes, but not step in them for fear of hurting them. One shoe was half off and every button of the other was in the wrong buttonhole. "Oh, Polly!" she cried scuttling over to her. "What was that dreadful noise?"

"Now you see, Joel," cried Polly, throwing down her work and gathering up Phronsie into her lap, "I've scared her most to death. 'Tisn't anything, Phronsie pet, but some bears and things Joel wanted me to tell of"—as Phronsie hid her yellow head on Polly's arm.

"Polly made that noise with her own mouth," said Joel, "and 'twas splendid, Phron. Make it again, Polly, do."

"No, I shan't," said Polly. "There, there, Phronsie, don't be scared. It was I made it, and not a truly bear."

"If it was you, Polly," said Phronsie, lifting her head, "and not a truly bear, I don't mind. But please don't make it again, Polly."

"I won't, pet," promised Polly. "Dear me, just look at your red-topped shoes. Take 'em off, or you'll spoil them. Mamsie doesn't like you to walk in them, you know."

"I want to go back to the bedroom," wailed Phronsie, "and show 'em to Seraphina. Oh, dear, can't I, Polly? I'll go on the tips of my toes."

"No, I'll carry you," said Polly, preparing to spring up, but Joel jumped to his feet—

"Let me, Polly. I'll carry her. Come on, Phron." He seized her and staggered off, depositing her on the bedroom floor, close to Seraphina lying face downward where she had been dropped in fright.

"Now go on," he cried, springing back to huddle at Polly's feet.

" 'I'll scrunch your head off,' " said Polly in a stage whisper. "I can't say it loud as I did before, boys, or Phronsie'll hear. 'Give me the pantry keys!'

"At hearing these dreadful words, the crocodile began to cry. 'I'm afraid, I'm afraid,' he said. But one of the wolves ran up and boxed his ears. 'Nobody dares to say he is afraid here,' he cried. 'Yes, we are going to have *those pantry keys.*' "

It was impossible to describe the excitement that now seized the two boys as they huddled closer and closer to Polly, as she hurried on—

"And when all the beasts and beastesses had promised to do just as the white polar bear should tell them, he roared at them in a perfectly dreadful voice: 'You must all say with me, "I'll scrunch your heads off if you don't give me those pantry keys."' So they all said it after him, the crocodile weeping great tears that ran over his cheeks as he repeated the words. And then every animal went to bed; and the next night the company came to the big house under the vines, and Adolphus's father sent for all the beasts and beastesses."

"And did they scrunch their heads off?" screamed Joel.

"Hush—you'll scare Phronsie again," cried Polly.

"Did they, did they?" cried Joel, lowering his voice. "Oh, make them, Polly, do, scrunch all their heads, every single one!"

"You must wait and see," said Polly. "And don't interrupt, or I never will get a chance to tell the story. Well, all the animals went up to Adolphus's house, two by two; and there, in the long hall, sat all the company in tall chairs, and Adolphus in the middle. And the first thing that anybody knew, before one of them was asked to perform a single thing, the white cat, that lived up at the big house and always slept on a white satin cushion and drank from a silver bowl, sprang into the center of the hall and made a bow and a curtsy. She had a green ribbon embroidered in silver tied under her chin, and she looked too perfectly splendid for anything.

" 'My master wishes me to say,' she announced with another low bow down to the ground, 'that you are asked over tonight not to show off but to eat mince pies! Behold!' And there right at her elbow were twenty-five boys dressed in green and scarlet, and all with big trays full of mince pies, with plums sticking out all over them, and—"

"Ugh!" grunted Joel, and kicking his heels in great disgust. "Now the white polar bear can't scrunch those people's heads off. Hoh! That's no story, Polly Pepper!"

VIII

The Cunning Little Duck

"THE little duck ran away," announced Polly, "to begin with," to the group around her chair.

"Then he was a very naughty duck," said Phronsie, shaking her yellow head.

"Tell about him!" cried Joel with a gusto.

"Yes, I'm going to," said Polly, setting her stitches with a firm hand. "But, children, you interrupt so much that it makes me forget all what I'm going to say, when I'm telling stories."

"Oh, we won't. We won't!" they all promised. "Do begin, Polly, do."

"Well, once upon a time," said Polly, with true storybook flourish, "no, when I was a little girl, years ago, that's the way Grandma Bascom begins her stories—"

"But 'twasn't years ago when you were a little girl, Polly," said little David thoughtfully.

"Well, 'tis in a play story," said Polly. "And all my stories

71

are make-believe, you know. Now, I'm an old lady, children, and I'm going to tell you about my little duck I had, oh, ever so many years ago!"

The little bunch of Peppers shouted at the idea of Polly's being an old lady and Joel got up and whirled around, clapping his fists together till the old kitchen rang with the noise. "Put on a big cap, Polly," he screamed, "just like Grandma's!"

So Polly, who dearly loved to dress up and play things, dropped her sewing and ran off into the bedroom. "There isn't anything I can tie on that's like a cap," she said, coming back, "but this. Wasn't it nice Mamsie had it?" It was a big piece of light brown paper that had done up the last batch of sacks brought home from the store for Mrs. Pepper to sew up.

"Hoh, that isn't *white!*" cried Joel in disdain, while the faces of the others fell.

"Well, we must play it's white," said Polly. "I'm going to; and all frilled with deep lace, too."

So the children began to smile with satisfaction once more. If Polly could play it was white and all trimmed with beautiful lace, it was all right.

"Run to the string bag, one of you children," said Polly, crinkling up the paper on her head to make it look as much like an old lady's cap as possible, and nearly putting out one eye with the corner of the paper, "and tie it fast while I hold it on."

"I will—I will!" cried little Davie, springing off.

"No, I will. I can get it twice as quick!" cried Joe, tumbling after him and seizing his jacket. Thereupon ensued a scuffle as to which should first reach the string bag in the

Provision Room. Joel did, and soon came racing back with a very red face, and bearing it triumphantly aloft. "Here 'tis—I got it, Polly. Now I'll tie you up."

Polly looked out from under her big paper—"Go and hang that string bag right up again, Joey," she said slowly.

"I got it," said Joel stoutly.

"Go and hang it up," said Polly.

"I—I—got—it," said Joel faintly—"I sh'd think I might keep it, Polly," he said in an injured tone.

"Go and hang it up this minute," said Polly, coming entirely out from under her big paper cap and fixing her eyes on him. When Polly looked like that, it always made them think of Mamsie, so Joel turned at once and went slowly down the steps to the Provision Room, dragging the string bag after him. He soon came back, twisting his small hands, and trying not to cry. "Now, Davie," said Polly pleasantly, "will you go and get me the string bag?"

Davie started to run on joyful feet, but seeing Joel moping in the corner, he stopped suddenly. "I'd rather Joe went," he said.

"No, I want you to go," said Polly firmly, "and if you don't hurry, I shall have to go and get it myself and you wouldn't want me to do that, I'm sure."

Thus adjured, David ran as fast as his feet could carry him and soon brought the string bag to Polly.

"Now says I," she cried, "somebody must tie my old cap on, and I'm going to ask Joel to do that." And she pulled out a long string. "Come on, Joey."

"I—didn't—mean—to," sobbed Joel, over in his corner. "Polly, I didn't."

"Well, see that you don't run and scramble and take away

Davie's things again when he starts first," said Polly. "Come on, Joe, I'm waiting."

So Joel tumbled out of his corner, wiping away the tears on the back of his little red hand; and soon Polly's cap was tied on in the most approved style, amid the shouts of the children who all escorted her to the cracked looking glass over the bedroom bureau, when she pronounced it "just too perfect for anything."

"Well, now," said Polly, drawing a long breath and racing back to sit down and pick up her sewing, "I must hurry and tell about my cunning little duck or I don't know what I shall do. Now, children, you know I'm an old, old lady, and—"

"How old?" demanded Joel, who dearly loved facts and figures.

"Oh, I don't know—most a hundred I guess," said Polly; "well—"

"Ho—Ho! Polly's most a hundred," laughed Joel, and Davie burst out laughing too. "Polly's most a hundred," echoed Phronsie with a gurgle.

"Now, see here, children, I shall never tell this story if you keep interrupting me like that," said Polly, pushing back her paper cap that settled over one eye. "Dear me, I didn't s'pose it was such trouble to pretend to be old—this slides all over my head and I can't see to sew. Well, I once had a cunning little duck, when I was a little girl years and years ago."

"Was he as big as that?" asked Phronsie, bringing her two fat little hands almost together in intense excitement.

"Yes," said Polly, "and a little bigger. Well, he was all

my own, you know; my grandmother gave him to me."

"Did you have a grandmother?" asked David. "I thought you were the grandmother," looking at the big cap with its nodding border.

"Well, so I am, but I had a grandmother too when I was a little girl. Everybody has a grandmother when they're little."

"Oh!" said Davie.

"Well, my grandmother gave me this little duck. Now, don't interrupt again," said Polly. "You see, he was so little when he was born that I s'pose he got lost in the grass, and no one saw him; and then the cat must have stepped on him, for his leg was bent, and—"

"What's bent?" demanded Phronsie, pushing an absorbed little face forward.

"Oh, doubled up like this," said Joel, suiting the action to the word, and twisting his leg into as much of a knot as was possible.

"Oh, Polly!" said Phronsie gravely. "Please don't let the little duck's leg be like Joel's."

"Well, you'll see, Phronsie," said Polly reassuringly, "I'll fix the little duck's leg all right. My grandma gave him to me, you know. Well, he was yellow and white, a cunning little ball, oh, so soft and puffy!"

Phronsie trembled with excitement and she put out her little hands as if she had the duck between them. "But please fix his leg, Polly," she breathed.

"Yes, yes, child," said Polly quickly. "Oh, dear me! I've sewed that seam wrong. Now that has all to come out."

"But please fix that little duck's leg first, Polly," begged

Phronsie, her lip quivering, "before you pick out those wrong stitches."

"Oh, dear me, was there ever such a peck of trouble!" cried poor Polly, picking frantically at the bad stitches. Then her old paper cap with its deep border slid down over her eyes, and her scissors tumbled on the floor.

"Look at Polly's cap! Look at Polly's cap!" screamed Joel.

"It's grandma," said little Davie, who dearly loved to carry out all Polly's make-believes, while Phronsie still insisted that the little duck's leg should be fixed before anything else was done.

In the midst of all this confusion the door opened suddenly, and there was dear old Mrs. Beebe, her round face smiling over a big basket.

"Well, well, my pretty dears!" she exclaimed. "Why, what's the matter? Polly got hurt? Oh, you poor creeters!" seeing the big paper flapping over Polly's brown head, and all the children crowded around her chair.

"No'm," said Polly, twitching off her big cap. And, "She's playing grandma," said Joel and David.

"But her cunning little duck has hurt his leg," cried Phronsie, with clasped hands, flying over to Mrs. Beebe, "and Polly is going to fix it right away."

"Yes," said Polly at sight of her face. "I must. Boys, go and tell dear Mrs. Beebe all about it, while I take Phronsie in my lap and fix that duck's leg." So Joel and David, very important at the piece of work set them, ran over and poured the whole recital into good Mrs. Beebe's ear, how Polly was playing grandmother, and they hadn't anything to make a cap of but an old piece of brown paper that came around the sacks from the store that Mrs. Pepper brought home to sew, and how the old thing kept tumbling over Polly's nose, so that she sewed up the seam wrong; and she was trying to pick it out, because, you see, she had to get it done before Mamsie got home, who had gone to the minister's to help Mrs. Henderson make her soft soap; and how Phronsie almost cried because Polly said the little duck's leg was bent in the grass, because maybe the cat stepped on it; and how that was the reason Polly was talking to her now, and fixing the leg up. And, oh, dear me, all this and much more, good Mrs. Beebe oh—ing and ah—ing at just the right times. "And that's all," announced little David at last, flushed and important.

Joel hung his head, "No, it isn't," he blurted out. "I was bad."

"You were bad?" echoed Mrs. Beebe. "Oh, no! I guess not," she said soothingly.

"Yes, I was," said Joel stoutly. "I scuffled Davie, and got the string bag first."

David shifted uneasily from one foot to the other. "He put it back," he said.

"Polly made me," said Joel, twisting his mouth not to cry, and with an eye to the big basket which was not for naughty boys. "Oh, dear me!"

Old Mrs. Beebe cast a puzzled glance at him, but was saved the necessity of replying, for old Mr. Beebe came in just then, rubbing his hands. "Well, how are you all, my pretty dears? I can't stay a minute, for my shop's all alone, an' folks'll be knocking on the door an' can't get in. Come, Ma, give 'em the things in the basket, and then come out an' get in the wagon."

Mrs. Beebe gave a sigh. "Dear me," she said, "I wish I

could set awhile; but then, there's the shop." So she got out of her chair and began to undo the basket. And Polly, with Phronsie radiant, and hanging to her hand, came running up and they all crowded around the good woman. And old Mr. Beebe laughed and shook his fat sides, and rubbed his hands together worse than ever. And at last all the things were out and on the table ready to surprise Mamsie with when she came home.

"And I guess if one of you will feel in my pockets," he said at last, when his wife clapped to the cover of the empty basket, "p'raps maybe, now, you'd find something you'd like."

"Let David," said Joel, swallowing hard.

"No, let Phronsie," said little David.

So Phronsie went up to old Mr. Beebe who lifted her into a chair to be on a level with the pockets in his greatcoat, and oh, oh! first she drew out slowly a pink stick, and then a great thick white one of peppermint candy! And then, midst a babel of thanks from the Five Little Peppers, and one or two kisses from old Mr. and Mrs. Beebe, away the big empty basket and the two good people went to their wagon.

"I'm sure," said Polly to herself, long after they had danced and danced around the table with its good things, "none of them care for the little duck now, so I can fly to my sewing and have a good time to pick it out and do it right." So she settled herself in the old chair in the corner, the children in great excitement still circling around the gifts which they were not to touch till Mamsie got home.

"I choose that," said Joel, smacking his lips, "that big fat doughnut, all crisp and brown. Oh, whickets!"

"Joel," said Polly over in her corner, "what did you say?"

Joel hung his head. "And I choose that," said Davie, pointing to some gingerbread, dark and moist, while he carefully licked the remnant of pink stick in his hand, for Phronsie had insisted on sharing her candy with them all, the minute the Beebes had gotten into their green wagon. "What do you choose, Phronsie?"

"I like this," said Phronsie, holding up a sticky wad of pink stick in her fat little hand, and smiling with a very much smeared face.

"Oh, deary me!" cried Polly at sight of her. "Well, I s'pose it's no use to wash her up till it's all gone. Well, I am thankful I didn't have to tell all the rest about that dreadful little duck."

IX

The Old Teakettle

THE rain dripped most dismally on the roof of the Little Brown House. It had rained just so, without any appearance of stopping, for three days, and Phronsie held a sad little face against the windowpane.

"Won't it ever stop, Polly?" she asked.

"Yes, I s'pose so," said Polly dismally; "though I don't know when. Mamsie, did you ever see it rain so long?"

"Dear me, yes," said Mrs. Pepper, looking up from her stocking mending over in the corner, "plenty of times, Polly. If folks don't worry over the weather and talk about it, it's all right. Fly at your baking, child, and let the rain take care of itself."

"It's so dark," said Polly discontentedly, "we can't see anything," as she went into the buttery for the flour.

"It's so dark," grumbled Joel, trying to make a box over in the corner, and catching her tone, "can't see anything."

Davie sighed, and went over to his mother's corner and stood there with a very long face.

"There, now you see, Polly," said Mrs. Pepper as Polly came back with the flour sieve and the bread bowl, and set them on the kitchen table.

Polly looked around the kitchen with a startled air. "Oh, I'm awfully sorry!" she cried, a wave of color flying up to her brown hair. "Mamsie, I truly am." Then she rushed over to Joel, who was banging petulantly at a refractory nail. "Look out, you'll pound your thumb," and she kneeled down beside him.

"Don't care," said Joel crossly. "Can't see anything. Mean old rain spoils everything."

"Joel!" It was Mother Pepper who spoke and her black eyes flashed sternly. "That's wicked. Don't you let me hear you say such things again."

"Oh, Mamsie!" began Polly.

"And a boy who talks about the rain in such a way is not only wicked but foolish. I think he had better go into the Provision Room and shut the door and sit down and think by himself for a while."

"Oh, *Mamsie!*" exclaimed Polly imploringly.

"Go straight along, Joey," said Mrs. Pepper; "and when you feel right about it, you may come back."

Joel laid down his clumsy hammer and, his round face working dreadfully, he stumbled off and down the rickety steps, and presently they could hear him shut the old door fast.

"Oh, Mamsie—Mamsie!" Polly sprang to her feet and rushed tumultuously across the room, and threw herself at

Mrs. Pepper's feet. "It's all my fault," she sobbed, burying her face in the blue-checked apron—"and I am the one who ought to be sent into the Provision Room."

"You're too big to send there, Polly," said Mrs. Pepper sadly. "Why, you're ten years old." She laid down her mending, and her toilworn hands smoothed the brown hair gently.

"But I made Joel say the bad things," cried Polly gustily, her shoulders shaking with her efforts not to cry aloud.

Phronsie, who had turned in her chair where she had been looking out of the window, at the unusual disturbance in the old kitchen, now got down very gravely and came over to Mother Pepper's corner.

"What is the matter with Polly?" she asked with wide, disapproving eyes.

"Mamsie will take care of Polly," said Mrs. Pepper.

"She's sick, I guess," said little Davie wonderingly.

At that Phronsie uttered a low cry, "Oh, don't let my Polly be sick—don't let her, Mamsie!" Then she screamed in dismay.

"Polly," said Mother Pepper, putting the stockings into the big mending basket with a hasty hand, and drawing Phronsie to her lap, "now I guess you'll have to do your best, my child, to set matters right. There, there, Phronsie, stop screaming. Polly's all well."

Polly felt for the first minute as if she could never lift her head and speak cheerily to the children. Oh, how much she would give to be Phronsie's age and be cuddled and allowed to have her cry out! But Mamsie's words! She swallowed hard the terrible lump in her throat, wiped off the tears, and said brokenly, "I'm all right—there, see, pet," and put up her head.

When Phronsie saw that Polly could really move, she stopped screaming, and Davie began to smile. "I guess she ain't sick."

"No, indeed," said Polly, finding it easier to control herself since she had begun, and hopping to her feet. "I'm going back to my baking," she cried.

"So do," cried Mother Pepper approvingly, with a little smile over at Polly that ran right down into the sad little heart.

"May I bake?" cried Phronsie, the last tear rolling off by itself in a lonely fashion. "May I, Polly, may I?" and she scrambled down from her mother's lap, and ran over to the table.

"Yes, indeed," cried Polly, delighted at the change in affairs.

"Then I shall," said Davie, "at least when Joel gets out. May I call him, Mamsie?" he begged.

"No," said Mrs. Pepper, picking up the stocking again, and attacking the biggest hole, "Joel must wait till he knows he's right."

"Then, I don't want to bake yet," said David with a sigh.

Polly flew around at her preparations for baking, making a great clatter with the things and keeping up a cheery little chat with Phronsie. But all the while her heart was sore over Joel sitting lonely and disconsolate in the old Provision Room. It seemed as if she could not bear it another minute longer when suddenly she heard the door open slowly and his feet coming over the rickety steps. Mrs. Pepper mended steadily on, and did not turn her head. Polly held her breath as Joel, without a glance for anyone else, marched straight past the baking table and over to Mamsie's side.

"I'm sorry I was bad, Mamsie," he began. But he never got any further, for Mother Pepper had him in her arms and there he was cuddled to his heart's content. And Polly deserted the baking table, leaving Phronsie to work her own sweet will among the materials, while she rushed over and dropped a kiss on Joel's stubby head, telling him it was she who was so naughty, and she never was going to do it again. And little David clasped his hands and beamed at them all in great satisfaction.

"Now you had better see what Phronsie is about," advised Mrs. Pepper wisely.

"I don't care," cried Polly in a glad recklessness and plunging over to the baking table, with both boys at her heels. "Oh, my goodness me! What have you been doing, Phronsie?"

"Baking a cake," hummed Phronsie, in a state of bliss. She had upset the flour pan in trying to pull it toward her, and what didn't fly over the floor was on her face and pinafore, while she patted the yeast in the cracked cup with her spoon.

"Hoh—hoh—how you look!" laughed Joel and David. "Just like the old ashman, with that brown flour all over your face."

But Phronsie didn't care, so while Polly shook off the flour and cleaned things up, taking great care to get the yeast cup the length of the table away from the little fingers, she was singing all the time, "I'm going to bake a cake—Polly said so."

At last the bread was made, and, covered with an old towel, was set down to rise by the stove; Phronsie's cake was set in her own little tin pattypan, and tucked into the oven; and then the three children stood and looked at each other. It was still dark, the rain going patter—patter—patter, worse than ever on the roof.

"Mamsie, do you mind if I tell them a story?" asked Polly, looking at them all.

"No, indeed," cried Mrs. Pepper cheerily. "Just the very thing, Polly. I'm glad you thought of it. I sh'd like to hear it too, myself."

"Would you, Mamsie?" cried Polly, quite delighted.

"Yes, indeed. Seems as if my needle would go in and out faster if I could hear something meanwhile," replied Mother Pepper.

So Polly, feeling quite important at being about to tell a story that Mother Pepper was to listen to, gathered the three children in a knot about her on the floor ready to begin.

"I wish Ben was here," began Joel.

"It's good Ben has wood to saw at Mr. Blodgett's," spoke up Mrs. Pepper quickly. "He's in that nice tight woodshed so the rain won't hurt him; and just think, children, of the money he'll bring home."

Polly couldn't help but give a little sigh. How perfectly lovely it would be if she weren't a girl but could go off and earn money just like Ben to keep the Little Brown House going! But Mother Pepper didn't hear the sigh, it was such a tiny one, as Polly saw by glancing over at her. And so away flew the storyteller as fast as she could, on her entertainment.

"Now, children," began Polly, hoping Mamsie would like the story, and racking her brains to make it up as she went along, "I'm going to tell you today about an old Teakettle."

"Hoh, hoh!" jeered Joel, knocking his heels together. "That isn't any story."

"That's funny," laughed little David, looking over at the Pepper teakettle humming away on the stove. "Was it like ours, Polly?"

"Yes," said Polly, "as like as two peas. Well, this Teakettle lived in a house where there weren't any children, only an old woman and a cat."

"It's Grandma Bascom she means," shouted Joel, very much disappointed. "Don't tell about anyone we know, Polly. We've seen her old teakettle lots of times, and—"

"And I sh'd think it would be better to let Polly tell the story in her own way," said Mother Pepper, "if there is to be any story."

"Oh, she may—she may!" cried Joel, casting an alarmed glance over his shoulder on the comfortable figure in the old chair, mending away. "Go on, Polly—do go on."

"Well, it isn't Grandma Bascom," said Polly, "this old woman isn't. My old woman with the Teakettle and the cat lived on the edge of a wood and—"

"And there were bears and hyenas and dreadful things there," cried Joel delightedly. "I know now—and you're going to have 'em come out nights and bite her."

"No," said Polly, "we've had so many bears lately, you don't want any more, Joe."

"Yes I do too," contradicted Joel flatly. "We can't have too many bears. I sh'd think you might give 'em to us, Polly," he added wheedlingly.

"Well, there aren't any in this story," declared Polly firmly. "Wait till I get through. You'll like it, I guess."

"Yes, wait till she gets through," echoed Davie. "Go on, Polly, please."

Phronsie patted her pink pinafore and pulled it into shape patiently. Polly hurried on.

"Well, this old woman who lived on the edge of the wood used to go out every single day and pick up pieces of branches of trees to burn. You see, she didn't have any children to go for her. And the cat stayed home to mind the house, and there was nobody to talk to but the old Teakettle."

"Oh, dear me!" said David.

"Now, the old Teakettle was cross sometimes," said Polly. "She was so very old."

"How old?" interrupted Joel.

"Oh! I don't know. Fifty years, I guess," said Polly at a venture.

"And she was black all over, oh, as black as she could be —blacker'n anything I see around here," said Polly, glancing at the rusty little shoes stuck out before her. "Well, and she was tired too, besides being black, because, you see, she had sung and hummed and buzzed every single day for all that long time just in that one spot. Oh, she was so tired she just wanted to roll down on the floor and off and away to see the world. And one morning the old woman put on her big black cap over her white one, and took down her thick stick with a knob on the end of it.

" 'Mind the house now,' she said to the cat, who sat by the fire. And off she went to the wood to get her branches and sticks.

"Suddenly there was a big noise just like this"—and Polly

gave a hiss as near like a bubbling-hot teakettle as she could manage—"and then a voice said, 'Hem.'

" 'Oh! That's you, Mrs. Teakettle,' said the cat, without turning her head.

" 'Who else would it be but me,' said the old Teakettle sharply, 'when there's not a soul comes in here day after day. Come, you cross thing, why don't you talk?' for the cat looked as if she were going to sleep that very minute.

" 'I haven't anything to talk about,' said the cat sleepily.

" 'Well, I have,' snapped the Teakettle—'puff—puff—and I'm very angry indeed. And I'm tired of staying in this old place day after day. And I tell you what I'm going to do. I'm going to jump right down and go off to see the world. Yes I am.'

" 'You can't,' said the cat, still not turning her head, 'for you haven't any legs.'

" 'As if that was any matter,' snorted the old Teakettle. Then she raised her lid and sent out angry little whiffs of steam so that the cat moved uneasily. 'I don't have to depend on legs, like you great lazy things. I can roll just as good.' With that she gave a great lunge and over she went on her fat side, and off with a bang to the floor. The cat, not knowing which way she might come, wisely sprang for the old table, and peered at her over the side. Like this," said Polly, hanging over an imaginary table edge.

The children screamed with delight, and Mamsie set a whole row of stitches briskly into place while she smiled contentedly over her needle. " 'Oh you bad, naughty thing!' cried the cat; 'Phif—spit—meow! To do such things and run away while the mistress is gone.'

" 'I can't help it,' said the old Teakettle, rolling busily on toward the door while a pool of hot water trailed off into little streams on the floor. 'I'm tired to death sitting in a hump on that old stove day in and day out. You can go out and see the world. It's all very well for you to talk.'

" 'I have to mind the house,' said the cat, sitting up stiffly on the table, her tail lashed around her body and her green eyes staring at the old Teakettle.

" 'Nonsense!' The Teakettle had got through puffing, because, you see, there wasn't any steam left in her, and now she began to roll along more slowly. At last she knocked up against the door with a bump.

" 'You can't get out,' exclaimed the cat, 'anyway, for you don't know how to open the door.' And she laughed softly under her whiskers to herself sitting there on the table.

"The old Teakettle lifted her long nose angrily in the air. 'Jump down this minute,' she cried, 'and open it for me. Come, I'm in a hurry, for I'm going to see the world.'

" 'I shan't open the door,' declared the cat with great composure," said Polly, feeling very glad she had slipped over the big word so well, " 'so there!' and she lashed her tail stiffer than ever around her legs.

"The old Teakettle cried and whimpered and begged, but it was no use. The cat sat up like a wooden cat, and just stared at her. At last the Teakettle rolled over on her side and laid her long turned-up nose on the floor.

" 'I'm afraid she's dead,' said the cat to herself. 'And—' "

"And was she dead?" asked little Davie. "Was she, Polly?"

"You'll see," she cried, "pretty soon. Well, so the cat was so awfully afraid the poor old Teakettle was dead that she stepped down from the table and went and bent over and looked at her. And no sooner had she touched her with her paw to feel and be sure about it, than the old Teakettle hopped up as quick as a wink; and the cat flew back, and then she had to run, oh, so dreadfully fast, because the Teakettle began to roll at her. And around and around the room they went, and the Teakettle kept always between the table and the cat, so she couldn't jump on that, and she couldn't hop on the stove because it was hot, so she had to open the door. And before she could shut it, there was the Teakettle close behind her!"

"And did she get away?" cried Joel; "clear off to see the world?"

"Yes," said Polly, "and she never came back. She screamed out as she rolled down the long hill before the cottage door, 'Goo-d—by—o-old—o-o-ld—cat.'"

"Oh, dear, dear!" said both boys. And "Go-o-d—by—ol-d —cat," sang Phronsie.

"And did she ever come—oh, see—see—" screamed Joel looking up, and nearly upsetting David as he jumped clear past him, "blue sky—see—come on, Dave, outdoors!"

X

The Pink and White Sticks

"Were they as nice as dear Mrs. Beebe's pink and white sticks?" asked Joel anxiously.

"And dear Mr. Beebe's," added Phronsie. "Were they, Polly?"

"Yes—no; that is, they couldn't be quite as nice, pet. No pink and white sticks could be, you know. But they were very nice indeed, and they all lived together in a candy jar."

"Oh—oh! Tell about it, Polly," they all begged.

So Polly got the little bunch of Peppers together in "the breathing spell," as the edge of the twilight was called, when it was too soon to light a candle, because Mother Pepper couldn't afford any light in the old kitchen except when it was absolutely necessary; and then she began:

"Yes, they all lived together in the big candy jar."

"Where was it?" cried Joel insistently, at which the others clamored immediately to be told the same thing.

"In the window of the little shop, just like Mr. Beebe's, only it wasn't Mr. Beebe's," said Polly.

"And was my dear, sweet Mrs. Beebe in there, and all the little shoes?" demanded Phronsie excitedly.

"No, no, pet. I said it wasn't Mr. Beebe's shop, so of course Mrs. Beebe wasn't there, nor the shoes," answered Polly, "but it was like Mr. Beebe's."

"Did it have a green door," asked Joel, "and a big knocker that went clang—clang—like this?" and he jumped up and sent out his arm after an imaginary brass knocker hanging on a big green door.

"Yes," said Polly. "I guess my shop door had a big knocker on it, all shiny like Mr. Beebe's."

"Your shop? Oh, is it your shop?" broke in little Davie incredulously. "Oh, Polly!"

"Of course it's my shop," cried Polly gaily, " 'cause I make it up out of my head, so I own all the things in it too."

"Oh! Give me some of the candy then," howled Joel, plunging into the middle of the group. "I want some right away, Polly."

"Why, I'm giving you some now," said Polly, laughing at his face. The children all looked puzzled enough.

"You see, you're getting some of the pink and white sticks in the story, and if I didn't make it up, you couldn't have any. Now you must just play you're eating candy. My, isn't it nice!" Polly held up long imaginary pink and white sticks, and took a good bite off from one of them.

Joel's sharp black eyes followed her closely. "I'd rather have the real sticks," he said slowly.

"Of course," said Polly, "but if you can't have real ones, it's better to have make-believe story ones. Well, now I'm going to begin."

"Yes, go on," said Joel, bringing down his gaze as Polly's hands fell to her lap. "You said they were in the big candy jar, Polly," smacking his lips.

"Yes—oh, and it stood on the shelf that ran along inside the window; and there was a little bit of a man who kept the shop, and he had a little bit of a wife who helped him, and—"

"Why ain't they big as Mr. Beebe, and big as Mrs. Beebe?" cried Joel, putting his hands out as far as he could reach in front of him. "I like 'em big. Why ain't they, Polly?"

"Because they aren't Mr. and Mrs. Beebe," said Polly. "Now, if you are going to interrupt every minute, I can't tell the story."

"I wish we could hear about those pink and white sticks," said little Davie patiently, and drawing a long sigh.

"Yes, you see the others want to hear about it, Joel," said Polly, "and it keeps us all back when you stop me so much."

"I want the pink and white sticks," said Phronsie, stretching out her feet. "Please hurry, Polly."

So Joel clapped one hand over his mouth to keep from interrupting Polly again, and she began once more.

"Yes, old Mr. Periwinkle and Mrs. Periwinkle were little and dried up, just like two little withered nuts; and they had ever so many little Periwinkleses, and so they had to work very hard to keep shoes and stockings on their feet, and to get them enough to eat. So Mrs. Periwinkle used to make candy and doughnuts and—"

"Oo!" exploded Joel, forgetting himself. Then he clapped the other hand, too, upon his mouth.

"And then Mrs. Periwinkle would run out into the shop and say to Mr. Periwinkle, 'Here's another batch of candy, my dear'; or 'Look what I've brought you,' sliding a pan of doughnuts on the counter just in time for the folks opening the green door and coming into the shop to buy things. Well, one day a perfectly dreadful thing happened!" Polly drew a long breath, and gazed at her audience.

"What was it?" cried little Davie breathlessly. Phronsie sat quite still with clasped hands, and wide eyes fixed on Polly's face. Joel was cramming his fists up against his mouth in great distress.

"Why, the pink and white candy sticks were gone, and there was the big jar all tumbled down on its side!" said Polly, with a very impressive air. "Just think of that, children!"

"Oh, dear!" exclaimed the two little Peppers, while Joel nodded his stubbly black head.

"Yes, they were," said Polly, still more impressively, "every single one of all those pink and white sticks."

"How many were there—ugh!" cried Joel, forgetting himself. Then he clapped his hands up to his mouth again.

"Oh, I don't know—yes, there were six—no, I guess eleven of those pink and white sticks," said Polly thoughtfully; "six white ones and five pink ones."

"I'd rather have had six pink ones," said little Davie reflectively.

"Well, I'll change them," said Polly accommodatingly, "and let the white ones be five. Yes, that's best after all— there were six pink ones, children. Well, and so—"

"I'd rather have the white ones be six," cried Joel in a

roar, and dropping his fists. "They're best, anyway. Mrs. Beebe's white ones were bigger'n the pink ones, and lots sweeter. Let the white ones be six, Polly, do!"

Thereupon an animated discussion began, as to which should be six and which should be five, between the two boys, little David taking an unusually firm stand as he insisted on the pink ones. So at last Polly broke in: "I'll tell you, children, what we will do. There shall be twelve sticks, six pink and six white ones. Now, that's fine."

"Yes, that's fine," cried Joel and David together. "Well, go on, Polly."

"Now, where do you suppose those pink and white sticks could have gone to?" cried Polly, clasping her hands. "Mr. Periwinkle and Mrs. Periwinkle hadn't sold them—what *could* have become of them?"

The little Peppers shook their heads. "And the little Periwinkleses hadn't touched them—oh, no indeed!" declared Polly in a tone of horror—"so what could really have become of them?"

"What?" It was Phronsie who asked this, and she crept into Polly's lap, and put her little hand up on Polly's neck.

"Well, nobody knew," said Polly, stopping only long enough to give Phronsie a hug and ever so many kisses. "And then, what do you think, children, they found had happened to the pink and white sticks?"

At this there was great excitement, the children protesting they couldn't guess, and wouldn't Polly hurry and tell them? So she dashed along—

"Well, Mr. Periwinkle said he was going to sit up that night and watch, and Mrs. Periwinkle said she was going to, and all the little Periwinkleses said they were going to do the same thing. So nobody went to bed at all."

"Oh, dear me!" said David.

"Didn't the littlest little Peri—what is it, Polly?" asked Phronsie in a troubled way.

"Periwinkleses," said Polly.

"Yes, didn't the very littlest get into the trundle bed?" asked Phronsie.

"No, not even the littlest of the Periwinkleses," said Polly. "She was the baby, and she sat up in Mrs. Periwinkle's lap."

"Oh!" said Phronsie.

"Well, along about ten o'clock—no, I guess it was about the middle of the night," said Polly, "all the Periwinkleses were keeping just as still as could be, you know, and there they sat on their chairs and crickets with their eyes wide open, staring at that big jar—oh, I forgot to tell you that Mr. Periwinkle and Mrs. Periwinkle had put some more pink and white sticks in it, so as to see what would happen to them, and—"

"Were there six pink and six white ones?" screamed Joel, before the others could say a word.

"Yes, I guess there were just exactly so many," said Polly, "and there they stood up, as tall and splendid in the jar."

"Oo!" Joel smacked his lips.

"Well, along in the middle of the night—nobody stirred but all the eyes were staring at those pink and white sticks, when suddenly there was a little wee, faint noise."

Phronsie snuggled up closer to Polly.

"It came from under the counter, and pretty soon they all heard a faint voice say, 'Is it time to come out and do it?'

" 'Yes,' said another voice; 'the clock has just struck twelve, and all the big Periwinkles and the little Periwinkleses are asleep.' "

"But they ain't, Polly," broke in Phronsie, suddenly sitting straight in Polly's lap.

"I know, pet, but these little things with the voices under the counter thought so, you see. And now I'm going to tell you all about it. Well, so out they crept—and they crept—and they crept—"

Joel and David huddled up as close as they could get to Polly, till they were almost in her lap—"And there, in the middle of the floor, were two little brown mice!"

Phronsie clapped her hands in glee.

"I'd rather have had a bear," said Joel, falling back disappointed.

"I hadn't," said David. "Go on, Polly, do."

"And those two little brown mice didn't seem to see Mr. Periwinkle and Mrs. Periwinkle and all the little Periwinkleses sitting round on their chairs and crickets, but they just danced off toward the big jar in the shop window."

"Oh, Polly! Are they going to take more pink and white sticks?" cried Phronsie, coming out of her glee and looking very sober.

"You'll see, pet. Well, and in a minute out jumped from their hole under the counter Father and Mother Mice, oh, just as big as you please, and just as smart, and they said, 'Wait, my children, you can't move the jar, you're too little,' and with one spring apiece they were up on the shelf; and then they ran up on the top of the jar and tumbled down inside among the pink and white sticks."

"Oh, oh!" cried the little Peppers.

"Yes; and 'Stand away there, my children,' came in very faint tones from the jar, 'or you'll be killed,' and one of the great big mice—it was Mr. Father Brown Mouse—stood on the very tipmost top of the jar, and let his tail dangle over.

" 'Now run down, my dear,' he said to his wife, Mrs. Mother Mouse, 'and stand on the ground—he called the shelf the ground, you know—'and pull my tail as hard as you did last night, you know. Then you must fly, just as you did last night too, when you see the jar coming, or you will be killed.' So Mrs. Mother Mouse promised she would do it all just as he told her, and she did. And over came the jar on its side on the shelf!"

"Oh, dear me!" exclaimed the little Peppers.

"Then in rushed the two little brown mice, and after them pell-mell the two big brown mice, to drag out the pink and white sticks. But Mr. Periwinkle hopped up, and so did Mrs. Periwinkle, and all the little Periwinkleses, and he said, 'No, sir, and No, ma'am, and no, you little Mousiekins, you don't take my pink and white sticks, and—' "

"Oh, Polly," cried Phronsie, grasping Polly's arm, "please do let the poor, sweet little brown mousies have the pink and white sticks. Please, Polly!" she begged, dreadfully excited.

"Hoh, hoh! Why, they were Mr. Periwinkle's pink and white sticks," cried Joel. "Oh, Polly! I hope he took a big stick and whacked 'em."

"Oh, no—no!" cried Phronsie, the tears beginning to come into her brown eyes. "Poor little brown mousies. Please, Polly, don't let him hurt them."

"Well, he shan't hurt them," said Polly, relenting. Davie twisted about very uncomfortably, longing for Polly to make the naughty little brown mice give back Mr. Periwinkle's pink and white sticks for Mrs. Periwinkle and the little Periwinkleses. But he couldn't go against Phronsie, so he swallowed his disappointment and said, "Do let the little brown mice go, Polly."

"Well, I will," said Polly, amid howls of disapproval by Joel. "Well, when Mr. Periwinkle said that, out jumped Mr. Father Brown Mouse, and Mrs. Mother Brown Mouse, and the two little brown mice, and each had a pink or a white stick in his mouth, and away they ran for their hole under the counter."

Phronsie leaned back in Polly's lap quite satisfied.

"Was it a white stick Mr. Father Brown Mouse had in his mouth?" asked Joel, smothering his disappointment as best he could.

"Yes, he had the white one," said Polly, smiling at him.

"Well, Mrs. Mother Brown Mouse got the best anyway," said Davie. "She got the pink one."

"Hulloa!" cried Ben rushing in, his face all aglow. "Well, I declare, if you are not all up in a bunch in this dark corner. Aren't you going to light a candle?"

Phronsie jumped out of Polly's lap, where she was nestling like a little bird, and rushed tumultuously up to him. "Oh, Bensie," she screamed, clasping her hands, "we've had pink and white sticks, and poor, sweet little brown mousies, and I liked 'em, I did," she cried.

XI

The Old Stagecoach

"G'LANG!" shouted Joel. " 'Twas just like Mr. Tisbett's, I know, Polly—wasn't it?" he screamed, coming up bright and shining after a race around the kitchen in which he cracked an imaginary whip and called to a make-believe pair of horses that were prancing this way and that and causing him no end of trouble.

"Yes," said Polly, "it was something like Mr. Tisbett's."

"Make it just *exactly* like his," begged Joel, crowding up to Polly.

"Take care, Joe," she warned. "You most made me upset that dish of potatoes. Go away now like a good boy, until I get ready to tell the story," and she bustled off into the pantry again.

Joel set up another prancing around the kitchen. This time little Davie joined in, and Phronsie came flying up in the rear, with very red cheeks and Seraphina upside down in her arms.

"Goodness me!" exclaimed Polly, coming out again with both hands full. "What a racket!"

"It's Mr. Tisbett's stagecoach," announced Joel with a flourish, and cracking his whip. "Hooray, there—get out of the way or you'll be run over! Any passengers?—want to get in, ma'am?"—with a bow to Polly.

"No," said Polly, "thank you, I'm not going away anywhere today, Mr. Tisbett."

"G'lang then!" and away they swept off rattling and lumbering along, and Polly was left in peace to get supper, for Mamsie would come home tired and hungry before long.

But at last everything was ready and the children, tired of play, began to tease Polly for the story she had promised them; and Joel drove Mr. Tisbett's big stagecoach into the corner, and tied the horses fast.

So Polly had to begin it right away. "Well, you know I told you it was a big stagecoach."

"Yes, yes, we know," said Joel, flopping down on a cricket, and folding his chubby hands. "Now go on."

"You see, there were four horses to this stagecoach," announced Polly, watching to see the effect of this on Joel.

"Whickets!" cried Joel, springing off from his cricket. "Oh, Polly—*four* horses!"

"Yes, there were," declared Polly, "four horses—two black ones and two white ones."

Joel stood perfectly still, and did not speak a word for several minutes, quite overcome at this. So Polly seized the opportunity to rush along as fast as she could in the story. "Well, and there was a funny old man who drove the stagecoach. He wasn't in the least like our Mr. Tisbett; he was little and round, and he had a squeaky voice; and he always said, 'Pay me your money before you get in, ma'am,' like this," said Polly, her voice going up in a funny little squeal, "which isn't the leastest bit in the world like our nice, good Mr. Tisbett."

"He lets me ride sometimes when I don't pay any money," said little Davie reflectively.

"And once," said Phronsie, pushing back her yellow hair to gaze into Polly's face, "he let Mamsie and me ride oh— away far off—up to the store, I guess."

"I know," said Polly, "he did, pet. Oh, our Mr. Tisbett is just as dear as he can be. Well, this stage driver was sometimes just like a snapping turtle. I guess he had the toothache, maybe."

"Oh, dear me!" said David, with a lively remembrance of his experience in that direction.

"Anyway, he was cross sometimes," said Polly, "so, you see, people didn't say much to him, but they just paid down their money into his hands and hopped in as soon as ever they could."

"How do you know two of the horses were black?" demanded Joel abruptly, and coming up behind her.

"Oh, goodness me, Joe, how you scared me!" exclaimed Polly with a jump. "Why, because I make 'em so in the story."

"Were they big, and did they dance and prance like this?" demanded Joel, kicking out behind, and then going through as wonderful evolutions as he thought his steeds could accomplish if he held the reins.

"Yes, I s'pose they could do everything," said Polly, "but I want to tell the story now."

"When I'm a big man I'm going to be a stage driver," announced Joel in a loud voice, "and I shall have six horses, so there, Polly Pepper."

"Well, one day this great big stagecoach I'm telling you about," said Polly, hurrying on with the story, as it was almost time for Mamsie to come, "was just as full as it could be, and there were two people upon the box with the funny old driver."

"That's me—one of 'em is," declared Joel; "and you—you may sit up there too, Dave."

"Yes, I'm going to sit there too," said little David, hugging himself in great satisfaction.

"There was a fat old woman who took up most of one whole seat; and she had a parrot in a big cage, tied over with a newspaper, all except a hole at the top so it could breathe. And the old woman kept leaning over and peeping into this hole, and asking, 'Hey, pretty Polly, how are you now?' and Polly Parrot always screamed back, 'Polly wants a cracker—Polly wants a cracker.' "

"And didn't anybody give her a cracker, Polly?" asked Phronsie.

"No," said Polly, "they didn't. Well, and—"

"Why didn't somebody give her a cracker?" persisted Phronsie gravely.

"Oh, because they didn't have any, and then—besides, oh, she had plenty of seeds in her cage. Well, so—"

"Did she like seeds?" asked Phronsie, pulling Polly's arm gently to make her pay attention.

"Yes, I guess so," said Polly absently. "Well, so you see—"

"Please let somebody give her a cracker, Polly," said

Phronsie in a grieved little voice that made Polly stop at once.

"Oh, I will, pet," cried Polly at sight of her face. "Yes indeed, that old green parrot shall have a cracker. The little thin man in the corner of the stagecoach felt in his pocket, and he found one, and he gave it to her."

"I think he was nice," said Phronsie, in great relief.

"Well, let me see—where was I?" said Polly, wrinkling her brows. "Oh! Well, in the other side of the stagecoach, sitting with their backs to the horses—"

"Two of them were black and two were white," said Joel.

"Yes," Polly hurried on to get him off from the horses, "well, there were three boys crowded into the seat, and they had a basket they were carrying to their grandmother, and there was a chicken pie in it."

"Oh, my!" exclaimed all the little Peppers together.

"Yes, and it was rich and fat and juicy," said Polly, for her life not being able to keep from saying it.

"Oh, Polly! I want some, I do," broke in little David imploringly. Joel was just going to say so himself, but he caught Polly's eye.

"Well, you can't have any," she said grimly. And she set her teeth together hard. How splendidly she could make a chicken pie if she ever had the chance! Why couldn't the Little Brown House ever have anything? And for a moment she drooped her shoulders in a sorry little fashion, and all the brightness went out of her round face.

"We never have anything," said little Davie plaintively.

"Never," said Phronsie sadly, shaking her yellow head. And there they sat, two sorry little figures, just ready to cry.

"Be still," said Joel, with a savage pinch on Davie's arm.
"Ow!"

"Well, you're making Polly sick."

At the word "sick" Phronsie raised her head. "Are you
sick, Polly?" she cried, getting into her lap.

"No, that is—I was naughty," said Polly, waking out of
her dream.

"Oh, you're not naughty, Polly," cried Phronsie, kissing
her. "You couldn't be."

"Yes, I was," declared Polly; "just as naughty as I could
be, and I ought to be put in the corner."

The idea of Polly's being put in the corner so astonished
the children that no one spoke, so she plunged into the story
as fast as she could. "Well, now, you know the little thin
man I told you about over in the other corner, who gave
Polly Parrot a cracker, had a—"

"Yes, I know," said Phronsie, patting her pinafore in a
satisfied way. "He was a nice man, Polly, and I like him."

"Well, he had a big black dog with him, and it was under
his seat."

"Oh, dear!" cried all the children together.

"Yes. Well, there were some other passengers in the stagecoach, and—"

"Never mind about them. Tell about the big black dog,"
begged Joel.

"Yes, tell about the big black dog," begged the other two.

"Well, I will. Now, the big black dog smelled the chicken
pie, you see, before the stagecoach had rattled on many
miles."

"Oh, dear!" cried the children.

"Yes. You see all these passengers were going down to Bayberry, and it was an awfully cold day, and everybody was all wrapped up in big woolen shawls, and they had their caps pulled down over their ears, and they all had mittens on. Oh, and the chicken-pie dish was hot when the boys' mother gave it to them to carry to their grandmother. It was just out of the oven, you know, so they took turns in carrying the basket on their knees. It kept their hands warmer, you know."

"That was nice," said little Davie reflectively.

"Wasn't it? Well, they were all going along as fine as you please," cried Polly, racing on in the story, "when all of a sudden—Whoa!—Gee—whoop—whoa-a!" called Polly in a very loud voice; and she pulled hard on an imaginary pair of reins and held in two pairs of fiery steeds.

"I can stop 'em better'n that," screamed Joel, springing to his feet. "Here, give me the reins." So he whoaed and pulled and roared and at last announced that the horses were brought up standing, and the big stagecoach was quite still.

"Thank you, Joel," said Polly. "Well, then, down jumps the fat little cross stage driver from his box, and he comes up to the door. 'Fly out of here,' he says, 'every one of you.'

" 'What must we get out for?' asked the woman with the parrot. You see, she was very fat and she didn't wish to be hurried out in this way.

" 'Get out this minute,' roared the little cross old driver, 'or I'll tumble the stage over, ma'am.'

"So she got out with a great deal of trouble, and set her cage, with the parrot in it, all tied up in a newspaper, except a hole in the top for him to breathe by—"

"Please don't let them spill out his cracker, Polly," said Phronsie anxiously.

"No, I won't, pet. You see, the little thin man stuck it in very tight in the bars over the seed cup, Phronsie."

"Polly, I like that little thin man very much, I do," declared Phronsie in a burst of enthusiasm.

"So do I, Phronsie. Well, and then the other passengers all got out. They had to, you see, because the cross little stage driver was screaming and roaring at them, you know, and last of all the three boys with the chicken-pie basket got out. And they set it on the grass, very carefully, under a bush by the roadside; and then they ran with all the rest of the people to see what the matter was with the stagecoach. Everybody ran but the big black dog."

"Now I know that he is going to eat up the boys' grandmother's chicken pie," cried Joel. "Oh, dear me!"

"Hush—don't tell things till I get to 'em, Joe," cried Polly, who dearly loved to announce all the startling surprises in her stories with as much of a flourish as possible.

"Well, I most know he is," said Joel, subsiding into a loud whisper. "Ain't he, Polly?"

"Maybe. Well, now, you know everybody was peering and looking this way and that, all over the big stagecoach. 'I don't see anything broken,' said the little thin man, getting down on his knees on the hard frozen ground to examine it underneath.

" 'And neither do I,' said the big fat woman very angrily, 'and I'm just going to get in again.'

" 'No you won't, either, ma'am,' declared the cross little

stage driver, 'for this is my stagecoach, and I tell you I heard something crack.'

" ' 'Twas a piece of a stone in the road, I guess,' said the thin little man, getting up from his knees, and brushing the dirt off.

" 'Or a stick you ran over most likely,' said another.

"But the little old stage driver said, 'No,' very crossly. 'It wasn't either of these things.' It sounded just like the bottom of his stagecoach cracking, and he wasn't going to have it smashed. And he kept them all out there in the cold till he looked over and under and around it very carefully. At last, as he couldn't find anything, not even the smallest, tiniest bit of a crack, he let them get in again. So the big fat woman picked up her parrot in the cage, with the newspaper tied over it, all except a hole in the top for it to breathe through, and everybody else got their things and clambered in—all but the three boys, who couldn't find the chicken pie they were carrying to their grandmother, that had been under the bush by the roadside."

"Oh, dear me!" they all exclaimed, while Phronsie clasped her small hands in despair, and sat quite still.

"No, it wasn't there," declared Polly, shaking her brown head—"not so much as a scrap of the crust or a bit of the dish or a single speck of the basket. And oh, how those boys did feel!"

"What did they do?" cried Joel, feeling such a calamity not to be borne.

"They just couldn't do anything," said Polly. "And down they sat on three stones by the roadside. And everybody had stopped getting in, and turned to help look for the pie. And pretty soon they all heard a dreadful noise."

"What was it?" asked Phronsie fearfully.

"Oh, now I know it is the chicken pie coming back, and those three boys can take it to their grandmother," exclaimed little David joyfully.

"Hoh—hoh—a chicken pie can't come back like that," said Joel with a snort.

"And the little thin man came scurrying out of the bushes and dragging after him his big black dog," said Polly with a fine flourish, "who smelled of chicken pie all over his face; and he wouldn't look at anybody, and especially the three boys sitting on their stones by the roadside; but he rolled his eyes up like this," Polly looked off sideways, and up at an imaginary sky, "and his master, the thin little man, said, and he dragged him by his collar up in front of those boys, 'Now, sir, say you're sorry you've eaten up all that pie'; and that dog said, 'Bark—bark!' just as loud, oh, you can't think!"

Phronsie screamed in great excitement, and clapped her hands together to think of the big dog. Then she grew very sober. "But what will the boys do, Polly?"

"And the grandmother?" finished Joel and David together.

"Oh, the little thin man said, 'Hold your hands, boys,' and then he dropped one—two—three—four—five—six gold pieces into them."

"Gold?" screamed Joel excitedly.

"Yes, real, true shiny gold," cried Polly, nodding away. "Enough to buy two dozen chicken pies, all richer and juicier and better than the one the boys were carrying to their grandmother."

" 'Now let's all hop into the stagecoach,' cried the little thin man—Why, here's Mamsie!"

XII

Mr. Nutcracker; the Story That Wasn't a Story

"Come on!" whooped Joel, rushing into the kitchen and tossing his cap in the corner. "My chores are all done. Now tell the story, Polly, tell the story!" he clamored.

"Oh, dear me!" began Polly in a vexed tone, and looking up at the old clock in the corner. Then she remembered what Mamsie had said once, "If you promise anything, do it cheerfully." "I will, Joey," she finished, a smile running over her face. "Just wait one minute," and she flew into the buttery.

"I can't wait a single bit of a minute," grumbled Joel.

But Polly was back almost before he could say another word. "Now, says I," she cried, "we'll have the story, Joe."

"It's got to be a long one," declared Joel, a remark he never failed to make on like occasions.

"All right," said Polly gaily. "Now, I thought up something you'll like, I guess, for this story. It's about Mr. Nut-cracker!"

"Jolly!" exclaimed Joel, hugely pleased. "I guess I shall, Polly," and ripples of satisfaction ran over his round cheeks. "Well, do hurry!"

"I've got to do some work," said Polly, pausing a moment to think. "I can't ever sit down to tell stories in the daytime without I'm working—ever in all this world, Joe Pepper. And Mamsie has just taken all the sacks home to Mr. Atkins; she finished 'em last night. Whatever'll I do?" she wrinkled her brows, and stood lost in thought.

"You might mend our stockings," said Joel, knocking one set of toes impatiently against the other. "Do hurry, Polly, and think of something," he implored, his face falling.

"Mamsie's done those," said Polly. "I peeked into the mending basket after breakfast, and they're all finished and rolled up into little balls."

"Well, come on, then," said Joel, thoroughly out of patience. "If there isn't any work, do tell the story, Polly."

"It doesn't seem right to be sitting down in the morning, without I am working," said Polly slowly. "I don't know when I've done it. But there really isn't any sewing and the biscuits I was going to make can be done just as well by and by, so I s'pose I can tell you the story now, Joey."

"Come on, then!" shouted Joel, throwing himself flat on the floor, and drumming with his heels. "Do hurry up, Polly Pepper!"

So Polly sat down on the floor, feeling still very queer to be telling stories in the daytime without a needle in her fingers, and Joel squirmed along and laid his head in her lap. "I'm glad you ain't sewing," he declared in great satisfaction, " 'cause now you can smooth my hair."

So Polly smoothed and patted his stubby head in a way that Joel liked to have Mamsie do, and presently she began:

"Mr. Nutcracker had a house—"

Rap—rap—came somebody's fingers on the old green door.

"Oh, bother!" cried Joel, jumping up. And Polly skipped, too, in surprise, for visitors didn't come very often to the Little Brown House door, and they both ran as fast as they could to open it.

An old man stood on the flat doorstone, leaning both hands on a knobby old stick; and his head, underneath his torn hat, was bobbing as he trembled with age. The children stared at him in dismay. "I'm very hungry," he said, looking at Polly. "I haven't eaten anything today. Can't you give me a bite?"

Oh, dear! Polly looked at Joel in dismay. There wasn't anything in the house except some cold potatoes that Mrs. Pepper was going to fry for dinner, and Polly's biscuits, as she called them by courtesy, that were still to be made, as the bread had given out.

"We haven't anything"—she began, in a faltering voice.

"Why, Polly Pepper!" exclaimed Joel loudly, and crowding past her to get a better view of their visitor. "We have too—lots and lots," for Joel never could bear to have people think they were poor.

"Where is it?" asked Polly, turning on him. Then she flew around again, for the old man was sinking down on the flat stone. "Oh, dear me! Don't please, poor old man," she begged, trying to help him up to his feet again.

"I'm very hungry," he quavered, shaking over his stick.

"Come into the house," said Polly, with both hands under his arm. "Joe, take his other arm—and you can sit in our Mamsie's big chair. It's splendid, and it will rest you."

The old man nodded, and set his poor trembling feet just where Polly told him to; and at last, Joel puffing and pushing on his side with a great deal of importance, he was helped into the kitchen, and set down in Mother Pepper's big calico-covered chair over in the corner.

"That's so nice," he said with a deep sigh, and resting his head on his shaking hands.

"Joel," said Polly, drawing off that individual into the entry with great difficulty, as he had no eyes or ears for anything but their visitor, "I'm afraid he's going to die, he's so very hungry. I must get him something to eat. Now I'm going to bake my biscuits; Mamsie'd let me give him some of those, I know."

"No, no!" cried Joel. "You've got to tell me about Mr. Nutcracker, Polly," seizing her gown.

"For shame, Joe," cried Polly warmly, "when that poor old man is maybe going to die because he hasn't had anything to eat. What would Mamsie say if she could hear you?"

Joel ducked his stubby head and kicked the floor with his toes in a shamefaced way. "Well, you may, Polly," he cried, "and I'll help you," he added, brightening up and running into the kitchen after her.

"So you shall," cried Polly briskly. "See if there's plenty of wood in the box, Joe, the first thing," as she hurried into the pantry to get the baking materials.

"Yes, there is," declared Joel, poking his head back of the

stove to investigate, "lots and lots, Polly Pepper. I'm going to put some more in," and he set up immediately a great clatter that told the work was well under way.

"Don't put too much in, Joe," warned Polly, knowing his energies in that direction. "You will have the house afire. Goodness me, do take out that last stick," as she came in with the bread bowl.

"Can't," said Joe. "It's got little sparks on the end."

"Then I'll blow 'em out," said Polly, setting down the bread bowl on the table; and running over to the stove, she pulled out, to Joel's extreme dislike, the big stick he had last crammed in, and suited the action to the word. "There, you've got plenty in already, goodness knows, Joe Pepper!" she declared, getting up with a very red face. "You know Mamsie doesn't like us to crowd the stove tight chock full. It burns splendidly, this new one does, and we'll have the chimney afire if we don't look out."

"The chimney ain't afire," grunted Joel. "I'll run out and see." And he dashed toward the door.

"Come back. Of course it isn't now," said Polly with a laugh, and flying over to the baking table. "Oh, dear me! I ought not to laugh when that poor old man is hungry." Then she suddenly dropped everything and ran over to him trembling away in Mamsie's big chair.

"We haven't anything in the house to eat but some cold potatoes," she said, the color all over her face, "and our mother is going to fry those for our dinner when she comes home. But I'm going to bake some biscuits, if you *could* wait, poor old man. They'll soon be done, for we've got a new stove and it bakes splendidly." Then Polly hurried back to her table, while the old man mumbled something down in his throat, she couldn't tell what, he shook so.

"It's good Phronsie and David are over to Grandma Bascom's," said Polly, flying at her work, "for she'd worry dreadfully over that poor old man, and she'd tease me to hurry and bake 'em fast, so I couldn't do a thing. There, now that pan's ready for the oven."

"Let me carry 'em and put 'em in," cried Joel, who, having given up his plan to rush out and investigate the old chimney from the small dooryard, was now hanging over Polly's baking table, and dividing his attention upon her work and the old visitor over in the corner. "Let me, Polly," springing up, and holding out both hands.

"Oh, I'm afraid," began Polly. Then remembering how he had to wait for the story, she added hastily, "Well, be careful, Joe," as she put the pan into his outstretched hands.

"I'll be careful," said Joe, marching off with his black eyes fastened on the pan which he was carrying carefully in both hands. "Now, says I, you're going into the oven, Mr. Biscuits."

Polly rushed back into the pantry to get another pan, when she heard Joel's voice: "Oh, I couldn't help it, Polly," and when she flew out, there was Joel sitting on the floor in a heap and the pan was upside down beside him, while several little lumps of dough seemed to be trying to get back of the stove.

"Oh, Joe, are you hurt?" cried Polly, flinging down her empty pan, and running up to him.

"No—no—no!" roared Joel in the greatest distress, "but

I've up—up—set—upset—upset"—and he screamed on worse than ever.

"Never mind," said Polly soothingly, and swallowing something in her throat as she looked at the poor little lumps of dough on the floor. "See, you didn't spill 'em all, Joe," and she turned the pan right side up. "There are some stuck fast."

Joel, at that, took out one black eye from under his arms, and regarded the pan through his tears.

"And you are scaring that poor old man most to death," said Polly, hastily gathering up the little lumps of dough. "Look at him, Joe."

Joel stopped instantly as he looked over at Mamsie's corner. There sat the poor old man, staring at them both and hanging to the arm of the big chair in consternation.

"Now you've got to go over and tell him that you won't cry any more," said Polly decidedly, "else I don't know what will happen. Maybe he'll go out on the doorstep again, and tumble straight down. Just think, Joel Pepper!" And with that she opened the oven door and popped in the pan that had a few lonely little dough lumps scattered in it.

Joel, thus adjured, scampered over to the poor old man. "I—I—won't—cry any more, sir," he blurted out, twisting his face dreadfully.

"Hey?" said the old man. "What's the matter?" So Joel told him the whole story.

And the old man, who hadn't heard the tumble and the upset of the pan, only Joel's roars, soon quieted down and leaned back in his chair.

"And now," said Polly, over by the table, "I shouldn't

wonder if this pan was ready for you to carry over and put in the oven, Joey."

"What?" exclaimed Joel, not believing his ears. "You going to let me put that one in?"

"Yes," said Polly, "to be sure. You won't stumble this time, Joe, if you look where you're going."

"I caught my toe in the rug," said Joe, racing over to the table. "I was looking at the pan and I didn't see where I was going."

"Well, you must use your eyes so you do see where you're going," said Polly with a merry laugh. "There now," and she put the second pan in Joel's happy hands. "This one will go all right, I guess."

And this one did. And it was presently shut up tight in the hot oven, along with the lonely little dough lumps, now puffing up finely; and Joel, proud as he could be, strutted up and down the kitchen floor. And Polly put away her baking things, and soon the old kitchen was spick span, it was so fresh and tidy.

"And now," she said, "we can't do anything for that poor old man till those biscuits are done. Oh, dear me, how perfectly splendid. Here comes Mamsie!"

And out through the old doorway, and over the flat stone, raced Polly, with Joel at her heels. And they seized Mother Pepper on both sides, holding her arms, while Joel took her big bundle, all the time pouring the story of the poor old man, and the dreadful state he was in, and the biscuits baking, and, oh! Joel must confess how he had upset the pan with the first ones, though Polly tried to stop him, and oh! couldn't Mamsie fry him some potatoes right away, and ever so much more, till they all three stood in the old kitchen.

"He must have some tea," said Mrs. Pepper, with a sharp look at him, and throwing off her shawl. "Run, Polly, and get the tea caddy."

"Oh, Mammy!" exclaimed Polly. Mother Pepper never had tea unless she had caught cold or was so tired she must take it or get sick, and there was now such a very little bit down in the bottom of the caddy. And Polly stood quite still.

"Run, I say, Polly," commanded Mrs. Pepper, and she pulled the old teakettle into a hotter part of the stove. "A fine cup of tea will do his bones good, more'n anything else."

"There's such a little bit left," gasped Polly, not moving.

"Polly!" Mrs. Pepper turned suddenly on her. "Why, Polly—hush, he'll hear you. For shame, child. He's such a very poor old man."

"And then you won't have any," said Polly, at her end of self-control. "Oh, Mamsie! I wish I hadn't brought him in," she added under her breath, and she burst into tears.

Mrs. Pepper only stopped to pat her head, and then she hurried into the pantry and brought out the tea caddy. And Polly, with the tears racing over her face, watched her as the precious tea was poured into the little black pot and set on the stove.

"Now run, Polly, child," cried Mother Pepper as cheerily as ever, "and get the big pink-and-white cup on the upper shelf." This used to be Father Pepper's, and was carefully laid away; so while Polly ran off with her tears, wiping them on her apron, Mrs. Pepper sliced up some cold potatoes, and set them in the spider to fry. Joel in the meantime had been opening his mother's big bundle, as he always tried to do whenever she brought home the fresh supply of sacks and coats to make, so he heard nothing of what was going on.

"And I guess you better have a look at those biscuits in the oven," observed Mrs. Pepper wisely, as she sliced away. So Polly ran and kneeled down before the stove, and drew out first one pan and then the other—the one with the lonely little lumps in it—

"Oh, Mamsie!" she exclaimed happily. "See, they're as fine as they can be!"

And sure enough they were; every biscuit had turned a lovely brown, and it had puffed up in just the right place, as much as to say, "You see, we did our duty."

"So they are," cried Mrs. Pepper, pleased to see Polly all right once more. "It beats all, Polly, to see how nicely you can bake things. Mother's proud of you."

Polly set down the two hot pans on the kitchen table and ran round back of her mother and dropped a kiss on the black hair. "I'm awfully sorry," she whispered.

"I know it," said Mrs. Pepper. "And now we just won't say any more about it, Polly, child." Then she briskly began to turn her potato slices that were sizzling away in the spider in the cheeriest fashion.

And Polly got a little old towel, very clean and nice, and spread it on the tray, and she put the big pink-and-white cup upon it, and Mamsie poured the tea into it, and dished out some crisp potato bits on a plate, and Polly put some little biscuits around it all, and there was a dinner fit for a king!

"Oh, my!" howled Joel, smelling the potatoes. "What

have you got?" jumping up, and nearly upsetting Polly and tray and all, as she carried it slowly across the kitchen to the old man's chair.

"Take care, Joe," warned Mrs. Pepper, following to help Polly.

"Oh—oh!" Joel seemed to lose sight of everything but Father Pepper's pink-and-white cup, and he pointed an astonished finger at it.

"I know it," said Mrs. Pepper, setting her lips together firmly; "Father'd like to have us let the old man take it. Now, Polly, you can feed him the potato, and—"

"No, let me," said Joel, crowding in between, and trying to get possession of the two-tined fork.

"No, I think Polly better, but you can break the biscuits apart," said Mrs. Pepper. So pretty soon the old man was sitting up quite straight for him; and after he had taken one or two good draughts of the steaming tea, he felt quite revived, and let Polly feed him the crisp potato bits, and the biscuits which Joel industriously broke apart, until Mrs. Pepper put down the empty cup, and regarded Polly's plate, on which there wasn't a scrap of anything left but the fork.

"I can't thank you," said the old man, quite heartened up, and looking around at them all.

"No, don't try," said Mrs. Pepper. "You can go to sleep now. Come, children," and she drew them off into the bedroom.

"Now, Polly," she said, when the door was shut, "you must run down to Parson Henderson's at once. He'll know what to do with the poor old man, for we can't let him go. He'll tumble down in the road."

"I will, mother," cried Polly, tying on her sunbonnet. "What'll I say, Mammy?"

"Say? Why, tell just what it all is—how he came, and ask Parson Henderson what we are to do. Run along, child, and don't let the grass grow under your feet."

"Will Parson Henderson know what to do with him?" cried Joel in a loud whisper.

"Yes, of course," said Polly quickly. "Parson Henderson knows everything. But s'pose he shouldn't be home and I sh'd see Miss Jerusha!" and Polly's round cheek turned pale with fright.

"Go along, child, and don't worry about things till you get to 'em," said Mrs. Pepper. "The Lord'll provide, and I believe He'll let Parson Henderson be home."

So Polly ran off on the wings of the wind and presently back she came in state, riding in the big old chaise that Parson Henderson had borrowed from one of his parishioners. And on the way the minister told so many pleasant things that Polly wished, if it hadn't been for Mamsie's anxiety over the old man, that that ride might last forever. And then they were in front of the Little Brown House, to which they drove up with a flourish, bringing Joel out with an envious whoop, and Mrs. Pepper to the window.

And then Parson Henderson and Mrs. Pepper and the children helped the poor old man tenderly into the big chaise, to go to the nice place that the parson knew about, till he would be well enough to go on his journey. And then home came Phronsie and David from Grandma Bascom's, down the lane, just in time to see the chaise go whirling off; and Ben, hungry as a beaver, came rushing in from his work for dinner. So Mother Pepper and Polly had to fly to get the midday meal ready, leaving it to Joel to tell the story in his own way, an opportunity that he improved to the utmost.

And after dinner Ben said that he wanted Joel to go back with him to work, for there was wood to pile and that meant ten cents more pay at night. So it was evening before Joel thought of the interrupted story, and he screamed right out, "Oh, Polly Pepper, you didn't finish about Mr. Nutcracker!"

"No," said Polly, "I didn't. And how could I?"

"Well, you must tell it now," declared Joel in a very injured fashion.

"Why, Joel Pepper, look at that clock!" cried Polly, pointing to it.

"It's only half—a little after seven," said Joel, looking every way but at the clock.

"Oh, Joe, it's twenty-five minutes to eight!" said Davie, running up to stand under the clock.

"Well, that isn't much," grumbled Joel.

"It's five minutes after your bedtime, Joel," said Mother Pepper, going into the bedroom for her big work basket, "so take yourself off."

"And I'll finish Mr. Nutcracker tomorrow, Joe," promised Polly, as Joel clattered upstairs.

XIII

Mr. Nutcracker

And so it came about that Polly began on the morrow, without any more ado, the story of Mr. Nutcracker, for Mother Pepper said that she might sit down as soon as the dishes were washed and tell it to Joel. So this is it:

"Mr. Nutcracker," began Polly in her gayest fashion, "was very high up in the world. In fact, he didn't like to have anybody above him. So he built his house clear up ever so far above everybody else. Then he was quite satisfied."

"What kind of a house?" broke in Joel.

"Never mind. You wait till you hear more of the story," said Polly. "Well, Mrs. Nutcracker liked her house that he built her very much indeed. That is, she would have liked it, but the children, the little Nutcrackerses, you see, wouldn't stay in."

"Oh, dear me!" exclaimed Joel.

"No, they kept jumping out as fast as they could. And those that didn't jump out, tumbled out."

123

"Oh, dear me!" said Joel again.

"Until it was very dreadful," declared Polly, shaking her brown head, "for it kept poor Mrs. Nutcracker running every minute to the door of her house to try to keep her children in. At last she said to her husband, Mr. Nutcracker, 'Pa, you surely must build me a house nearer to the ground.'"

"And did he?" cried Joel, absorbed in interest.

"No, he said, 'Oh, never! No Nutcracker has ever lived lower down in the world than we are! I can't do it, my dear!'"

"That was bad of him," exploded Joel with very red cheeks. "Bad, mean old man not to do as Mrs. Nutcracker wanted him to do. Wasn't he, Polly?"

"Well, you'll see," said Polly, hurrying along as fast as she could. "And the little Nutcrackerses kept jumping and tumbling out of the house at a great rate, until one day something very dreadful happened."

"Tell about it," cried Joel, hugely pleased.

"Yes, I'm going to. Well, Pa Nutcracker had gone off about his business and Mrs. Nutcracker was doing the work, when suddenly there was a loud noise down on the ground and two or three of the little Nutcrackerses jumped out to the door, and leaned over, and said they were going down to see what it was, and then away they rushed with a hop, skip, and a jump. And six of them, brothers and sisters, said they were going, and they were in such a hurry they didn't look straight before them, and they tumbled through the air—whiz—whiz—"

"Did they come on their heads?" cried Joel excitedly.

"No, they stuck their feet out, and they came right down

on them," said Polly, "just as good as could be. So you see they weren't hurt a bit. Well, and then as Mrs. Nutcracker was all alone, why she thought she might as well go too. So she went down. And there was the Nutcracker house left all by itself. Then came the dreadful thing."

"What was it?" asked Joel fearfully, and snuggling closer to Polly.

"Well, at first it was just as still," said Polly, dropping her voice to a little whisper, "you can't think how still it was, Joey Pepper. Not a creature was stirring and—"

"Why didn't she shut the door," cried Joel, "when she went out, and put the key in her pocket? Say, Polly?"

"Why, there wasn't any key," said Polly, racing along. "Now, you mustn't stop me any more, Joe, else I never'll get through."

"Mr. Nutcracker wasn't a nice man at all, I think," said Joel in great disapproval, "if he couldn't give 'em a key. Was he, Polly?"

"You'll see," said Polly, redoubling her speed.

"Well, when Mrs. Nutcracker ran along so swiftly, being in such a hurry, you see, her great long train to her dress swept out and—"

"Is it a train of cars?" asked Joel, his eyes sticking out as far as possible. "Oh, Polly! I've never seen 'em, 'cept in a picture."

"No," said Polly. Then she burst out laughing, "How could a train of cars be hanging on Mrs. Nutcracker's dress, Joe? Dear me, that would be funny!"

"You said train," declared Joel, dreadfully disappointed.

"I know, but this is different. It's something made like

the rest of the dress, and it hangs off when the one who's got the dress on walks, and she can swish it around perfectly splendidly; just like this, Joel Pepper," and Polly hopped to her feet, and began to parade up and down the old kitchen floor, holding an imaginary trailing gown and then letting it fall like a peacock's tail as it swept the ground, while she held her head high and sailed off.

"Hoh, how you look!" cried Joel in disdain.

"Joel," she cried, coming up to him, with sparkling eyes and her cheeks rosy red, "it must be perfectly lovely to have a train to your dress. Oh, don't I wish I had one just like that picture in Mr. Beebe's book! Then I'd have a fan, a red fan just like that lady—no," said Polly, wrinkling her brows as she tried to decide, "I b'lieve I'd rather have a pink fan, Ben does so love pink. Yes, my gown shall be pink, too, pink satin with sweet little white flowers all over it, and shiny. Oh, Joel, it shall shine just like everything!" and Polly swept up and down again like a lady of fashion.

"Well, that isn't Mrs. Nutcracker," called Joel loudly, in an injured tone.

"Oh, I forgot!" exclaimed Polly, all her airs and graces tumbling off from her in a flash, and she scurried back to Joel. "Oh, let me see! Where was I?"

"You said Mrs. Nutcracker's long train swept out," supplied Joel.

"Oh, yes, so I did. Well, and you know the dreadful creature that was always watching to see if he could find the Nutcracker house left all alone caught sight of her long train sweeping away, and he snapped his green eyes with delight, and he laughed a perfectly dreadful laugh, and he said, 'Now I have it, now I have it!'"

"Oh! Who was he?" screamed Joel, flinging himself forward almost into Polly's lap.

"Wait, and you'll see," she replied, laughing. "Well, so, sure enough, just as soon as Mrs. Nutcracker was fairly off, in hurried this dreadful creature, right in the doorway of the Nutcracker house."

"Did he get on Mr. Nutcracker's bed?" cried Joel.

"Wait and see," said Polly again.

"You say, 'wait and see,' every single time I ask anything," grumbled Joel.

"And I am going to all through this story," said Polly coolly, "so it won't be any use for you to ask me, Joe. Well, and there he was as quick as could be, inside that dear little house, and all those Nutcrackerses away."

Polly spread her hands in a sad little way.

"Oh, dear me!" exclaimed Joel in distress.

"Well, now you know when Mrs. Nutcracker went down she didn't mean to stay long, but she met a friend—"

"Who was it?" asked Joel abruptly.

"Oh, it was—dear me!" said Polly, bursting into a little laugh. "It was her cousin, and—"

"You said it was her friend," corrected Joel.

"Well, and so it was," said Polly merrily. "I'm sure a cousin is a very nice friend, indeed."

"I wish I had a cousin," said Joel. "I've never had one. Why don't we have some, Polly?"

"Some what?" asked Polly absently, with her mind on the story, wondering how she should end it.

"Some cousins," said Joel, twitching her gown. "Why don't we ever have any; say, Polly?"

"Oh, some folks don't have any," said Polly, stifling a

sigh as she thought how very nice it would be to have a houseful of cousins to go and see.

"I s'pose poor folks don't have any," said Joel reflectively.

"Um—maybe," said Polly, her chin in her hands, and only half hearing what he said.

"Well, do go on," begged Joel in alarm lest he should never get the end of that story, and jogging her elbow. "What next, Polly?"

"Oh!" Polly started suddenly and rushed on again. "Yes, there he was, that dreadful creature right in the—"

"You said that," cried Joel. "Mrs. Nutcracker met her cousin, you told already. Now what next?"

"So I did," said Polly brightly. "Yes, she met her cousin, and so they stopped to talk and to ask after each other's families, and that took a good deal of time, you know; and all this while there was that dreadful creature in Mrs. Nutcracker's little house."

"Oh, dear me!" cried Joel.

"Yes, and there were all the little Nutcrackerses having such a good time running around, trying to find out what the noise was all about, and Mr. Nutcracker, too, he—"

"Polly," asked Joel suddenly, "what was the noise about?"

"Oh, it was nothing but a boy driving a lot of pigs to market, and they wouldn't go the way he wanted 'em to so he chased 'em, and he switched his stick over their backs and they squealed awfully. And the little Nutcrackerses were so sorry that they had taken the trouble to come down just for that, so they said they'd race up home again and see who would beat."

"Oh, Polly!" cried Joel, in great excitement. "And did

he'd like it, he was quite sure he should. And so, on Polly hurried. "Well, there was Mr. Nutcracker with Mrs. Nutcracker and all those little Nutcrackerses hanging on to him, oh, so tight and fast! So he couldn't get away you see, although he begged and begged. And then Mrs. Nutcracker spoke up loud and sharp, 'Children, you hold tight on to your Pa and don't you let him go, while I run down and get the cousins to come and help us.'"

"Oh, Polly! Now I know," exclaimed Joel in great glee. "There's going to be a big, big fight. I like it a great deal better to have all those cousins come and help. I do, Polly, truly."

"So I thought," said Polly bobbing her brown head. "Well, I must hurry. So Mrs. Nutcracker ran as fast as her feet would carry her down to the ground, and she called every one of those cousins she'd been talking to such a little while ago, and the big tears rolled out from her eyes and she couldn't speak for a whole minute.

" 'Dear, dear, dear!' cried all the cousins, huddling around her. 'What is the matter, Cousin Nutcracker?'

"And then she finally told them all about it and every one of those cousins promised he'd go up with Mrs. Nutcracker and help to drive out the bad, wicked creature who had stolen into her house.

"Oh, that was nice!" screamed Joe, in a joyful tone. "Now there's going to be a big, big fight," and he wriggled all over in great satisfaction.

"And so up they all came in a troop—I guess there was a dozen of 'em," said Polly.

"Oh, my!" exclaimed Joel.

"Yes, and Mrs. Nutcracker rushed up ahead of 'em all to her husband. 'Pa,' she cried, 'here we are—we'll help you to drive out the bad, naughty, wicked thing from our house.'

"And every single one of those cousins said, 'Yes, we'll help you, Cousin Nutcracker.'

"So the little Nutcrackerses let their pa go and they were very glad to do so, for they ached all over holding him so long—he was very big, you know, and he kicked dreadfully, and bit and scratched, whenever he didn't like things, and—"

"That wasn't nice in a man," observed Joel. "I ain't going to bite and scratch when I'm grown up, Polly."

"Hey?" said Polly. "Oh!" and then she laughed. "Well, don't interrupt again, Joel," she warned, holding up her finger. "Well, Father Nutcracker, he said, 'Now, Ma and children,' turning to the little Nutcrackerses, 'and you, cousins, let's plan how we'll do this thing. Since you've come, you might as well help, though I could have done very well alone. Now, I'm going ahead and just as soon as my nose sticks in the doorway, do you jump in and scream, "Now we got you!" and we'll all hop on that dreadful horrid creature, and beat him, and pitch him out of our house.' "

Joel gripped Polly's arm in speechless enjoyment.

" 'All right,' said the cousins, bobbing their heads. And, 'I approve of your plan, Pa,' said Mrs. Nutcracker very proudly. And the little Nutcrackerses hopped and skipped in joy, and so they started."

Joel's eyes got very big, but he didn't say a word as he clung to Polly's arm.

"And don't you think," said Polly, "that the hateful, bad old thing in the Nutcrackers' house didn't hear them coming; they all stepped on the tips of their toes, you know; and he just winked and blinked his green eyes as he said to himself, 'I'll catch 'em every one pretty soon.' And then he looked up, and there was Mr. Nutcracker's nose in the doorway."

Joel jumped as if he were shot. "Oh, Polly!" he screamed.

"And after him came all those cousins and Mrs. Nutcracker. She was slower, 'cause she was so big, you know. Yes, and every single one of those little Nutcrackerses, they just ran in between all the others, and all together they jumped and hopped onto the great big dreadful creature, and—"

"Make him hop at them, and kick, too, Polly, that big man with the green eyes!" howled Joel, quite gone in excitement.

"Oh, it was very dreadful," exclaimed Polly, holding up both hands, "for about a minute or so. And instead of the great, dreadful thing crying out, 'I've got you!' he began to whimper and beg, 'Oh, let me go! Let me go!' And pretty soon all the whole bunch of Nutcrackerses, and their cousins who had come to help, just lifted up that bad, wicked, horrid thing with the green eyes that had stolen into their house, and they pitched him head over heels through the doorway, and down—down. And he was ten feet long so he was dreadful slow in—"

"Oh, Polly Pepper!" roared Joel. "What you saying? Why, there isn't any man so big as that."

"It wasn't a man," said Polly coolly.

"Wasn't a man?" fairly squealed Joel. "What was it?"

"A great brown, striped snake," said Polly. "He was lovely, but he was bad you know, to steal into the Nutcrackers' house when they were all away."

Joel tumbled back and thought a minute. "Was Mr. Nutcracker a man, Polly?" he asked, fixing his black eyes upon her face.

"Oh, no!" said Polly with a little laugh. "Why, didn't you guess, Joey Pepper? He was the sweetest dear of an old gray squirrel you ever saw, so of course he had to have a brush train just like Mrs. Nutcracker's, you know."

XIV

The Runaway Pumpkin

"I DON'T see," said Van as they were all seated on the rug before the library fire, listening to one of Polly's stories, "how you ever do think of such splendid things, Polly Pepper."

"That's nothing," said Jasper, "to the stories she has told time and again in the Little Brown House in Badgertown."

"Oh, tell us one of those now!" begged Van eagerly. "Do, Polly Pepper." And, "Do, Polly Pepper," cried Percy and little Dick together. And, "Do, Polly," said Jasper pleadingly, "if you are not all tired out."

"Oh, I'm not tired!" said Polly, shaking back the little fluffs of hair from her brow. Then she sat looking into the fire a minute. "I guess I'll tell you of The Runaway Pumpkin."

"Do," cried Jasper in great satisfaction. "I remember that; that's fine. Now, keep still, you three chaps, or else Polly can't tell it. You're worse than the menagerie any day," as the boys began to express their enthusiasm in such a babel Polly could scarcely get a word in by way of beginning.

"Well, once upon a time," began Polly, trying to frown at them, but instead the brown eyes were laughing as she hurried on with quite a flourish. "You must know that my story is all about the time when animals talked, and pumpkins walked, and—"

"Oh, don't have any poetry!" began Van in alarm. "That's perfectly horrid. Don't, Polly."

"Why, it isn't in poetry," she said.

"Yes, 'tis," contradicted Van.

"Look out," cried Jasper. "The first chap who contradicts will get off from this rug, and have no story at all."

"I didn't mean," began Van.

"No, he really didn't mean to contradict, I believe, Jasper," said Polly. "But what did make you think I was going to tell you a poetry story, Vanny? Why I couldn't if I wanted to. Tell me—"

"Why, you said the animals talked and the pumpkins walked."

"Oh, dear me!" cried Polly, almost tumbling over on the rug, and laughing merrily, in which they all joined, "I didn't know I made a rhyme. So I did say that, didn't I? Well, you needn't be frightened. I won't do so any more. I don't believe I could if I wanted to. Now, then," and she sat straight and wiped her eyes, "I'll begin again."

"And if you interrupt another time, old fellow," said Jasper in his fiercest fashion, and he pretended to make a dive for Van's coat collar, "out you go, sir, neck and heels. Go on, Polly; I'll keep this chap straight."

"Well, pumpkins did walk and talk too," said Polly,

plunging on in her gayest mood, "in those days I'm telling you about. Now, Farmer Stebbins had a big field of them— oh, it was as big as this house and the grounds, and way, way off—I don't know how far, and every single bit of it was full and running over with pumpkins."

"How many?" cried Van thoughtlessly.

"Sh!" Jasper held up his hand, and made a great show of springing in Van's direction, which made that individual duck suddenly behind Percy's back.

"You see, he had to have a great many pumpkins to take to market, because there were such lots of children at his house and that was all they had to live on."

"Did they *eat* pumpkins?" cried Percy in a tone of disgust.

"They didn't exactly eat them," said Polly, "at least not all the while; but they ate the things their father bought with the money he sold them for at the market."

"Oh! Well, go on."

"And every day all those children would climb up to all the windows in Farmer Stebbins's house and watch to see the pumpkins growing bigger. And the first thing they did in the morning was to run out and count them to see if anybody had run off with any in the night."

"How many were there?" asked Van, bobbing up from his retirement.

"*Sh!*" cried Jasper.

"Oh, I don't know; about a million, I suppose," said Polly recklessly.

"Oh, Polly Pepper!" exclaimed Percy in astonishment. "Why, that can't possibly be true."

"Of course it isn't," said Polly coolly. "This is a make-believe story, you know."

"And if you two chaps don't keep still, you'll get no story," declared Jasper again. "Here's Dick, now, is as quiet as a mouse. You might learn manners from him."

"I want to hear Polly Pepper tell the story," said little Dick, folding his hands tightly together.

"Of course you do—so we all do; and that's the only way we can hear it, by keeping quiet. Well, go on, Polly, please."

So Polly began again: "Well, the pumpkins grew and grew. First they were green, you know, and funny little things, and the vines quite covered them. And then they grew bigger, and swelled all up fat and round, and ran their heads through the green leaves; and the frost came one night and bit the grass and all the tender things everywhere, and the next morning when all the Stebbinses ran out, it didn't seem as if there was anything in the world but big yellow pumpkins. All the vines were just puckered and shriveled up. But the pumpkins were just as proud as could be, and they said, 'Now we've got the whole world to ourselves.'

"And Farmer Stebbins went up and down among them all, rubbing his hands just like this," and Polly looked so like him that everybody burst out laughing, "and he said, 'Now, says I, my fine pumpkins, we'll put you in a pile very soon, and when your coats get yellow, away you go to market.'"

"What did he mean?" demanded Percy.

"Be still, and she'll tell you," said Jasper.

"And sure enough, what do you think! Every single one of those million pumpkins soon found himself in a great big pile against the barn, and there they were to stay until the farmer said they were yellow enough. Then away they would drive to the market!

"Well, one cold night everybody had gone to bed in the farmhouse, and even Snap, the great brindled dog, was asleep, and all was as still as it could be when one yellow pumpkin up top of the very tip of the pile whispered, '*Hist!*' and every other pumpkin listened with all his might to hear what he was going to say.

" 'We are all very foolish,' said the Tip Top Pumpkin, 'if we stay here to be carted off to that old market where somebody comes along to buy us to carry us home to eat up.'

" 'What can we do?' cried all the others straight through the big pile.

" 'Hush—don't make such a dreadful noise,' warned the Tip—Top—Pumpkin, 'or we shall have the whole house after us. I'm not going to be made up into a Thanksgiving pie, I can tell you.'

"At the word 'pie,' all the other pumpkins shivered so that down came the pile, rolling and clattering to the ground; and some of them were going so fast they couldn't stop but kept right on and were never seen more.

" 'Let's all run,' said the Tip Top Pumpkin suddenly. 'Come on.' With that he tumbled himself down with a will and set off down the road toward the village. The other pumpkins didn't dare to follow, but they huddled together just where they fell. And so 'Tip Top,' I'm going to call him, went on alone. But he didn't care and he sang to himself as he rolled along just as jolly and gay. And the first thing he knew an awful thing came thwacking on his back, and a big hand said, 'Here, stop there! You're coming with me.' And he looked up and saw a giant."

"Oh! oh!" screamed the three boys.

" 'Oh, no, I'm not going with you,' gasped poor Mr. Tip Top. 'I'm going by myself, thank you.' And he wished a thousand times he was back again on the snug pile with the other pumpkins.

"The great big giant only laughed, and he slipped the pumpkin into his pocket, where he rattled round no bigger than a hickory nut."

"Oh, dear me!" exclaimed Percy, while Van struck his hands together in delight. "And then the giant stamped on the ground, and poor Mr. Tip Top thought it thundered, and he began to beg with all his might to be let out. And in a minute some boys, three or four times as big as Farmer Stebbins in size, came running up. 'What do you want, master?' they cried.

" 'Catch me a young elephant,' roared the giant at them. 'A juicy, tender one, and half a dozen young lions for sauce. And then run home and heat the pot boiling hot, for I've got a juicy pumpkin in my pocket for a nice little morsel to go with them.'

"Oh, how poor Mr. Tip Top trembled down deep in that giant's dreadful pocket! It was as black as a well, and however much he struggled, he knew he never could get up.

" 'Please, Mr. Giant,' he said in a very weak voice, he was so afraid, 'do let me out. You are so big I could only make you a mouthful, and I want to go home.'

" 'Be quiet!' roared the giant at him, 'or I'll chew your head right off in one bite now.'

"So poor, miserable Mr. Tip Top had nothing to do but to roll into the farthest corner of the pocket, and shiver and shake, and hope for some means of escape. And away sped the giant across the fields. Then the poor pumpkin knew he was being carried to the castle underground where the giant lived, and that he would never come out alive—oh, dear, how he shivered and shook!

"And pretty soon, down went the giant over a long pair of steps, two at a time, then down some more, till the poor pumpkin's head became quite dizzy. And at last he stopped and stamped on the ground, and Mr. Tip Top was very sure this time that it thundered.

" 'What ho!' screamed the giant. 'Is everybody asleep that you do not come when I call?' And there was a great scampering, and all the little giants and Mrs. Giant and all the servants came running as fast as could be. And the ground shook like everything till poor Mr. Tip Top thought he should die of fright.

" 'See what I've brought,' cried the giant in a dreadful voice, and he tipped up his pocket and out rolled the yellow pumpkin. All the giants and giantesses and Mrs. Giant raced after him with dreadful big steps, but he rolled under a big stone chair, cut out of the side of the rock that the cave was made of. 'Oh, save me—save me!' he cried, and he began to cry as hard as he could.

" 'I'll catch him,' cried every one of those dreadful creatures hunting for him. And at last one great big giant boy seized him and carried him off in triumph, but the others ran after him, trying to get the pumpkin away, and there was such a dreadful time as they tossed poor Mr. Tip Top back and forth like a big yellow ball that his head spun around and around on his shoulders, until old Father Giant roared out, 'Stop playing with him for the pot is boiling hot now, and I'm going to have him for my supper. I won't wait for the elephant and the little lions, for I'm very, very hungry.' And the pumpkin was so scared at that, that he gave a great jump and rolled away into a crack in the floor; and although every one of those giants and giantesses got down on their knees and flattened their faces to see him, they couldn't get him out. And old Father Giant, in great anger, said he would have to stay there till the next day when he would send for the carpenter to take up the floor. Then he should be boiled in the pot for a sweet morsel with his dinner. Oh, how poor Mr. Tip Top shivered and shook!

"And about the middle of the night, when not a single person was awake and everything was as still as a mouse, there came a little call just beside the crack: 'Pumpkin! Say, Pumpkin, don't you hear me?'

" 'Oh, I guess I do!' said poor yellow Mr. Tip Top; 'it's Johnny Stebbins.'

" 'Yes 'tis,' said the voice, 'it's Johnny Stebbins, and I've come to save you.'

" 'If you will only get me out of here,' said the yellow pumpkin, 'I'll go home and be just as good. I never'll run away in all this world again, never. You can take me to market, and I'll go along as nice as can be.'

" 'Yes,' said Johnny, 'you must go along good, for you see all the pumpkins have to be carried to market for we shouldn't have anything to live on if they didn't.'

" 'I know it,' said Mr. Tip Top quite humbly. 'Oh, do get me out!'

" 'Well, I will,' said Johnny, 'but you must do just as I say.' So the yellow pumpkin promised he would and Johnny ran around the outside of the cave, and pretty soon Mr. Tip Top heard him say, 'Roll over here.' So the yellow pumpkin rolled in the direction of the voice and there was a hole big enough for him to get out of, and oh, in a minute there he was out in the fresh air! And then Johnny said, 'Roll home now as fast as you can. I'm going to stay and scare the big giant and Mrs. Giant and all the little giants, and cut their heads off.'

" 'Oh, dear, Johnny!' cried Mr. Tip Top, and he burst out crying. 'Do come home. He'll kill you and chew your head off.'

" 'Pshaw! No, he won't,' said Johnny, 'and I've got to kill that old giant and Mrs. Giant and all those dreadful giant-esses, else they'll steal all our pumpkins. See what I've got,' and he ran behind a big tree, and came out again with a perfectly horrible head of a wild beast with flaming eyes and a big mouth and—"

"Oh, a jack-o'-lantern!" screamed Percy and Van and Dick together.

Polly nodded gaily and dashed on. "Mr. Tip Top took one look at it, and he said very bravely, 'I'm going to stay too, and help you. Make me look like that.' So in two minutes Mr. Tip Top had flaming eyes in him, and a horrible big mouth, out of which he kept saying, 'Now we'll scare them twice as soon. Come on, Johnny!' And in they crept into the cave.

"Oh, dear! You never heard such screams and roars! The giant called for his sword and his servants, and then he huddled under the bedclothes and pulled them up over his ears. So Johnny cut off his head easy enough. And Mrs. Giant ran screaming out of the cave, and she was going so fast she couldn't stop herself running down the hill, and so she rolled into the pond at the bottom. And all the little giant boys and girls ran this way and that and climbed into the trees, so they were all caught, and the servants too. And then Johnny took a great piece of sealing wax he had brought along in his pocket, and stuck the stone door fast so it couldn't be opened. And then away he and Mr. Tip Top went home.

"And Farmer Stebbins was so pleased with Mr. Tip Top that he said he should sit up on top of the big old clock in the kitchen. And there he is now, I suppose!" finished Polly with a flourish.

XV

The Robbers and Their Bags

"Oh, dear me," exclaimed Polly. "What shall I tell about?" She had just run into the library after her music lesson was over, and Monsieur had tripped off on the tips of his toes, his waxed mustache-ends trembling with delight in his enthusiasm over Mademoiselle Peppaire and her progress. "I can't think of an earthly thing to make a story of," and she wrinkled her brows in dismay.

"Let her off, Van," cried Jasper.

"No, no, no!" cried Van, in alarm. "She said she'd tell a story as soon as she got through her music lesson."

"Yes, she did," said Percy; "and it rains, and we can't go out, you know, Jasper," and he gazed dismally from the long window.

"Oh, I'll tell it!" Polly made haste to say. "I did promise it, boys, and you shall have it, so come over here," and she ran to the corner with the cushioned seats under the windows. "Now, then, let me see—oh, I'll tell you about The Robbers

145

and Their Bags," she announced, saying the first thing that came into her head.

"Oh, oh, oh!" screamed the boys in the greatest glee, while little Dick, quite overcome with the idea, rushed out in the hall to proclaim the fact to the first person he might meet, who chanced to be his grandfather.

"Polly's going to tell us a story about robbers, and she's got bags, and just everything," he screamed excitedly.

"Hoity-toity, Dick," exclaimed old Mr. King, whose plans for the day had all been set aside by the rain. "You must look where you are going, child, and not run into people so," as little Dick stumbled up against him.

"But she is, Grandpapa, she really and truly is," cried Dick positively.

"Who is? And going to do what?" demanded Mr. King.

"Polly; and she's going to tell us a perfectly splendid story." And then away Dick dashed back to the library again.

"In that case," observed the old gentleman to himself, "I might as well add myself to the youngsters; and Phronsie will probably be there." So as he had been waiting till Polly should be through with her music lesson, for Phronsie always sat patiently with one of her numerous dolls in the long drawing room on these occasions, he marched to the scene of the hilarity over the story, which was now fairly launched.

"And so you see," Polly was saying, as he opened the door—"Oh, boys, here comes dear Grandpapa!"

All the boys were on their feet in an instant to get old Mr. King the best chair in the room, an attention which pleased him immensely, and he was soon seated in their circle, Joel planting himself down on the floor at his feet. Phronsie looked over from Polly's lap, where she was snuggling. "Does your head ache, Grandpapa?" she asked gently.

"It feels as if it were going to, all the while, Phronsie," said the old gentleman artfully.

Phronsie put up one little hand and patted Polly's cheek. "I must go and sit with Grandpapa, Polly," she whispered, "and keep him from being sick." And she got down and hurried over to climb in his lap. "Now I guess it won't ache, Grandpapa, dear," she said, smoothing his white hair gently.

"It won't now you are here, Phronsie," said old Mr. King, holding her close. "Now, then, Polly, my girl, let us hear that wonderful story."

So Polly began again. "Well, you see, it's all about some robbers, and—"

"Make 'em be big, and ever so many of them," cried Joel.

"Oh, Joe, be quiet!" warned Jasper. "Polly can't get on at all if you are going to interrupt every minute."

"Joel's always breaking in," cried Percy wrathfully. "Do stop him, Grandpapa."

"I'll stick a pin in him," said Van pleasantly, who sat next.

"Oh, Van!" exclaimed Polly.

"Here, you two boys," cried the old gentleman, "you mind what you're about, both of you. Joe, don't you let me hear of your stopping Polly; and do you, master Van, keep your pins to yourself. Now, then, Polly, begin again."

So Polly, with a nod and a reassuring smile for him, rushed on. "Well, you see, these robbers lived in a cave dark and big. It was against a mountain, around which ran a lonely road. Nobody ever went that way who could help it, because for years and years robbers had been there, and scared all the travelers away. So, you see, the robbers had it pretty much to themselves. Well, at the end of the long and lonely road was a little village. It was about as big as Badger-town, but not nearly so pretty," said Polly, with a light in her brown eyes.

"Bad—ger"—began Joel.

"Ugh!" exclaimed Van at him, while Grandpapa held up a warning finger.

"Yes, it was just about as big," said Polly. "Well, there were some men who were pretty rich lived there in fine smart houses, about six—no, I guess a dozen of them, and the robbers had waited a good while to see if they would come down their long and lonely road. But they never had, for you see, whenever they had to get to the next place, they went clear away the other side of the mountain, and so kept off from the dreadful robbers and their cave. Well, so one night, all the robbers sat and made up a plan, and—"

"How many?" began Joel abruptly. But one look at old Mr. King stopped him.

"Well, there were just about a hundred robbers," said Polly, seeing it was expected of her to have a good number.

"Oh, my!" exclaimed Percy.

"And they all decided that as the splendid rich men who lived in the big houses wouldn't come to them, they would go after them."

"Oh, dear!" said little Dick.

"Yes, and so the head robber—oh, he was too perfectly splendid to look at—" cried Polly, waxing enthusiastic, as she looked at her absorbed audience, "he was all dressed up in red velvet, and a white plume in his hat that trailed off in the air, and he had a long sword in his belt, and it clanked every step he took, and two or three knives and pistols—oh, and other things stuck in around his waist, so he was perfectly dreadful too. Well, he told twelve of his robbers to go and catch the splendid rich men, and get all their money, and—"

"How did they get it, Polly?" cried Percy.

"Ho! Ho! Who's interrupting now?" cried Van, bursting into a laugh.

"Hush!" said Jasper, over at Percy who ducked immediately.

"You'll see," said Polly gaily. "Well, so one dark night—oh, you couldn't see your hand before your face hardly—don't you think, all the twelve splendid rich men got twelve letters—I mean each man got one—saying he was to go off, just as quick as he could go, over to the big house where the minister lived, 'cause he wanted to see him on very important business indeed, and he couldn't wait a minute. So every single one of those twelve splendid rich men started from his home and ran as hard as he could. And before he had gone very far, he met a man—he didn't see him, it was so dark, but he ran up against him, and they nearly knocked each other over.

" 'Stop, there!' roared the man, that the man who was running knocked up against. 'What are you doing, tumbling me down in this fashion?'

" 'Oh! I didn't mean to,' said the poor man very humbly; and he couldn't breathe very well, because, you see, he'd been running so fast, and he'd bumped into the other one so suddenly. 'I won't do it again, but the minister, I expect, is sick, so excuse me,' and he tried to go by.

" 'No, you don't go any farther,' roared the other man at

him in a dreadful voice, and he pulled out from under his arm a big bag, and popped it over the head of the poor man who had been running, and then he tumbled him upside down and shook him around in the bag down into the bottom of it, and then he tied up the neck."

"Oh, Polly! Tied up the man's neck?" asked Ben.

"No, I mean the neck of the bag," said Polly. "Then he set the bag with the man in it on a big stone by the roadside. 'Now there you must stay, till I come for you' he said, and he laughed as hard as he could, and hopped off in the darkness."

"Oh, oh, oh!" cried all the group, with smothered exclamations.

"Yes, and away he went to find the other eleven robbers; they each had a bag, you know, just like his. Well, every time one of them met one of the splendid rich men running to the minister's house, why the robber pulled out his big bag from under his arm and popped it over the other man's head, and turned him upside down and shook him into the bottom of the bag, and then tied up the neck—the neck of the bag, I mean—and then put him on a big stone by the roadside, and told him to stay there until he came back for him. And then those twelve robbers just looked at each other and said they wanted to sit down and rest."

"I should think they'd want to," said Ben, under his breath.

"Well, and then one of them said suddenly, 'Come, now, let's go to the first house belonging to those men in the bags. We'll find bushels of gold I expect in the cellar, and—'"

"And did they?" screamed Van, forgetting himself.

"Ho, ho! Who's talking now?" cried Percy, with a disagreeable little laugh.

"Hush!" said old Mr. King, holding up a warning finger at both of them.

"And so they ran softly off on the tips of their toes," said Polly, hurrying on; "and before any one could breathe, hardly, there they were in the house of one of the perfectly splendid rich men. Now, there was a wise old cat there, living in that very house. She was all black but two green eyes —no, I guess this cat had yellow eyes, yellow with long black stripes in them that grew big when she was angry. Now, she knew everything almost, and she was as good as she was clever. Well, she just softly tripped along to her mistress's bed, and hopped up and whispered in her ear, 'Don't you be afraid, mistress dear, but lie perfectly still, and I'll take care of those robber men and won't let them hurt you.' So the mistress turned over and went to sleep again."

"She was a nice cat," said Phronsie, pausing in her work of patting old Mr. King's white hair to turn and look at Polly, "and I like her, I do," as Polly sent a smile over to her, and then raced on.

"Well, the cat ran off on the tips of her toes, and hopped up to the kitchen shelf, and took down in her mouth a long, sharp knife; and then she flew out of the back door, I tell you, oh, so fast, and away off. And pretty soon she came up to a big bag with a man inside it, sitting on a stone by the roadside. 'Master, dear,' she cried, hopping up to put her mouth close to the bag, 'is that you?'

" 'Oh, dear me, yes!' said the poor man in the bag, in a muffled voice, 'and I should like very much to get out.'

" 'Well,' said the wise old cat, 'I'll let you out in a minute.'
So she took the sharp knife in her paw, and she just slashed
it good through the string that tied up the neck of the bag,
and in a minute out popped the man and stood up on his
feet. And then they heard a cry, 'Oh, dear me, I'd like to get
out!' and, don't you think, right around the corner was another big bag with a man inside it, all tied up around the
neck, and sitting on a stone by the roadside. And so the man
that had just got out and his wise old cat, who slipped the
sharp knife into her mouth again, rushed around the corner.
The cat took the knife in her paw before her master had a
chance to, and she just slashed it through the string that tied
up the bag, and in a minute that man, too, was out and
standing on his feet on the ground."

Phronsie laughed in delight, and clapped her hands.
"Polly, I like that cat, and she's good," she cried again, dreadfully excited.

"So she is, pet," cried Polly, nodding away to her. Then
she raced on.

"Well, those two men stared into each other's faces, and
one said, 'Well, I declare, how do you do, Mr. Brown?' and
the other man said, 'Well, I declare, how do you do, Mr.
Smith?' And just then they all heard a little cry. Around another corner was another bag all tied up just as the other two
had been, and sitting on a stone by the roadside. And then
the wise old cat did just as she had done before, and pretty
soon there were three men standing up quite straight on the
ground, and they all said, 'This is perfectly dreadful, isn't it?'

" 'Now, I tell you, sirs,' said the wise old cat, sitting down before them and staring at them very hard, 'I've got a plan in my head, and you must do as I say.'

" 'Indeed you must,' whispered her master to the others, 'because when she looks like that she knows how to do things. And she's got something on her mind.'

" 'Just as soon as we find all the men in this town who are tied up in bags and set on stones by the roadside, and get them out,' said the wise old cat, 'we must hurry right home. But we've got to have twelve men,' and she bobbed her head to herself; but she didn't tell her master that there were twelve robbers in his house, for, you see, she had counted them.

"And all this while those twelve robbers were eating up the mince pies that belonged to that cat's mistress, and there she was going to have all the cousins over to dinner the very next day. And those dreadful robbers sat on the kitchen table and ate, and ate, and ate. And then they drank up all the milk."

Phronsie stirred uneasily, and looked very sad over this, so Polly hastened to say, before she could ask the question, "except some in the pitcher up on the top shelf, that was put there for the littlest little girl."

But still Phronsie's face was very grave. "Won't there be any left for that nice old cat when she gets home, Polly?" she asked.

"You must make some be reserved for that cat, Polly," said Grandpapa, nodding furiously over at Polly.

"Dear me, yes. We wouldn't let that wise old cat go without hers!" exclaimed Polly, quickly. "Such a dear as she is!

Oh, there was a whole bowlful, Phronsie, on another shelf, clear way back, that the robbers didn't see!"

Phronsie leaned back and put her head on old Mr. King's breast while she drew a long sigh of relief. "Please tell some more, Polly," she begged.

"Well, so the wise old cat gave three nods over to the three men waiting there for her to tell them things, and she said to each of them, 'Now put your bag under your arm, you'll want it before long, and follow me'; and away she trotted on the tips of her toes, till she had found and untied nine other men inside of big bags and sitting on stones on the roadside.

" 'Um—' said the cat, her paw on her mouth, 'I guess this is all; anyway, we've got twelve. Now we must run, for master has a dozen robbers in his house. Now, says I, see who gets there first.' "

"And which did?" cried Percy, and Van, and Joel, and David, all together, Jasper and Ben laughing to hear the babel.

"Oh, the wise old cat, of course!" said Polly, laughing too. "You didn't think I'd let anybody beat her, did you? Well, she was waiting there on the front doorstep as they all came puffing and panting up. 'Now do just as I say,' she whispered into their ears, 'and each of you pick out the robber you see first, as you go in, and rush up and pop your bag over his head, and tie it down fast with your string, before he can scream. They're just getting through eating mince pie'; for, you see, while she was waiting for these men to come, she had taken the time to creep along the window sill and peep within the kitchen.

" 'Oh, oh!' cried her master. 'Eating up my wife's mince pies, the villains!'

" 'Now follow me!' the cat commanded. 'Have all your bags ready!' and in they rushed. And every man caught a robber by flopping his big bag over his head before he saw him coming, and then they every one tied the neck of the bag up just as it had been done before, and while the robbers wriggled and screamed, and beat and kicked, as the bags were shaken up and down, they couldn't get out. And the wise old cat went around to each bag. 'Yes,' she said, quite satisfied, 'the knots are all fast.' "

"Oh, wasn't that perfectly splendid!" shouted Joel. And everybody was so delighted with the capture of the robbers that they forgot to reprove him. And Phronsie clapped her little hands and crowed and laughed with the rest; and Mrs. Whitney heard the noise and ran in to see what the fun was. "Well, I declare," she exclaimed, hurrying over to their corner, "to think I've missed this splendid time!"

"Oh, Mamma!" cried little Dick, hopping out of the center of the circle closing around Polly, "she's been telling us beautiful things about robbers and—cats—and—"

"No, she hasn't," contradicted Van, "it's only one cat. Dick's so little, he doesn't know anything—"

"Oh, Vanny!" reproved his mother.

"And I'm not little," cried little Dick wrathfully, and standing very tall. "And she did tell about robbers—Polly Pepper did."

"Well, you said *cats*," said Percy, "and 'twasn't but one."

"Never mind," said Jasper, "this one was wise enough for

a dozen cats. Do stay, Sister Marian; it's a fine story," turning his kindling face toward her.

"Indeed I will," she cried; so he jumped up, and pulled forward an easy chair, and Polly waited till she was seated in its comfortable depths.

"Now, Polly," said Mrs. Whitney, with her sweetest smile, "I am as anxious as any of these young creatures for this enchanting story." So Polly hurried on.

"Where was I? Let me see——"

"The robbers were tied up in the bags," they all shouted at her.

"Don't you know?" added Joel, not very politely. "Why, Polly Pepper, have you forgotten?"

"Hush!" said Jasper warningly.

"Oh, yes, indeed!" exclaimed Polly. "Well, and then the cat cried in a very loud voice, 'Now I must go and wake mistress.' So she ran up into the bedroom and she skipped upon the bed and called close to her ear, 'Wake up, mistress dear, the robbers are all caught and waiting for you.' And so her mistress turned over and opened her eyes; and she looked at the cat, and said, 'Is that so?' And then she sat up straight, and then she hopped off from the bed and ran down the stairs after the wise old cat.

" 'Shoulder your bags, every one of you!' commanded the cat, running into the kitchen, and she jumped up to the table to see that they obeyed. And every man picked up the bag that had the robber inside it that he had caught, and he swung it off up on his shoulder.

" 'Now away to jail!' shouted the cat."

"Hooray!" screamed Joel, beating his hands together in great excitement.

"At the word 'jail,' every robber inside of a bag began to scream and beg to be let out, and—"

"Oh, do let them out!" begged Phronsie. "Please do, Polly."

"Oh, Phronsie, I can't!" said Polly. "They are bad, naughty, wicked robbers, you know; and they'd kill that nice, dear old cat, maybe, if they got out."

"Would they?" asked Phronsie anxiously.

"Yes, indeed," cried all the little circle together.

"I really think, Phronsie," added Grandpapa decidedly, "that it is not safe for Polly to let those bad robbers out."

"Don't tie the bags up very tight, then, please, Polly," begged Phronsie.

"Polly will fix it all right, Phronsie," said Jasper, with a smile. Polly thanked him with a little nod, and hurried on. "Well, so you see, off they all went to jail. It was a great big stone house, oh, as big as three or four houses that folks live in, and there was a row of pens that—"

"Pigpens?" asked Joel abruptly.

"Dear me, no," said Polly, with a little laugh. "They were prisoners' pens. And the wise old cat just raced along as hard as she could, all the twelve men with their bags on their backs coming after. And she spoke up as bold as you please to the man at the gate who had a big iron key in his hand, oh, as big as could be: 'I've got a dozen robbers for you to shut up and keep fast.'

"At that the man at the gate put his big key in the lock—

open flew the gate, and in went all the dozen robbers in their bags on the twelve men's backs, with the wise old cat at the head of the procession; and in a minute they were each in one of the little pens, and—"

"Couldn't they take off the bags then, Polly?" cried Phronsie. "Please let them for a very little bit of a while."

"Yes," said Polly, "they did. The wise old cat asked the gateman who locked them all in to undo the bags.

" 'But you can have only your heads out,' said the gateman to the robbers, clanking his big key against the wall, 'so you can see things.' And he tied the bags all up around their necks; each head stuck out, you know, and the bag was drawn up in a ruffle, and tied fast."

"Oh!" exclaimed Phronsie.

"But that was much better," said Jasper cheerfully. "Just think, Phronsie, to get their heads out."

"Yes," said Phronsie slowly.

"And the next day the judge, the man who sat on a platform at the end of the big hall, told one of the servants to bring a big bell and call everybody in, and to scream as loud as he could, 'Twelve robbers in bags to be sentenced.' And the people kept coming in, and coming in, and coming in until there was only a little path in the center for them to bring the robbers in. Pretty soon the man with the bell went up and down, and roared out, 'Bring the robbers in!' And twelve other servants went out and got them and set them up in a row right in front of the judge on the platform—"

"And were their heads out?" asked Phronsie.

"Yes, their heads were all out, the bags were tied in ruffles, you know, around their necks. And they tried to get on their knees to beg the judge not to kill them, but instead they flopped over and the servants had to go around among them and set them up straight again. Well, oh, I forgot to tell you that the wise old cat sat up on the platform—the judge invited her, you know. And the judge whispered something to the man with the big bell and he ran out and came racing back with a long knife; and after him came another man, wheeling and trundling a big grindstone—"

"Oh!" screamed Joel, in the greatest glee, "they're going to chop off all the robbers' heads, I know."

"Oh, Polly," began Phronsie, just ready to cry.

"Wait, and you'll see, pet," said Polly reassuringly. Old Mr. King put his hand over Phronsie's small ones, and whispered something in her ear, so she snuggled up against his breast once more.

"Well, oh, let me see! Where was I—oh—"

"You are going to chop off all those robbers' heads," howled Joel and Van together.

" 'Now,' said the judge, in a perfectly awful voice, and looking at all those dozen robbers, 'you've got to promise to show the way to your cave, or off go your heads!' and he pointed to the man sharpening up the long knife on the grindstone.

"The robbers shook so in their bags they all flopped over again and rolled on the floor. So somebody had to go and set them all straight in a row once more. 'Hurry up,' cried the judge, 'and say "Yes," for the knife is ready.'

"The man sharpening up the long knife began to brandish it in the air over the head stuck out of the bag of the robber first in the line.

" 'Ow!' screamed the robber, trying to draw his head under the ruffle. 'I say, "Yes." '

" 'And I say, "Yes," ' screamed every one of the rest of the robbers, huddling as best they could under their ruffles.

" 'Very well, then,' said the judge. So the man with the knife laid it down by the grindstone, and the judge gave his hand to the cat. 'You must go to the cave,' he said, 'and capture the rest of the robbers.' "

Joel and Van, who were horribly disappointed when the man put up his knife, now brightened up at prospect of livelier work, and more to their taste, at the cave. "Do hurry, Polly!" they clamored.

"Well, then the judge told the man who had rung the bell to jingle it again and scream out 'Eighty-eight men wanted at once' because, you see, he knew there were just one hundred robbers in all. And when they came in he told them to go out and get a bag apiece, just like the ones the twelve robbers were in. And pretty soon they were all ready and off they started, with the wise old cat at the head; and after her came the twelve men with the robbers in the bags, all but their heads, because, you see, those would have to be out, for them to see the way. And the robbers said, 'Left, right,' as they had to turn, all along the way to the cave, down the long and lonely road. Well, and finally they reached the place, and they stopped and listened. 'They are boiling their hasty pudding for supper,' said one of the robbers, because, you see, all the men made them tell things.

" 'This is the time, then,' said the wise old cat to the first robber. 'Now do you call out big and loud to let you in.' So the robber did it; he had to, you know; and a voice inside said, 'Oh! that you, Jim, back again?' and the great stone door flew open. And just as quick as you could think, there they were all inside; and every man pulled out a bag from under his arm, and flopped it over the head of a robber, all except the robber who was stirring the hasty pudding over a big iron kettle—he fell into the kettle instead, because he ducked his head when he saw the bag coming. Well, and oh, they were all hauled off to jail, but first the nice old cat took some sealing wax she had been wise enough to bring with her from the jail, and she stuck the big stone door all up tight so that no more robbers could use that cave.

"And the judge sentenced all the hundred robbers, in a bunch, to a desert island where there wasn't any cave, nor anybody else—not a single person besides themselves. So they were all taken off in boats the next day, and—"

"And could they get out of their bags then?" asked Phronsie, with a long breath.

"Yes, after they got to the island," said Polly, "but not a single minute before. And as soon as they rolled them out of the boats, the men who brought them untied the bags and said 'Scat!' And away ran the robbers and were never seen again."

XVI

Polly Pepper's Chicken Pie

"YES, indeed, Jasper," cried Polly, "I'll tell about the chicken pie I made; only 'twasn't a chicken pie at all," and she broke off into a merry laugh.

"Hold on," cried Ben, "you'll spoil it all, Polly. Tell the story first, that's best."

"So I will," said Polly. "Well, in the first place, none of us in the Little Brown House ever knew where it came from, to begin with. Ben found it one day in a swamp down by the meadow as he was digging sweet flag to sell, to get some money to buy a pair of boots for the winter. It wasn't hurt in the least, only it was so small it couldn't get out. The wonder is how it ever got there at all. However, Ben didn't care for that, so long as he could get Master Chick in his possession. So he took an old fence rail, and by dint of poking and urging the chicken, which didn't want to come, and by floundering and tumbling around in the bog till he was pretty wet himself, at last he caught it.

"Oh, you must know it was a fine black chicken—a Shanghai; and Ben grasped it, oh, so tightly, under one arm, and he flew home, and bursting into the door, he scared us and he most upset me—I was helping Mamsie to pull out the basting threads of the coat she had just finished. And goodness me, how that chicken did scream!"

"Yes, and so did you, most as bad," said Ben, bursting into a laugh. "I never will forget. You said I'd scared you most to death."

"Well, and so you did," declared Polly. "We didn't see that dreadful chicken till you flapped it in our faces. It was lucky that the children weren't there or I don't know but what the roof of the Little Brown House would have flown off with the noise."

"Where were the children?" demanded Percy.

Joel twisted uneasily. It had always been a great trial to think of his absence on such a momentous occasion.

Polly answered briskly, "Why, the two boys were down in Farmer Brown's cowyard. There was a little hole full of water, something like a pond, you know, and they were sailing boats, and—"

"Oh, dear me, I wish we hadn't been!" grunted Joel. "I'd rather have seen the black chicken come in."

"And Phronsie had been put to bed early. It was almost dark, you know, and she was tired out; so Mamsie and I were all alone."

"And Mamsie thought it was a crow," said Ben to Mother Pepper, who still was at work over her mending basket the same as ever. "Didn't you, Mamsie?"

"Yes," said Mrs. Pepper, with a smile at the remembrance. "He was more like a crow, children, I'm sure, than anything else, he was so black."

"Oh, how I wish we could have seen it!" exclaimed Percy and Van together.

"And Ben said he'd give me half of the chicken," ran on Polly, "and then we could have him for Thanksgiving, and I could make my pie—"

"Oh, you ought to have seen Polly dance when I told her that!" said Ben, laughing again.

"Oh, dear, you did have such good times in the Little Brown House!" cried Percy enviously. "Why couldn't we have been there!"

"And then we began to count up how long it would be to Thanksgiving. We'd never had one, you know," said Polly.

"Never had a Thanksgiving!" cried all the Whitney children together.

"Hush!" exclaimed Jasper, with a warning pull at the jacket nearest to him.

"I remember," said Mrs. Pepper, laying down her work. "It was July then, and there were four months to wait; but if we could find out where the chicken belonged, I told you, we must give it back."

"And did you give it back—did you—did you?" clamored the Whitney boys.

"No," said Polly, "because we couldn't find anybody who had ever seen him. So we put him in the shed where the old gray goose was, and—"

"Oh! did you have an old gray goose, Polly Pepper?" cried Van. "Tell about him, do."

So Polly dilated at great length on the old gray goose— how it was the only living thing they had because they were too poor to buy a cow or a pig, or even a chicken, and how the old goose had lived there ever since they could remember, and how cross it was, so they couldn't play with it, and how it bit Sally Brown one day when she came over with an errand from her mother, and—"

"Tell about how it bit Sally Brown," interrupted Van eagerly.

"If you stop for everything, Polly never'll get that chicken pie baked," said Ben.

"Yes," said Jasper, "now don't interrupt again. It's a shame to have to tell stories and be stopped every minute."

"Oh, I don't mind it!" said Polly brightly. "Only if you have all about Sally Brown and everything else, why I shan't get through with the chicken pie."

"Go on about the chicken pie, then, do, Polly," said Van reluctantly, mentally determining to have the whole of Sally Brown and the old gray goose some time. And so Polly ran on again—how they always fed the old gray goose every day most carefully, and Phronsie saved something from her dinner for it most especially and—"

"It used to eat awfully," grumbled Joel.

"Hush!" said Ben.

"And so you see," cried Polly gaily, "how perfectly fine it was to have such a splendid chicken come to us. Seems as if it was just on purpose for Thanksgiving, for you must know that Mamsie had promised us a chicken pie as soon as she could manage it, and it was to be all wings, and drumsticks, and wishbones and—"

"Oh, Polly Pepper!" exclaimed Percy, with a little laugh. "Chickens don't have but one wishbone apiece."

"I can't help it," retorted Polly recklessly. "Seems as if this chicken pie was going to be better than any other that was ever baked in all this world. Oh, and the crust was to be thick, and the gravy was to be just lovely, and Phronsie was to have the wishbone."

"Yes, I was," said Phronsie, with a small sigh, and folding her hands.

"And so, you see, when Mr. Shanghai dropped down from the clouds in the way he did, why we were just as happy as we could be. Well, every day when the work was done up we talked over just how that pie was to be baked; and when it was too dark to see, for we didn't light the candle any earlier than we could help, and—"

"Why didn't you light the candle early?" asked little Dick, pushing forward into the middle of the group.

"Why, because we were poor," said Polly, "and we had to save the candles as long as we could. Well, and we used to play it really was Thanksgiving, and the table was set, and—"

"And Polly always played that she had a bunch of flowers to trim the chicken with," said Ben.

"Well, and now something very dreadful happened," said Polly, "very dreadful indeed. I won't tell you what it was, but—"

"Oh, tell, tell, Polly Pepper, do!" cried all the Whitney boys in a clamor.

"No, not just yet," said Polly, shaking her brown head decidedly, "because that would spoil the story. But I'm going to pretend that the old gray goose and the black chicken could talk together, and tell you what they said."

"And then will you tell us the perfectly dreadful thing

that happened?" asked Van anxiously, while the others cried delightedly, "Oh, that will be fine!"

"Yes," said Polly, with a reassuring nod over at him, "I will Vanny, tell it all. Well, so here is what they said. The old gray goose began it:

" 'Humph!' she said, with a very knowing look. 'You don't know as much as you will in a short time—say in November.'

"Now, what November was, the chicken, of course, couldn't tell, for he had never seen a November. So he asked the cross old goose very plainly, but very politely, one day, to tell him exactly what she did mean. This was the week before Thanksgiving, and it rained, and it was cold and dreary, and the two were perched on a rail, shivering with the cold. But what the old gray goose was saying made Shanghai shake and shiver worse than anything else, only he pretended that he wasn't frightened a bit.

"Now, you must know that the old gray goose was very angry at the Shanghai chicken for coming there at all, and when she saw us all feed it, she got angrier and angrier till she tried to say very bad things indeed to that poor little black chicken."

"That was naughty," little Dick burst out vehemently.

"Yes, she was very naughty indeed," said Phronsie, shaking her head gravely.

"So she was," declared Polly. "Wait, and you'll see what happened. Well, she went on and on, and talked and talked about how the chicken was to be baked in pieces in a pie, and all that.

" 'I've seen 'em!' she said with the air of one who knew

everything. 'Year after year, hens and chickens, yes, and geese, stepping around in the morning, oh, so happy and smart, and then at evening they would go past here to market, all stiff and stark, with their heads off and Mr. Brown's boy holding them by their legs! All for pies, and so that people may eat themselves sick. And they call it a Thanksgiving!'

"Oh, how the chicken shook! It seemed as if it would fall off from its perch; but it was very dark, so the old goose didn't notice it. Shanghai wouldn't for all the world have had her, so he controlled himself and, being a brave little fellow, he stopped the beating of his heart, and he spoke up loud:

" 'Well, why weren't you baked in a pie, then, along with the others?'

" 'What! Why—well—' stammered the goose, 'they were going to kill me time and again—but—well, the fact is, they thought so much of me they couldn't bear to.' In spite of its fright, the chicken couldn't help laughing softly to itself.

" 'Well, come, you'd better go to bed!' crossly snapped the goose. 'They'll come for you bright and early in the morning. I heard 'em saying so.'

" 'Well, then I say,' declared the chicken, drawing himself up on his long legs till he looked, oh, so tall, 'they won't find *me* here. That's all I've got to say!'

" 'Why, where will you go?' demanded the goose, seeing that she had gone too far in the desire to make the poor little chicken as unhappy as possible.

" 'Oh, I'm going to set out for my own fortune!' gaily replied the chicken. 'At any rate, it can't be any worse than to be baked in a pie. I think I see myself staying here for *that!*

No. Good night, Mrs. Goose. Thank you for all your kindness. I'm off!'

" 'Yes, and be stuck in a bog for your pains!' scornfully hissed the old goose, seeing it was useless to advise or to urge further. But the chicken's long legs were going at a pretty smart pace down the hill, and it was soon out of sight, and it was never seen by any of us in the Little Brown House again."

"Oh, dear me!" screamed Percy and Van together. "Then, you didn't have any chicken pie. Why, Polly Pepper— And you said you had one!" While little Dick roared steadily, only the words, "chicken," and "pie," and "Oh, dear! oh, dear!" could be heard.

When the noise was quelled as best it could be by Jasper and Ben, Polly was saying, "Well that was the very dreadful thing that happened, you know I told you about, and—"

"And didn't you have anything?"

"Any pie—any pie at all," screamed and wailed the Whitney children, beside themselves with distress. So Polly hastened to reassure them. "There, there, don't feel so, boys. You'll see it all turned out beautifully, after all."

"How could it," exclaimed Van, horribly disappointed, "if you didn't have any chicken pie, after all?"

"You'll see," was all that Polly would tell him by way of comfort as she hurried on.

"Well, 'twas a beautiful morning, wasn't it, Ben," cried Polly, "when you went out to kill the chicken?"

"Yes," said Ben, "but what I remember most of all was how you all screamed and cried, and said you'd rather go without the pie than to have the chicken killed."

"Oh!" exclaimed the little bunch of Whitneys.

"I know it," said Polly. "And so, after all, it was better that that black Shanghai ran away."

"Oh, Polly Pepper!" cried all the children but Phronsie.

"Yes," said Polly stoutly, "I really think it was. Well, never mind, let us go on and hear the rest of it. Joel was the first one to tell us the chicken had gone. He rushed screaming in, 'Oh, Mamsie! Mamsie! the chicken isn't there!'"

"Oh, dear me!" interrupted Joel, "I remember."

"And after him came Davie flying in, and then I can't tell you how we all acted in that kitchen."

"You didn't, Polly," said Ben hastily. "All the rest of us did."

"I know I was just as bad as any of us," said Polly. "Well, anyway, then we all went out and hunted for the chicken, and—"

"And didn't you ever find him?" demanded Percy.

"No, she said so before," said Van. "She said they never saw him again, don't you know?"

"No, we couldn't find him," said Polly to Percy, "though we hunted high and low—in the woodshed, and the Provision Room, and all about the house, and down in the pine wood, oh, and over by Cherry Brook. Well, you can't think how we searched for that long black chicken. Yes, and Ben ran down to the swamp where he had found it, when he was digging sweet flag, to see if perhaps Mr. Shanghai had run back there, and got stuck in the bog; but no, he wasn't there, not a bit of him, so finally we all had to come home and tell Mamsie that we couldn't find him. And it rained dreadfully all that afternoon. And there was the flour bag standing up all ready in the pantry, oh, dear, and so we had to tell stories to keep the children from being too sorry and forlorn, and—"

"You did, Polly," corrected Ben. "I couldn't, but you told some splendid stories."

"Oh, will you tell us some of those splendid stories, Polly Pepper?" cried Percy radiantly. "Will you? That you told that rainy afternoon, when the black chicken ran away?"

"She's going to tell us how the old gray goose bit Sally Brown, too," declared Van positively, not losing sight of this future bliss.

"And so I will, Van," promised Polly; "and I'll tell you one of the stories I told the children on that dreadful afternoon when it rained, and the black chicken ran away. But not now. I must finish about the chicken pie."

"Tell more than one, Polly," begged the children. "*Please* tell us all the stories you told then."

"We'll see," said Polly brightly. "I'll tell you some, but I don't know as I could tell you all the stories I told that dreadful afternoon. I had to tell a good many, you know; it was so very hard to get over. Well, now we must hurry. Where was I? Oh—"

"You said you were telling stories," shouted Van, first of all.

"Yes, I know. Well, it was Ben who first proposed the best thing you could think of in all this world. All of a sudden he jumped up and waved his hand like this." Polly sprang to her feet. "See here, children, why not let's have the old gray goose?" she shouted.

"And you all screamed at me, 'The goose,' in great scorn," said Ben.

"I know we did," said Polly humbly, her hand falling to her side, "but that was because we weren't as smart as you were, to see what a wise thing it was to have the old gray goose. I remember you said, 'If we can't have chicken pie, why we must take the next best, and that's goose.'"

"Well, you all came around finely in a little while, though," said Ben, smiling at her. "And Mamsie said: 'I think Ben is right; and the old gray goose is really too cross to be allowed to live, for it isn't safe to have her around any longer, so she really ought to be killed, anyway, and we can boil her a good while to make her as tender as possible. So you can have your pie, Polly!'"

"Oh, dear me!" said the Whitney children.

"And Polly said: 'But why couldn't the old gray goose have run away, I wonder?' and that made us all laugh," said Ben, "instead of crying any more."

"Oh, I'm so glad!" screamed Van, and he rolled over and over on the floor in a ball. "Now the old gray goose, the bad, naughty, hateful old thing, is going to be killed, instead of the chicken she scared so."

"So am I," cried Percy; but he sat quite straight and dignified in his chair, only clapping his hands by way of approval. "Oh, do tell on, Polly!" he begged.

"And so the old gray goose, huddling in from the rain and chuckling to herself at the state of affairs, didn't dream what was coming. And on the next morning, chop—off went her head—and we had our pie."

"And Polly had some flowers on it, after all," said Ben, "for at the last minute a neighbor ran in with a bunch of posies, and she said: 'I'm real sorry you had such a time about your pie, children.' So, you see, the old gray goose was decked up fine after all, for Polly stuck them in her bony, tough old breast."

"And Mamsie baked us such a beautiful pudding," cried Polly, looking over at Mrs. Pepper with a bright smile.

"Most all plums," said Joel, smacking his lips at the remembrance. "My! Wasn't it good, though!"

"And did Phronsie get her wishbone?" asked little Dick anxiously.

"Why, how could she, when the black chicken ran away with it?" cried Polly.

XVII

Phronsie Pepper's New Shoes

"It was such hard work to make the fire burn that morning," said Polly. "Something was the matter with the old stove worse than usual. The big cracks seemed bigger than ever, although Ben had stuffed them up with putty the week before, and—"

"What had he stuffed them up for?" demanded little Dick, plunging into the center of the group.

"Hush!" said Van, laying a violent hand on his jacket. "Do be still. You crowd so, and ask questions."

"I don't 'crowd so and ask questions,'" said little Dick tartly, and he turned a very red face to Polly. "What did he do so for, Polly?"

"Why, we were very poor, you know," said Polly, "and the old stove was all tired out, it had been baking so long— oh, for years and years. And it had big holes and cracks come in it that let the air through, and then that put the fire out."

"Oh," said little Dick.

"We weren't so very poor," said Joel uneasily, who never could bear to be pitied.

"No, not when our ships came in," said Ben soberly; but his eyes twinkled, at which Polly laughed merrily.

"Oh, dear me!" she cried, wiping her eyes. "Joel's ships were always coming in."

"What do you mean, Polly Pepper?" cried Van quickly. "You say so many funny things. What were Joel's ships? And when did they come in?"

"Now, see here," said Jasper, "if you ask so many questions, Polly never can get to the story how Phronsie got her new shoes. And to think how you three chaps have been teasing her to tell it! If I were Polly, I wouldn't give you a single scrap of it."

But Polly tossed him a bright smile over her shoulder and dashed off again as fast as she could.

"You see, boys, when the putty that Ben had stuffed into the old stove tumbled out that morning, I was just going to put my pans of bread into the oven. Think of that!"

"Oh, dear me!" exclaimed the Whitney boys.

"Well, there wasn't any more putty. Oh! I forgot to tell you that Ben was away at his work, so he couldn't fix it, and besides, there wasn't any."

"Why didn't you take some cotton wool?" cried Van.

"Dear me!" exclaimed Polly with a little laugh. "We never had cotton wool. That would have been splendid— most as good as having a new stove. But sometimes Davie used to give us a boot top, and—"

"A boot top!" cried both of the Whitney boys together.

"Yes, when anybody gave him an old boot top, he'd save

it for the stove. The bits of leather stuffed it up just finely, and—"

"I'd have given a boot top too, if I'd had it," said Joel grimly, and his chubby face lengthened.

"Oh, Joel was splendid too," said Polly, turning a radiant face on him. "He gave things too, and helped to do the stuffing. I don't know what I should ever have done in all this world without those two boys," and she beamed at them. "Well, I must hurry, or you never will hear about Phronsie's new shoes. Oh, where was I?"

"Why, you were stuffing up the old stove to make it burn," said all the Whitney boys together. "Don't you know, Polly Pepper?"

"Oh, yes! Well, and I was in the midst of it, when Phronsie came out of the bedroom and said, 'Oh, I am so hungry, Polly.' Dear me, and there I was. My hands were just as black as could be, and Joel and David were away, you know, and so Phronsie begged to go to the Provision Room herself to the bread pail that always hung under the steps, and I told her she might.

"Well, when she went along," said Polly, hurrying over this part of it, as she thought she saw Phronsie's head droop a bit, "she took the big bread knife out of the cupboard; she thought, you know, it would help me; and the first thing anybody knew, down she rolled over those dreadful old rickety steps!"

Every one in the group sat perfectly still, as if not daring to breathe, and little Dick threw his arms around Phronsie while his mouth worked dreadfully as he tried not to cry.

"And I cut my thumb," said Phronsie, holding it up.

"Yes," said Polly, hurrying on, "it was only her thumb she cut, but how it did scare me! I don't know how I ever got down over those stairs. And there she was in a little heap at the bottom, and that dreadful old bread knife lying down on the floor a little way off. Oh, dear me! I can't bear to think of it even now. And there were little dabs of blood on her pink apron, and all over her face. But she said it was only her thumb."

"Yes," said Phronsie gravely, "it was only my thumb."

"And so it was surely, as I soon found out," said Polly, drawing a long breath. "Well, we soon got Phronsie upstairs, all right."

"Yes," said Joel, "and the first thing Polly did, she said to the old stove, 'Oh! you old naughty thing, now think what you've done this morning'—that's what she told us."

"And then I had to get some court plaster to stick the cut together with," said Polly. "So Phronsie sat in Mamsie's old rocking chair, while I ran over to Grandma Bascom's for it; for you know, of course, that if any of us got into any trouble, why, the first thing we did was to get into Mamsie's chair, if she wasn't home."

Phronsie put one soft little hand on Mother Pepper's lap, and patted it.

"And she had cake," said Joel. "Mamsie's chair, and a piece of cake too."

"Yes, there was a piece that had been given Mamsie, and we were saving it up for a treat that we were to have had that very night, but when Phronsie got hurt, why, of course she must have it. Well, I thought Grandma Bascom never would find that court plaster. She wanted so to hear all about how Phronsie got hurt in the first place, and then she didn't know where she had put the court plaster, and, oh, dear me, I thought I should fly, to think of poor Phronsie curled up in the big chair waiting for me. But at last Grandma found it in the cupboard drawer; and she cut off a piece, and then it wasn't but a minute or two and the cut was stuck together and tied up in an old handkerchief, and Phronsie's pink apron was taken off and she had a clean one on, and I brushed her curls, and everything was getting all right again. And then in popped Ben!"

"And Ben whistled 'Whew!' " said little Davie, "just as loud as he could. Polly told us he did."

"And they both kissed Phronsie all around again, and Ben kissed her the most because he hadn't been there at the first," said Joel; "Polly told us—oh, and then Polly said—"

"Oh, let me tell," begged David in great excitement.

"No, I began first," said Joel. "I want to myself, Dave."

"Yes, he did begin first, Davie," said Polly, smiling into his little eager face. "Joel ought to tell." So Joel began again triumphantly, in a loud voice, "Well, Polly said—oh, I'd rather Dave told—you may," he broke off suddenly, looking over at David.

"No," said Davie. "You began first. You tell—"

"But Joel wants you to, Davie," said Polly, smiling over at Joel in a way to make the color fly up on his round cheeks in his delight, "so I would."

"Let Phronsie tell," said Joel, "that's best. Go on, Phron. Tell what Polly said."

"She said," began Phronsie, "right in Bensie's ear, she

told me so, that I ought to have my new shoes. Yes, she did—"

"Just think of that!" exclaimed old Mr. King, who hadn't spoken a word, but had sat quite still, holding Phronsie cuddled up in his arms. "I should say so too. It was just the time for those new shoes to be bought."

"But Polly didn't tell me then," said Phronsie, twisting around to look into his face. "She whispered to Bensie, and he whispered in her ear, and they told me to wait."

"Just think of that," said Grandpapa, patting her small hand as it lay confidingly in his big palm.

"Yes," said Phronsie, "they did. And Polly said, 'Sh, sh! If Mamsie will only say yes.'"

"Well, and at dinnertime in flew Joel and Davie hungry as bears—they were always hungry," said Polly, laughing, "and the bread was not done, and—"

"And we had to eat the old crusts in the pail. We always had to," grumbled Joel.

"And Joel said he could have rolled down the stairs without getting hurt," said David, "and he was going to take the bread knife, and try it."

"But I got that away from you, sir," said Ben. "We'd had enough cuts for that day."

"And I showed them my thumb," said Phronsie with an important air.

"Yes, and Polly took off the handkerchief, but she wouldn't let us peek under the court plaster," said David.

"Well, I guess not," said Polly.

"And then she told us lots and lots of stories," said Joel.

"Oh! Will you tell them to us, Polly Pepper, when you get through about Phronsie's new shoes?" begged the Whitney boys all together.

"Oh, not today," said Polly. "I will some other time, maybe."

"They've got to be lots and lots of them," declared all three together.

"Well, do let Polly finish this one first," cried Jasper. "Father, can't you stop these chaps from interrupting her every minute," appealing to old Mr. King.

Instead of this, the old gentleman leaned back in his chair and laughed so long and so heartily that every one in the room joined. And when they sobered down, Polly was saying, "And then Mamsie came home, and everything was all right."

"And Mamsie said I could have my new shoes, all-to-my-self shoes," declared Phronsie, very much excited and sitting very straight in old Mr. King's lap; "she did, Grandpapa."

"So she did," assented the old gentleman, bowing his stately head gravely.

"That's nothing," said Percy Whitney in a dissatisfied way, "to have a pair of shoes given you. Why didn't they give you something better than that?"

Phronsie opened her eyes very wide. "I never had a pair whole mine before," she said simply.

"Never had a pair of shoes before," screamed Percy and Van together, while little Dick made a big O of his mouth in utter astonishment.

Jasper leaned forward and tried to pull all three jackets together.

"Gently, boys," said Mrs. Whitney, laying a soft hand on the shoulder nearest to her.

"Don't you understand," said Polly, "that we were very poor, very poor indeed; and Phronsie had never had a pair of shoes all to herself before."

The Whitney boys had no words to offer at that, but sat quite speechless.

"And Mamsie had promised them just as soon as she could get the money."

"And I never had any new shoes," said Phronsie, shaking her yellow head. "No, I never did."

"And one day I heard her asking Seraphina, her doll, 'Do you suppose I'll ever get my new shoes? Not till I get to be a big woman, I guess.'"

"And did you say 'Yes,' Mrs. Pepper—did you—did you?" cried Van, jumping out from the center of the group to precipitate himself at Mother Pepper's elbow.

"Yes, I did," said Mrs. Pepper, smiling at him. "I thought, seeing Phronsie had got hurt it was just the right time for those new shoes to be bought."

"She did—she did say 'Yes,'" proclaimed Van, flying back again, as if bearing a wholly new fact.

"And I should say so too," declared old Mr. King positively, and gathering Phronsie up closely in his arms again.

"Well, and so it was all 'really and truly,' as Phronsie said, settled," ran on Polly once more. "And now, just think, Phronsie was to have her new shoes, and all to herself!"

It was impossible to describe the effect of this announcement upon her auditors as Polly made this statement most impressively, and she rushed on, "and Ben was to run over and ask Deacon Brown if we couldn't have his green wagon, and—"

"And we were to sit in behind," shouted Joel—"Dave and me. Oh, g'lang! Didn't we have fun, though!" cracking an imaginary whip.

"Oh, dear me," exclaimed Van discontentedly, and rolling over on the library rug. "Why couldn't we ever have lived in a little brown house and sat in behind in a green wagon."

"Mamma," screamed little Dick, with cheeks all aflame, and plunging up to Mrs. Whitney's side, "can't we? can't we?"

"What, dear?" asked Mrs. Whitney.

"Sit in behind in a green wagon? Can't we, mamma, just like Polly and Phronsie, and—"

"Ha, ha! Polly and Phronsie didn't sit in behind," shouted Joel. "They sat on the seat with Ben. Dave and me sat—"

"I sat with Polly and Bensie," announced Phronsie, clasping her hands in delight, and drawing a long sigh of satisfaction; "and I could see the horse, and we were going to get red-topped shoes."

"Yes, she wanted them," said Ben, nodding to the others. "Oh, it just scared me, for I was afraid we couldn't get them."

"But we did," declared Phronsie, shaking her yellow head positively—"oh, beautiful red-topped ones, Grandpapa," and she turned to him confidingly.

"Bless your heart!" exclaimed old Mr. King suddenly, and patting her little hands, "so you did. Dear me, yes, to be sure."

"Well, it was *such* a time to get Phronsie ready the next day," said Polly with a long sigh. "Dear me, I thought I never should get through. And then she had to sit in her little chair and wait for the rest of us, and for Ben to bring the horse and the green wagon from Deacon Brown's. Oh, and we were so afraid it would rain—just suppose it had!" and she brought up suddenly at the direful prospect.

"And did it? Did it rain?" cried Percy anxiously, pulling her sleeve.

"No, it was clear as a bell," said Polly. "Oh, you can't think how beautiful that day was! Seems to me I never saw the sun shine any brighter. 'Twas just as if it were made for us. And Mamsie stood on the doorstep to see us go, and the last thing she said was, 'Be sure not to get them rights and lefts, they'll wear longer,' and 'Get them plenty broad.' And I had her purse with the money in it."

"And Joe and David were just dreadful," said Ben, as Polly stopped a minute to take breath. "They dangled their legs out the back of the wagon, and they screamed and made an awful racket—we couldn't keep them still. They scared the old horse most to death."

"Well, he wouldn't go unless he was scared," said Joel. "Would he, Dave?"

"No," laughed Davie. "And then Ben said he'd turn around and drive home again if we didn't stop, so that scared us. And then Polly thought she'd lost Mamsie's purse with all the money in it, and that was worse than ever."

"Yes," said Polly with a long breath; "how frightened we all were. That was perfectly dreadful."

"But she didn't lose it—Polly didn't," cried Phronsie,

shaking her yellow head positively at them all. "No, she truly didn't. And I had my new shoes, and they were red-topped ones," she brought up triumphantly.

"Yes," said Ben, "that was the hardest part of it all. Phronsie wanted red-topped ones and that scared Polly and me dreadfully, for there was only a little bit of a chance that Mr. Beebe would have any, you know, and—"

"But he did," interrupted Phronsie eagerly, and leaning forward to look into old Mr. King's face. "My dear Mr. Beebe did have red-topped shoes. He did, Grandpapa."

The only answer the old gentleman gave was to clasp her closer to his breast, while Polly hurried on.

"Well, *such* a time as we had getting into old Mr. Beebe's shop," she cried, holding up both hands. "Dear me! I thought we never should begin to try on those shoes, and then—"

"And there were, oh, so many shoes," cried Phronsie, clasping her hands, "hanging up in the window, and—"

"Yes, and rubber boots," broke in Joel. "I always wanted them, Dave and I did. But we never got them," he added under his breath.

"Yes, just lots and lots of shoes," Polly was saying; "but that wasn't anything to the ones inside. Why, they hung up all around the shop, just every place a shoe could hang. Oh, and there were ever so many in boxes too. And old Mr. Beebe keep pulling out one after another, and he had them tucked under the shelves and everywhere else. And it did smell so nice and lovely of beautiful leather," she sighed in delight at the remembrance.

"Tell about the pink and white sticks, Polly," begged Davie, pulling gently at her sleeve.

"And the doughnuts," said Joel. "I liked them best."

"Well, I didn't," said David decidedly. "I liked the pink and white sticks best."

"So did I," said Joel, "when I was eating them. But the doughnuts lasted longer, so I liked those best."

"And of course we couldn't get rights and lefts," said Polly, "because, you know, Mamsie told us they wouldn't wear as good; so it seemed as if we never could get Phronsie fitted in all this world."

"And I couldn't see any red-topped shoes in all that shop," declared Ben to the group hanging on every word, "although I walked around and around, and stared at everything with all my eyes."

"Oh, dear me," exclaimed all the auditors in great distress.

"No, I couldn't, and I was just going to give it up, and make up my mind to go home without getting Phronsie any, when don't you think old Mr. Beebe said—you tell them, Polly, what he said," and Ben stopped quite tired out.

"No, you tell," said Polly, delighted to get Ben to talking, and she leaned back and folded her hands restfully.

"Well, he said," began Ben, seeing that Polly was not really to tell it, " 'I made a pair once for the squire's little daughter down to the Point; but her ma didn't take them, 'cause they were too small.' Well, you can just think how we didn't dare breathe, for fear they wouldn't fit."

"But they did," cried Phronsie greatly excited. "My dear Mr. Beebe made them fit me, he did."

"Yes," said Ben, drawing a long breath, "on the shoe went just as nice, and he buttoned it up as snug as could be, and he said, 'But perhaps you'll object to 'em, 'cause they're red-topped.' Just think of that!"

The Whitney boys screamed right out at this stage of affairs, and even Jasper shared in the general excitement, until Phronsie's red-topped shoes seemed to be the same little specks of color before their eyes as when she danced around the old kitchen to show them to Mrs. Pepper.

"Well, now," said old Mr. King at last, in a lull, "we must let Polly tell the rest of it. Go on, Polly my girl, what next?"

"Well, then Phronsie had to get off from the little wooden chair old Mr. Beebe made her sit down in, and stamp in the red-topped shoes real hard, to see if they really were a good fit; and then I paid him out of the money in Mamsie's purse, and he rolled up the old ones in a newspaper; and then he gave her—don't you think—the most *beautiful* buttonhook —oh! you can't think, it shone just like silver, and—"

"And was it silver?" demanded Van, who, seeing the story on the wane, was jealous of every bit of statistic by which to spin it out. "Was it really silver, Polly Pepper?"

"Sh—be still, Van," said Jasper with a little nudge. "Polly cannot possibly get on if you interrupt her all the time."

"No, it wasn't really and truly silver," said Polly, with a bright smile for Jasper, "but it was just as good. Oh, and then dear old Mrs. Beebe gave us another doughnut apiece out of the big stone pot; and then we came out of the shop, and climbed into the old green wagon and drove home."

"And I had my new shoes on, Grandpapa," announced Phronsie, turning to the old gentleman as if a wholly new fact were to be stated; "and they were red-topped, they were!"

"Yes, she kept sticking her feet out from under the shawl Mamsie had told me to tuck her up in every minute, to be sure the shoes were really there," laughed Polly. "Oh, dear! Such a time as I had to get her home, and it was most night too."

"She stuck them out just like this," declared Joel, running out his feet spasmodically, regardless of his neighbors.

"Look out, Joe," said Ben, "and keep your feet to yourself. Goodness me! There's some difference between them and Phronsie's."

"I think she put them out like this," said little Davie, making gentle thrusts with his shoes, "and she didn't knock folks over."

"Well, I don't care," declared Joel, pulling in his feet as suddenly as he had sent them out. "The doughnuts were good, anyway," veering off to safe ground.

"So they were," said Ben, smacking his lips.

"And it was nice to get home to mother," said Polly with dancing eyes—"and she had two candles lighted in the kitchen. I don't know when we'd had more than one at a time before; and she said she couldn't have done better about Phronsie's shoes if she had gone herself—I always remembered that," and Polly turned a beaming face over at Mother Pepper, busy darning the Whitney boys' stockings.

Mrs. Pepper looked up and sent her a bright smile in return. "And Phronsie said she was going to take her shoes to bed with her."

"Ha, ha!" laughed the Whitney boys.

Jasper tried to pull all the three jackets, but only succeeded in reaching Van who was nearest. "Be still, can't you?" he said under his breath, with a glance at Phronsie sitting dewy-eyed and radiant in Grandpapa's lap.

"Yes," said Polly, dashing on quickly, "and what do you think I saw when I went to bed with Mamsie?"

"What—what?" cried the boys.

"Why Phronsie in the trundle bed. One shoe was held tightly in her well hand, but the other, she couldn't hold it very well, you know, because of the cut thumb, and there it was, tumbled right down over her nose."

XVIII

The Old Gray Goose

"You promised," cried Van in a loud, vindictive voice. "Now, Polly Pepper, you did, just as true as anything."

"Well, she didn't promise she'd tell it now," said Jasper. "You two boys would tire her to death, if you had your way. Polly, I wouldn't oblige them. They're perfect tyrants."

"Well, she did promise," repeated Van positively, shaking his brown head, "and when she says she'll do anything, Polly Pepper always does it," he brought up triumphantly.

"Yes, I did promise them, Jasper," said Polly, stifling a sigh, as she thought of the hole in her time that the story would cut. "So I'll do it, boys."

"Oh, goody!" exclaimed Percy, who had kept still through fear of not standing well in Jasper's eyes. Van turned a somersault in the middle of the library floor and came up bright and smiling, but speechless.

"Let her off, boys," begged Jasper, seeing Polly's face. "She'll tell you just as good a one some other time."

189

"No, no," howled Van in alarm. "It's got to be now. You said so, Polly, this very morning at breakfast—that you'd tell it just as soon as you got through with your music lesson, so there!"

"And so I will, Vanny," said Polly brightly. "I'm going to begin it this very minute; that is, as soon as you've called Joel and David and Phronsie and Ben. We couldn't ever in all this world have a story without them."

"We might without Joel," said Van, making lively progress toward the door, having certain reasons of his own for a cooling off toward that individual since the contest in strength with the fists of the little country lad.

"For shame!" cried Jasper after him. "We all want Joel."

"Van doesn't like Joel since Joe beat him," said Percy pleasantly, who dearly loved to take Van down.

"Well, I could have beat him as easy as not," shouted back Van, rushing out into the hall with a very red face to execute his errand, "but he was company, and I didn't want to hit hard."

"Ha, ha!" laughed Percy in derision, and doubling up in amusement.

Polly stood quite still, and looked at him long and intently. As far back as she could remember no one had ever talked so in the Little Brown House, and over her came at this moment an intense longing to be back in the dear old kitchen, where all was bright and cheery and sunny. Percy, being unable to get away from her gaze, grew very red and uncomfortable. At last he said, "Van is such a nuisance," as he fidgeted from one foot to the other. Still Polly didn't say anything.

"And he's always boasting of what he can do." Percy now was in such distress that he had no more words at his command, and he looked ready to cry as he stood helplessly before her. But there was no chance for Polly to say anything, for in burst Joel and David, with Phronsie flying along in the rear. Van having gone to look up Ben, both of them presently made their appearance.

"Now, that's good of you, Polly," said Ben, beaming at her, "for it's raining so dismally it's just the thing to have a story." So that Polly felt quite cheered, and glad already that she was to tell the story.

"Isn't it?" cried Van quite importantly. "Well, I made her."

Percy made a movement involuntarily as if he were about to speak, but thinking better of it he went to the outside of the group, and sat down quietly on the corner of the sofa, the others drawing up chairs and crickets to a circle around Polly.

"Well," said Polly with a flourish—then she looked over and saw Percy. "Oh, come over here," she cried to him. "Here, Jasper, let Percy sit next." So Jasper moved away from Polly's side and pretty soon Percy, dragging up a chair, was sitting close to Polly, and she was smiling down at him as if nothing had happened.

"Now, I thought I would tell you about the old gray goose," she began, but a shout interrupted her. "Oh, that's fine!" cried Van, when the noise died away.

"Because it rains just about as badly as it did on that November day when the black chicken ran away and spoiled our Thanksgiving pie," said Polly, with warm little thrills at her heart to see the happy faces before her, "so you see it's just the time to have the story."

"Do begin," urged Percy, unable to keep still longer.

"Well, the old gray goose had lived with us, you know, ever since I could remember," ran on Polly, "so she was awfully tough—why, we never thought of killing her to eat—"

"But you did," cried little Dick with big eyes. "You said so, Polly Pepper."

"Dear me, yes," said Polly, bobbing her brown head. "But that was afterward, when we had to. But before the black chicken ran away, why, no one ever in all this world thought of killing that old gray goose to eat. Well, she was so old and tough, and she had grown cross, and one day she bit Sally Brown."

"Tell about it, Polly, do!" begged Van, Percy so far forgetting all unpleasantness that he begged eagerly too.

"Yes," said Polly, "I am going to. Well, you know Sally Brown was Deacon Brown's daughter, and she lived in—"

"Did her father let you take the big green wagon when Phronsie had her new shoes?" asked Van abruptly.

"Yes, he did."

"Oh! I do so wish we had a Deacon Brown, who would let us have a big green wagon and go off to places," said Percy enviously.

"Well, 'twouldn't be Badgertown, I can tell you that," said Joel, swelling up importantly, delighted to see Percy's face.

"No, you needn't expect to have such good times as the Peppers had in their Little Brown House," said Jasper decidedly, "because you can't, no matter where you are. I know, for I've been there."

"Jappy always feels so big," said Van irritably, "because he's seen the Little Brown House. Well, do go on, Polly," he added quickly.

"So I will," said Polly with a merry laugh, "if you boys will let me, but you interrupt me so all the while that sometimes I don't know where I am."

"I should think so too," said Jasper. "Polly, I wouldn't tell them another thing unless they'd promise to keep still."

Thereupon such an alarm lest Polly should stop altogether seized the group that everybody kept still as Polly ran on—

"Well, you see, Sally Brown lived in a big red house. Her father was awfully rich, and he had two barns—oh, and a big henhouse, and a great pen where the pigs were kept."

At this there was every appearance of an outbreak, but a glance at Jasper made them clap their hands over their mouths.

"Yes, oh, and there were cows and sometimes cunning little calves, and everything just nice and splendid at Deacon Brown's, till you couldn't think of anything he didn't have. Why, they had milk every single day to drink— the Brown children had. Well, one day Sally Brown's mother sent her to our house to ask Mamsie to come over to help Mrs. Brown to make soft soap."

"What!" exclaimed both Whitney boys together. But Jasper shot them such a keen glance from his dark eyes that they both ducked simultaneously without another word.

"Yes," said Polly, hurrying on. "You see, Mamsie was always so very glad whenever anybody wanted help about anything, because we were very poor, you know, and the money got us some Indian meal and molasses."

"Oh!" said the boys.

"Well, Sally Brown says she ran across the meadows—you see, Deacon Brown's house was off on the road to Cherry Brook, and so whenever we went to the Browns', or they came over to see us—that is, we children—why, we would run 'cross lots, and—"

"What's 'cross lots?" broke in Van.

"Ha, ha! don't know what 'cross lots is," laughed Joel heartily.

"For shame, Joe!" said Ben, and—"Why, Joey, how could they know what 'tis to run 'cross lots, when they've never lived in the country," said Polly.

"Well, 'cross lots is just prime!" exclaimed Joel lustily. "It's to jump and race and tear and holler over the grass and the corn, and through folks' orchards, and over the stone walls, lickety-split—whoop-la!"

He jumped up, and began prancing through an imaginary race, down the long apartment, steering clear of the oaken furniture and damask furnishings, with a keen eye for the distance.

"Come on, Dave," he shouted over his shoulder, "let's show them what it's like," while the Whitney boys sat transfixed with longing at every step.

"No, you don't, Joe," commanded Ben sharply, "in the house. Stop this minute." And little Davie said quietly, "We ought to wait till we get out of doors."

"Well, come on out now, then," cried Joel, whirling around in his tracks, and looking like a race horse held up against his will.

"Why, Polly's telling about how our old gray goose bit

Sally Brown," said David, getting closer to Polly. "We can't now, Joey."

"I don't want to hear about Sally Brown," grumbled Joel, very much out of sorts, "and I wish the old gray goose had bit her worse, I do."

"Oh, Joey!" reproved Polly; "think how good Deacon Brown was to us, and Mrs. Brown too."

"Well, Sally wasn't," said Joel shamefacedly, digging his toes into the soft carpet. "She bit me once, and scratched my face."

"Well, then, I suppose you were bad to her," said Ben coolly. "So come back, Joe, and don't interrupt this story again. Besides, it's raining like everything."

"Well, we can go on the veranda," said Joel, but he came reluctantly back and sat down again.

"Well, so Sally ran 'cross lots," said Polly, picking up the narrative again. "She told us all about it, you know, and she says she never saw the old gray goose till just as she ran into the lane, down by Grandma Bascom's. And the first thing she heard was a 'Hiss—hiss!'" exclaimed Polly, suddenly stretching up her neck as much like a goose as possible so that every one of her auditors jumped; and the Whitney boys looked at the door involuntarily, as if expecting to see an old gray goose walking in, at which they all laughed right merrily so that old Mr. King popped his head in the door to see what it all meant.

"Sally Brown is biting the old gray goose," piped out Phronsie, flying to him, at which they all laughed worse than ever, so that it really seemed as if Polly never would finish that story in the world.

At last everything quieted down, and Polly was under way again in the midst of the narration. "So just as she turned into the lane down by Grandma Bascom's, '*Hiss— hiss!*' came something after her, and looking over her shoulder she saw our old gray goose running on its sticks of legs as fast as it could, with its long neck stuck out straight at her, and screaming and hissing like everything. Oh, dear me! And Sally was so frightened she couldn't run another step, and so she just sat down on the grass, and covered up her eyes with her two hands."

"She always was a silly," declared Joel in scorn. "Why didn't she just turn and stare at that old goose? That's the way I'd done, and then, says I, I'd taken a stick and run after her, and whacked her over the head."

"And what did the old gray goose do then?" demanded Van Whitney, with one ear out for what Joel would have done.

"Why, that dreadful old bird just climbed up into Sally Brown's lap, and nipped a little bit of her arm into her bill, and bit it. And Sally squealed perfectly awfully, and Grandma Bascom heard her, and she came out of her door and shook her broom at the old gray goose, so then she went away—"

"Who did—Sally?" asked Percy with a puzzled air.

"No, the old gray goose did," said Polly. "She took her sticks of legs out of Sally's lap, and she pulled her long neck in, and went off; and Sally came crying over to us, and—"

"And she *always* was a silly," said Joel again with a snort of disdain, "and a crybaby too."

"And Mamsie tied up Sally's arm with opodeldoc," said Polly, glad she could do so well with the long word.

"What's opodel, and the rest of it, Polly?" asked Percy, who was always uncomfortable if he couldn't get the smallest detail of a story.

"Oh! I don't know," said Polly, wishing very much that she had learned all about it so as to be able to tell now. "It's green stuff, like herbs, you know, and Mamsie always soaked some and tied it on us when we got hurt."

"I thought you said Phronsie had her toe tied up in worm something," said Percy in a literal way, "when it was pounded."

"Wormwood? Oh, yes, so she did," said Polly. "Well, Grandma Bascom gave us that. I suppose we didn't have any opodeldoc in the house that day. But sometimes Mamsie would have wormwood too, because we used to get hurt, some of us, pretty often, of course, and we had to be tied up, you know, till we got well."

"What were you tied up to?" broke in little Dick with big eyes.

"Oh, we weren't tied up," said Polly with a little laugh. "I mean our fingers and toes were tied up when they got cut and pounded."

"Oh!" said Van.

"Why, it's cleared off!" screamed Joel, springing up and pointing to the window. "See the rainbow! Come on Dave. Now let's run 'cross lots outdoors!"

XIX

The Green Umbrella

POLLY was at her wits' end to think of anything to make a story out of. She was longing to run out into the conservatory and be with Turner in his work among the flowers, and it seemed as if her feet must carry her off in spite of herself. But there were all four of the boys standing in a row before her, and Phronsie's little face expectantly lifted waiting for Polly to begin.

"Oh, dear me!" she exclaimed with an impatient little flounce, "I do wish—"

"Is that the story, Polly?" asked Phronsie wonderingly.

"No, it isn't," said Van. "And I don't believe she means to tell us any." The faces all fell dismally at that.

"Don't you, Polly?" asked Phronsie anxiously.

"Well, you see, pet," Polly began, half ashamed of her ill humor.

"No, she doesn't mean to," declared Joel, scanning Polly's

face closely. "She's going off somewhere, maybe with Ben, and she won't tell us where. I'm going to tag them."

"Oh, no, I'm not, Joe!" said Polly quickly. "I was going into the conservatory to help Turner work over the flowers."

"Oh, bother that old conservatory!" exclaimed Joel, who was always lost in wonder over Polly's love for flowers. "It's mean not to stay and tell us a story," he added in a dudgeon. "We haven't heard one for ever so long."

"Polly wants to work over the flowers," said Phronsie. Yet she looked very grave as she said it.

"Yes, I do," said Polly, and she turned back and regarded the little group of boys most decidedly, "and I'm tired to death of telling you children stories. I want to have a nice time once in a while myself," and a little red spot began to come on each cheek.

The boys all stared at her without a word, and Phronsie crept nearer and put her little hand against Polly's dress.

"And you tease and tease the life out of me," cried Polly, who, now that she had begun, found it impossible to stop herself, "and I wish you'd go away and let me alone." And there stood Mother Pepper. How she got there, no one ever knew, but there she was in the doorway.

"Polly," said Mrs. Pepper, and there was a look in her black eyes that made Polly's brown ones droop, "you needn't tell any story just now."

"Oh, Mamsie!" cried Polly, all the color gone from her cheek, and bursting into a torrent of tears she rushed to Mother Pepper's side. "Please let me—oh, do! I'd rather tell a story than do anything else. I would, truly."

"Oh, we don't want any story!" screamed Joel, breaking

away from the others to precipitate himself into Mrs. Pepper's arms, his face working frightfully in his efforts not to cry. The other boys stood helplessly by, lost in astonishment.

"No, Polly," said Mrs. Pepper firmly, "not now. The story must wait. And now, children, you can go away and shut the door."

"Can I stay?" begged Phronsie, two tears rolling down her round cheeks, as she came up and stood imploringly by Mother Pepper's side.

"No, dear." So Phronsie crept off like a hurt little thing after the others, and carefully shut the door. Then they all sat down on the lowest stairs to think about it.

"Was that really Polly Pepper?" asked Van in an awe-struck whisper, after a long silence.

"Who did you think it could be if it wasn't Polly?" demanded Percy crossly, and turning on him.

"Some old witch dressed up in Polly's clothes," said Van stoutly. Little Davie laid his head down on the stair above him. "Nobody could get into Pol—Polly's clothes," he sobbed convulsively.

"Of course not," said Percy gloomily. "It's only because Van is such a silly, that he says so."

"And if you say that again about an old witch getting our Polly's clothes, I'll pitch into you," cried Joel with a very red face; and doubling up his stout little fists, he made a lunge at Van.

Van pretended not to be afraid but managed to get on the other side of Percy.

"Oh, dear—dear!" wailed David steadily.

"And you've made Dave cry," cried Joel, "and I'll pound

and bang you for that." This time he managed to reach Van, but in the same moment, "Hoity-toity!" exclaimed a voice above them; and there at the top of the stairs, and looking down at them, was Grandpapa.

"What are you all doing?" he asked, regarding them fixedly.

"We're just sitting here," said Percy, who was the only one to find his tongue, and looking up sidewise.

"So I perceive," said the old gentleman.

"Joel was pitching into Van, Grandpapa," cried little Dick in the most cheerful of tones, and scrambling upstairs at a very rapid rate, "and Polly—"

"Ugh!" screamed Joel after him. "Don't let him tell, Grandpapa," he begged, bounding over the steps to rush past Dick and reach the old gentleman's side first.

"You pushed me," cried little Dick savagely, and coming up red-faced and shining. "He pushed me, Grandpapa," and he doubled up his fists at Joel.

"Hoity-toity!" exclaimed the old gentleman again. "You mustn't be so free with your fists, my boy."

"It's my fault," said Joel. "I was going to pitch into Van. Don't let Dick say anything, Grandpapa," he begged anxiously.

"Polly said"—began Dick, but Joel clapped his hand over his mouth—and there were the two boys whirling around and around, the old gentleman in the center looking at them helplessly.

Meantime Phronsie had come over the stairs to put her hand into the old gentleman's. "Please stop them, Grandpapa," she begged piteously.

"Goodness me, dear!" exclaimed Mr. King. "There, there, Phronsie child, don't cry."

At the word "cry" Joel's hand fell helplessly down from Dick's mouth and he stood quite still while little Dick slid out from under his arm triumphantly.

"If you do speak, you'll be a mean little beggar, Dick Whitney," cried Van, flying over the stairs, "and Polly Pepper won't ever tell you a story in all this world again."

At these words Dick closed his mouth and concluded not to say what was on the tip of his tongue.

"And I was just as bad as Joel, Grandpapa," went on Van, crowding up to the old gentleman's side, "for I said bad things about—"

"Ugh!" exclaimed Joel, turning on him suddenly. "Don't let him tell, Grandpapa. Make him stop."

"Phronsie," said old Mr. King, turning to her very much puzzled, "I can't make anything out of these boys. They're in a bad way. You come with me, child," and he seized her little hand, and moved a step or two away. But Phronsie gently pulled him back.

"I think I ought to stay here, Grandpapa," she said, regarding the boys gravely, while the tears went slowly over her round cheeks.

"Nonsense, child, you can't do them any good. If they want to pound each other's heads they'll do it, and I think myself it might be a good dose for them both."

"But they ought not to, Grandpapa," said Phronsie in distress. "Polly wouldn't like it."

At mention of Polly's name Joel left pursuit of Van, and plunged up to old Mr. King. "I won't touch either of them," he cried. "I don't care if they pound me; I'll let them."

"And I'm not going to pound him," declared Van with a positive air.

"I am," announced little Dick magnificently. "I shall knock Joel flat," and he beat the air with his fists.

At this old Mr. King burst into such a laugh, in which Percy and Van and Joel joined, that the tears forgot to roll down Phronsie's cheeks, and David got off from the lowest stair and came up to add himself to the group.

"Well, now," said Grandpapa cheerfully, "seeing everything is so nice and comfortable, you would all do well to come into my room and see what I've got for you. Put up your fists in your pocket, Dickybird, and save them for next time." With that he marched the whole bunch of children before him into his own writing room. And there, behind the table and waiting for them, was Polly Pepper.

The children all stared at her a moment; then Phronsie piped out, rushing tumultuously over behind the table to get into Polly's lap. "It is Polly. She's got back."

"Yes, Polly has got back," said the old gentleman. "Now, Polly," before any one had a chance to say a word, "I think you would better set right to work about that story." And he bustled about in such a lively manner, getting everybody into chairs, that almost before the children knew it, there was Polly in the very midst of—

THE GREEN UMBRELLA

And it began like this:

"Ever and ever so many years ago," said Polly, "there was a queer little man and he lived in the middle of a big city, in a perfectly funny little house, with only one window in it besides the door, and he had a little daughter. She was only so high"—Polly put her hands up above the table top a little way—"and she could speak thirty-seven different languages."

"Oh, Polly!" exclaimed old Mr. King under his breath.

"And there wasn't anything that would make music that she couldn't play on," said Polly, "so they didn't have to have the hand organs stop in front of the house. The queer little old man used to climb up the tree in front of the perfectly funny little house, and if he saw a hand-organ man coming along, he would scream out, 'Go right away! My daughter makes all the music I want.'"

"Even if there was a monkey with him?" asked Joel, breaking in.

"Yes, even if there was a monkey," said Polly. "That made no difference; he made him go away all the same. Well, and then down the queer little man would slide along the tree till he got to the ground, and then he would rush into the house in a great state, and he would cry out, 'Come, my daughter, and play me a tune,' and then he would begin to dance. Round and round and round and round he would spin until his feet were all twinkling in and out underneath his coat, for I must tell you that he wore a long coat that flapped around his heels every step he took."

"Ha, ha!" laughed Joel, in which the others joined, Polly smiling at them to see their brightness restored. "Well, and there he would keep Araminta Sophia, for I forgot to tell you her name, playing away till she almost tumbled down she was so tired. And at last, when he had danced as much as he wanted to, he said, 'Now take the green umbrella and go out and buy me some fish for breakfast.'

"So Araminta Sophia hopped up from the piano stool, and ran out into the shed that was tacked onto the perfectly funny little house. And there, hanging on a gold peg, was the green umbrella."

"Real gold, Polly Pepper?" cried Van.

"Yes," said Polly, "real true gold, and it was—oh, so big, you can't think, and ever so thick through. Well, and on it dangled the green umbrella, for that was the place where it always had to be kept whenever Araminta Sophia brought it home. I don't know what would have happened if she hadn't hung it up there."

"Didn't anybody ever carry it but Araminta Sophia?" asked Percy.

"Dear me, no," said Polly, "for if they should, it would run away with them."

"Oh! Make the queer old man carry it, and have it run away with him," screamed Joel. "Do, Polly."

"No, no," said old Mr. King, seeing Polly hesitate. "I shan't have any such work as that. This story is begun, and I'm going to hear the rest about Araminta Sophia. Go on, Polly, my girl."

"And some other day I'll tell you how the queer old man did carry the green umbrella, and it did run away with him," said Polly, with a bright smile for all. "Well, so Araminta Sophia took down the green umbrella from its golden peg, and then she hung a little basket on her arm to bring the fish home in, and off she started, as nice as you please. And just as soon as she got outside the door of the perfectly funny little house, all the birds in the tree that hung over it and in the trees all around whispered to each other, and piped and trilled, and sang it over and over, 'Here comes the green umbrella! Here comes the green umbrella!' "

"What did they all say that for?" asked Joel.

"Oh, you'll hear," answered Polly, "if you wait. Well, that is just what all the birds did say. They always said it whenever they saw Araminta Sophia come out under the green umbrella. You see, if she hadn't got it, all the birds would have flown at her, and jumped down on her head, and made a nest in her hair."

"Oh, dear me!" cried all the boys together.

"And so she had to take it every single time she went out to walk," said Polly decidedly, "else it would have been perfectly dreadful. Well, off she went, with the little basket that she was to bring the fish home in, hanging on her arm, when as she turned a sudden corner, an old woman with a big brown cloak on, and her face all hidden in the back of a big hood, stepped up to her and said, 'Pretty little lady, what have you there?' Now Araminta Sophia had always been told by her father, the queer little man, not to talk to strangers, and she was going right on under her green umbrella when the old woman said again, 'Pretty little lady, how your eyes shine! What have you there?'

" 'I am going to buy some fish, good woman, for my father's breakfast,' said Araminta Sophia, stopping just a moment. And before she could say another word, the old woman put her hand under her long brown cloak, and drawing it out, she bent over the little basket. 'Look within! Look within!' she screamed."

"What was it?" shouted Joel and, the others demanding to know the same thing, old Mr. King's writing room was presently the scene of great confusion. When it cleared away, Polly was saying, "And so Araminta Sophia peered into the basket, and the more she looked she couldn't see anything. And so she said pretty soon, 'Good woman, I see nothing.'

" 'Give me the umbrella a minute, stupid creature,' said the old woman. 'I'll hold it over your head and do you tip up the basket with both of your hands, and then you will get the pretty gift I have thrown within it for you.'

"Now, Araminta Sophia wanted dreadfully the beautiful gift the old woman had put in the basket. 'Hold the umbrella carefully over my head,' she said, giving it into the skinny hand. And in a minute, as soon as the words had left her mouth, away flew the old woman, the green umbrella and all, into the sky."

"Oh, dear me!" howled all the boys together. Phronsie snuggled down into Polly's lap, and held tightly to her.

" 'Pretty creature with the shining eyes, look out for the birds!' screamed the old woman in the brown cloak, mounting the sky and holding the green umbrella tightly in her skinny hands. And then she laughed a dreadful laugh. And Araminta Sophia sat down on a big stone by the roadside and put her face in her two hands and cried as hard as she could."

"Oh, dear me!" said the boys again, while Phronsie gave a long sigh, and crept within Polly's arms closer than ever.

"Don't feel badly," said Polly, "but wait and see if perfectly splendid times don't come to Araminta Sophia. Well, there she sat, crying away on her stone, her little basket dangling on her arm, and the birds flying about her. And as soon as they saw the old woman mount up to the sky carrying the green umbrella, every single bird screamed right out, 'Oh, come, the green umbrella's gone! The green umbrella's gone!' And they all hopped down on Araminta Sophia's head, till you couldn't see anything but a heap of birds, and—"

"Oh, dear me!" cried all the boys again—and, "Do make somebody come out and shoot them," cried Joel in great excitement.

"Wait and see," said Polly merrily. "Well, when Araminta Sophia felt all the birds hopping down on her head, she spoke up very humbly: 'Oh, if you please, little birds, I should like to have you get off from my head.'

" 'We can't,' said one of the birds, peering at her with one eye, 'for the old woman that has gone up into the sky won't let us.' "

"She's a bad old woman," shouted Joel vindictively. "Make something come and eat her up."

" 'Please get off from my head,' begged Araminta Sophia, and 'We can't, because the old woman up in the sky won't let us,' the birds kept saying, when suddenly when no one was looking, along came a man with a big gun over his shoulder. "Ah, ha!' he said, 'now I'll have those birds.' "

"Goody!" cried Joel, slapping his hands together smartly. "Oh, make him catch every single one, Polly."

"Don't let him hurt Aramin—what is her name, Polly?" begged Phronsie.

"Araminta Sophia. No, pet, she's not to be hurt," promised Polly, patting Phronsie's yellow hair. "Well, up went the man's big gun, and bang! bang! every single bird fell dead to the ground."

It was impossible to describe the excitement now, and Polly felt warm little thrills at her heart to see it all.

"And don't you think, boys and Phronsie," she ran on gaily, "that the old woman in the brown cloak, who had mounted the sky carrying the green umbrella, peered down from under it, and when she saw what was going on she was very angry, and she cried great big tears, and she couldn't stop, but kept crying and crying, and the tears grew bigger and bigger, and they fell all over her skinny hands, and washed the handle of the green umbrella out of them; for the tears fell over them so fast she couldn't hold it, you know. So away it fell down to earth again, down, down, till it came right on top of Araminta Sophia's head."

"And Ara—what is it, Polly?" cried Phronsie, greatly excited, "got her green umbrella again, didn't she, Polly?"

"Yes," said Polly, nodding her head briskly. "There it was, just as good as ever. So Araminta Sophia jumped up, and was just going off with her little basket she was to bring home the fish in, and carrying the green umbrella over her head, when the man with the big gun said, 'Stay!' So Araminta Sophia stopped right straight off where she was.

" 'Is that old woman in a brown cloak any relation of yours?' for the old woman was coming down from the sky, and they could just see her cloak.

" 'Oh, no!' said Araminta Sophia, looking out from under her green umbrella, and getting up closer to the man with the big gun. 'She ran off with my green umbrella.'

" 'Flew off, you mean,' said the man. 'You should always say what you mean, child. Well now, old woman with the brown cloak, you have flown up there, and there you must stay.'

" 'Let me come down,' squealed the old woman angrily. 'Get out of the way, and let me come down.'

" 'No, indeed,' said the man, and he put his big gun to his shoulder. 'You flew up there, and there you must stay, or I'll shoot your head off.' "

"Whoopity-la!" howled Joel, springing to his feet, followed by Davie and the Whitney boys. "This way," and he put an imaginary gun to his shoulder and took aim at a fanciful old woman in a brown cloak up in the sky. "Bang! Bang! There you go, old woman, and your head's off."

"No, no, he didn't say so," cried Davie, running up to Joel. "The man with the big gun said he would shoot her head off if she came down, Joe."

"I don't care," said Joel, banging away. "I'm going to shoot her, anyway. She's a horrible old woman, and I shan't let her come down. Bang! bang!"

"Well, that isn't the way to do it," said Van, twitching at the imaginary gun. "You don't aim high enough."

"And couldn't the old woman *ever* come down, Polly?" asked Phronsie, a troubled look beginning to settle over her face.

"No, dear," said Polly, "there she had to stay."

"Not *ever* come down?" persisted Phronsie.

"No; that is," as she looked at Phronsie's face, "I guess the man with the big gun would let her come down once in a while, and then Araminta Sophia could stay in the perfectly funny little house and shut the door, you know, so the old woman couldn't let any more birds get in her hair. And then back she would have to fly up into the sky again —the old woman with the brown cloak, I mean—for the man with the big gun said if she didn't he should know it, and he would come and shoot her head off."

"Polly," said Phronsie, laying her cheek against Polly's rosy one, "I am so very glad you let that old woman come down sometimes, because maybe she had a little girl and she wanted to see her. I am so glad, Polly."

XX

The Green Umbrella and the Queer Little Man

"Come on," shouted Van at the bottom of the stairs, "Polly Pepper is going to tell the story of The Green Umbrella and the Queer Little Man. Come on!" and in two minutes the bunch of the youngest Peppers, with Percy and little Dick, precipitated themselves over the stairs, and raced along at his heels until they all brought up in Jasper's den.

"Now, that's fine!" exclaimed Jasper, jumping out of his chair behind the writing table, as they all plunged in, Van having made the appointment in advance. "But where's Polly?"

"Oh, she's coming!" cried Van, rushing around and tumbling over everybody else in his eagerness to draw up the seats. "She's up in Ben's room, and they're both coming in a minute or two. Here, you fellows," to Percy and Dick, "help along with these chairs, will you?"

Percy, who didn't like to move quickly at anything that was like work, slowly managed to draw up one chair into which he planted himself, drawing a long sigh as he sat down.

"That's nice," growled Van, quite red in the face from his exertions. "You feel smart, don't you, to leave us to do all the work as usual."

Percy pretended not to hear, which so enraged Van that he ran up and planted a smart rap on Percy's back as he leaned back composedly in his chair.

"Do that again, will you?" he cried, whirling around to glare at Van. "I'll knock your head off, if you do."

"Here, here!" exclaimed Jasper, looking up quickly from the corner where he was piling away his schoolbooks till it was time to fly to work on them again. "You'll march out of this room if you carry on like that, I can tell you. Up and apologize to each other, now, both of you chaps."

"He's always pitching into me," cried Percy, his face getting a lively red, for he hated above all things to miss Jasper's approval, "and I'm tired of it."

"Apologize, I say," commanded Jasper, with a bob of his head that Percy knew meant business, "or out you go. While as for you, Van, I don't know but what I much better pitch you out neck and heels, as it seems you began it."

"Oh! I'll apologize. I'll say anything you want, Jappy," cried Van in alarm, for invitations to Jasper's den didn't come often enough to be lightly regarded; and not waiting for a reply, he ran around Percy's chair, and stuck out his hand. "I'm sorry, but I wish somebody else would pitch into you, for you're so mean and lazy."

"Hold on!" roared Jasper at him. "That's no apology."

"I don't mind it," said Percy carelessly, and he extended his hand with a patronizing air that made Van furious and sent him back to his work over the seats in anything but a sweet frame of mind.

"How Polly Pepper ever gets along with you, I don't see," said Jasper in despair, as he retreated to his corner.

"Oh, we don't act so before her," observed Van pleasantly, pulling and pushing some refractory chairs into place.

"Well, I should be ashamed to act worse when she is not by," retorted Jasper scornfully. "Think how dreadfully she would feel to see you chaps going on so."

Percy hung his head, and Van cried out in alarm: "Oh, don't tell her, Jappy, don't tell her!"

"As if I'd want to tell her," exclaimed Jasper in greater scorn than ever.

Meantime Polly, who had taken her recreation hour the day before to plan out this story of The Green Umbrella and the Queer Little Man, was sitting down on the floor, her head in Mother Pepper's lap, while Mamsie's hands softly smoothed the brown hair.

"I don't see how I came to say it," she mourned for about the fortieth time. "The words seemed to slip out, Mamsie, without my saying them, and then I couldn't stop."

"No, that is generally the way," observed Mother Pepper. "When anyone lets ill temper say the first word, good-by to all peace of mind. So watch the first word, Polly."

Down went Polly's head lower than ever in Mother Pepper's lap.

"I know you were tired of telling stories to the children,"

went on Mrs. Pepper, "but that's no excuse. And besides, you had promised."

"I know it," mumbled poor Polly into Mother Pepper's stuff gown.

"And if a body is going to do a kindness for another it's best to do it cheerfully, remember that, Polly."

Polly didn't say anything and the kind hands kept up their stroking of the brown hair, and the clock on the shelf ticked away busily as much as to say, "Remember that, Polly."

"And now," said Mrs. Pepper at last, quite cheerily, "I wouldn't ever say anything more about this. We've talked it over, you and I, a good many times, and you've told Mr. King, so it's no good to keep it alive. Just do the best you can now, Polly. Only remember never to let it happen again."

"Mamsie!" exclaimed Polly, lifting her head from Mrs. Pepper's lap suddenly, and sitting quite straight on the floor, her brown eyes shining through her tears, "I just hope there'll be, oh, lots and lots to do for those boys. I love to tell them stories, and I'm going to do everything else I can think of for them too."

"There'll be enough you can do for them, I guess, Polly," observed her mother wisely, "and that's the better way to show you're sorry than talking about it. There, here comes one of them now for you," as Van bounded in, holding out both hands, much as if Polly Pepper were a parcel and he was to bear her down to the waiting group below.

"Oh, Polly, we're ready," he began; but she sprang to her feet and interrupted him. "Oh! For the story, Van? All right, I'll go," and she ran to the door but came flying back.

"Good-by, Mamsie," and she tried to set a kiss on the smoothly banded black hair, but Mrs. Pepper lifted her head quickly, so the soft little kiss dropped on the end of her nose, which made them all laugh merrily.

"Here she is!" cried Van, throwing open the door of Jasper's den, and handing Polly Pepper in with a flourish, "and Polly wasn't in Ben's room after all. I had the greatest time to find her."

"No," said Polly, her cheeks as red as a rose, "I was in Mamsie's room."

"Well, where is Ben?" cried Percy from the depths of his comfortable chair.

"Go and find him for yourself," Van was on the point of saying, but a glance at Jasper made him send the words back.

"Sit here, Polly," Jasper was saying, conducting Polly to the big chair back of the table.

"Oh, Jasper! That looks as if I was going to give a lecture," laughed Polly. "Dear me, how pompous!"

"Well, you must sit there," declared Jasper, clearing a better space on the table. "Dear me, I make no end of a mess with my papers."

"Never mind," said Polly brightly, "I'll help you, Jasper." So together they piled the papers up neatly, and Jasper crammed the whole budget into the table drawer. Then he rapped with the paperweight.

"The meeting will come to order. Does anybody know anything about Ben?" when the door opened, and in stalked that individual.

"Had to go downtown to carry my boots to be mended,"

he said. "Whew, didn't I run home, though! Nearly knocked over an old woman with a basket coming around the corner."

"Did you knock her over, Bensie?" asked Phronsie, leaving the chair she was tugging at to draw it closer to Polly, and coming up to look at him gravely.

"No, I didn't," said Ben, getting into the nearest chair. "I put out both arms, and I screamed, 'Hi, there!' and the old woman and basket and all walked right into them."

"That was nice," observed Phronsie in great satisfaction. "Then she didn't tumble," and she went back to her chair, and mounted it to fold her hands in her lap.

"Polly Pepper is to tell a special story by request," announced Jasper with a grandiloquent air as if addressing a large assembly, "and if the audience will be so good as to come to order, she will begin it at once. If you don't stop talking and be quiet, I'll pitch you all out of the window," he added in his natural voice.

"That's a great way to address an audience, I should think," said Ben in pretended indignation.

"I can't help it," said Jasper recklessly. "Now then, Polly, they're still for just a minute, so you would better begin."

"I promised to tell you the story," began Polly brightly, "of The Green Umbrella and the Queer Little Man, and how it danced away with him."

"Yes, yes!" cried all the roomful. Phronsie smoothed down her white apron in great satisfaction.

"Well, so here it is. Now, you know Araminta Sophia got the green umbrella all safely back again when the man with the big gun—"

"Scared the old woman in the"—began Joel, but Ben plucked him by the jacket collar. "Go on, Polly," he said coolly. "I'll hold this chap still through this story."

"Well, she hung it up on the big golden key when she got home," ran on Polly. "You know she had to buy the fish for her father's breakfast before she could go home, and—"

"What was in the basket, Polly?" asked Phronsie suddenly, stopping the smoothing process to look at Polly.

"Why, the fish," said Polly, "of course. I just told you that, child."

"No, no," said Phronsie, shaking her head, "I don't mean the fish. I mean the other thing, Polly."

"I don't know what you mean, Phronsie," said Polly, looking around on the group in a puzzled way.

"The other thing," persisted Phronsie, clambering down from her chair to come to Polly's side. "What the old woman said she put in, Polly."

"Oh!" said Polly. Then she burst into a merry laugh. "None of you boys remembered to ask me that, and I forgot it myself. Oh! 'twas just her fingers, Phronsie. That was all."

"Whose fingers?" asked Phronsie very much mystified.

"Why, the long skinny ones that belonged to the old woman," said Polly. "She put them in the basket, and just pulled them out again."

"But she said she put in a gift for Ara—what did you call her, Polly?" said Phronsie.

"Araminta Sophia," said Polly. "Well, she said that because she was a naughty old woman, Phronsie. There wasn't any gift at all. Now go and sit in your chair again, that's a good girl. Then I'll go on with the story."

So Phronsie clambered into her chair, and laid her hands in her lap. But her mind was busy over the naughty old woman, and the absence of the gift in the little basket that was to bring home the fish.

"Well, where was I?" began Polly again. "Oh! I know. Araminta Sophia was hanging up the green umbrella on the golden hook, when suddenly the door of the shed opened wide, and in came her father, the queer little man. 'What a time you have been away, daughter,' he squeaked out.

" 'I couldn't help it, father,' said Araminta Sophia, and then she told him the reason why and all about it. But the queer little man only said, 'What a tiresome story. Tell me some other time.' "

"I don't think that was very polite," began Joel, but Ben took another hold of his jacket collar.

"He was more polite than you are," whispered Ben.

" 'And you needn't take the trouble to hang up that green umbrella, daughter,' said the queer little old man, 'for I am going out to walk with it myself.'

" 'Father!' exclaimed Araminta Sophia, turning pale with fright. 'Why, you've never done such a thing in all your life,' and she clasped her hands tightly together around the green umbrella.

" 'Silly chit!' cried the queer little old man in a terrible passion. 'Do you think you are going to tell me what to do? Give me that umbrella this very second.'

"Araminta Sophia tumbled down to her knees, holding on to the green umbrella, and besought him that he wouldn't take it from her but would let her hang it in its place on the golden hook.

" 'The man out there with his gun will shoot you,' at last she said. 'He's most dreadfully big too,' which was the very worst thing she could have said, for the queer little man always fancied that he was as strong as a lion and it made him very angry to hear of anybody bigger than he was. So now he squeaked out in what he fancied was a terrible voice, 'Give me that umbrella this instant, or I'll put you up in the corner with your face to the wall.'

"After this terrible threat, Araminta Sophia handed him the green umbrella without a word; and then she tumbled over on the floor in a dead faint, and the old white cat, who caught all the spiders and mice in the perfectly funny little house, crept in and licked her face until she came to and sat up straight."

"That was nice of the old white cat," said Phronsie to herself, smoothing down her apron again in satisfaction.

"But by that time the queer little old man was gone, and the green umbrella with him. At first he walked along quite fiercely, taking what he thought were very big steps, but they were little bits of mincing steps like—"

"Show us, Polly, do," begged Van. So Polly hopped out from her seat behind the table, and amid peals of laughter she minced up and down like a tiny, queer little man, until she nearly tumbled over on her nose.

"Dear me!" she exclaimed, as she hopped into her seat again. "It's perfectly dreadful to be so little. Well, where was I? Oh, well, off he stepped, holding up the green umbrella as proudly as possible and wishing there was somebody to see how nice he looked; but there wasn't, only a pig behind a fence looking out through the holes, and he didn't care in the least, for he was grunting for something to eat, so you see the queer little old man had to go mincing and nipping on quite alone.

"Well, and before he knew it, he was stepping off very briskly. 'Dear me, how young I feel!' he exclaimed to himself. 'It all comes of carrying this green umbrella. Now I mean to take it out to walk every day.' And as he finished the last word, he found himself running.

" 'This is perfectly splendid!' he cried joyfully. 'I don't know when I've had such a good run. Now I'll enjoy it till I get to that tree yonder but then I must stop, for I shall be quite tired.'

"And in a minute he was close to the big tree, but just as swiftly, before he could draw another breath, he was whisked by. He stuck out his arm, the one that wasn't carrying the green umbrella, you know, and he tried to catch hold of the tree. But alas, he was running by at the top of his speed, and now the big tree was clear way behind, and—"

"And couldn't he stop?" cried Phronsie with wide eyes. "Do make him stop, Polly."

"I can't," said Polly, "because this is the story, you know, of how the green umbrella ran away with the queer little old man."

"This queer little old man has got to run, Phronsie," said Jasper, "so we shall have to let him."

But Phronsie sighed as she folded her hands.

"And the queer little old man knew, too, by this time that he had got to run," Polly was saying, "and he began to sigh and to groan, 'Oh, I wish I hadn't taken this green umbrella.' And all the while he was going faster and faster till his head began to spin and he thought he should drop down in the road. But he couldn't, you see, for his little bits of feet kept hopping and skipping along, so of course there was no time for him to tumble flat. And in a minute he came to a great big pond and—"

"Like what you said Cherry Brook was?" cried Van, breaking in.

"Dear me, no," said Polly with a little laugh; "this was ever and ever so many times bigger, like—"

"Oh, I know," declared Joel in an important way, quite delighted to show Van his superior knowledge. "It was like Spot Pond, Polly, over by Badgertown woods."

"Yes," said Polly with shining eyes, "it was, Joel, just like dear old Spot Pond by Badgertown woods," and she leaned her cheeks on her two hands and her elbows on the table, lost in delightful reminiscence over Joel's words.

Van got out of his chair, and slipping away from the reach of Jasper's fingers, he plucked Polly's sleeve. "You said the queer little old man and the green umbrella came to a big place just like Spot Pond," he whispered in her ear.

"What—oh!" said Polly, lifting her head up suddenly. "Yes, so I did. 'Well now,' said the poor little queer old man to himself, 'I shall surely stop. I am so glad to see this water, for I am really almost run to death.' But the green umbrella made him hop clear across the pond, and there he was on the other side, running for dear life through a brambly wood and up the side of a mountain."

Van ran back to his seat, hugging himself joyfully at this entrancing stage of the story. "Now, there were some people living on the top of that mountain," said Polly quite impressively, "who were very funny people indeed. They were thin and tall—oh, just as thin as bean poles, and as high; and when they went out they always pulled on seven-league boots, and—"

"What are those boots, Polly?" asked Phronsie quickly.

"Oh! let me tell her," cried Van eagerly, delighted to think there was something he could show off in to advantage. "I know. My fairy book tells all about it."

"Well, I shall tell," declared Percy for the same reason. "You see, Phronsie—"

"No, indeed you shall not," exclaimed Van in a dudgeon and forgetting all about Polly Pepper being there. "I began first," and deserting his chair again, he ran over to Phronsie's side and tried to take her hand, but she kept it folded over the other one in her lap and looked gravely at him.

"And I say I shall," cried Percy in a passion and forgetting the same thing. "And as for your beginning first, you are always crowding in, so that's nothing."

Polly leaned back in her big chair and looked at them in dismay.

"And I think you would both better go out of my den," said Jasper coldly.

"Oh, Jasper!" exclaimed Polly quickly. At the sound of her voice both boys turned and looked at her. "I didn't mean to!" exclaimed Van, wilting miserably. "And I didn't either," cried Percy, wishing he wasn't so big, and could creep into a corner.

"And please don't," cried Polly at them, and she clasped her hands and her cheeks got rosy red again.

"We won't! We won't!" they both promised. Van slipped back to his seat and Percy said, "You may tell Phronsie, Van, if you want to."

"No, I don't," said Van, getting down as small in his chair as he could, feeling Polly's brown eyes looking him through.

"I would rather have Polly tell me," said Phronsie with grave eyes for both of the boys.

"Yes, you tell her, Polly, do," said Jasper. "That is best."

So Polly told Phronsie all about what seven-league boots were, and how the people who wore them could take great big steps, longer than anybody else in all the world, and how they could jump from the top of a mountain to another one just as easily as anything, and nothing could catch them. "And so you see," said Polly, winding up her description, "when these tall, thin people heard the little queer man with the green umbrella coming up, they all burst out laughing. 'We'll show him what running is. Get on your boots,' said everyone to each other.

"And every single one of them hurried and pulled on his seven-league boots."

"Oh, goody!" howled Joel, slipping away from Ben's hand.

"Now the queer little old man tried to stop when he got up to them, but instead of that he whisked along by them and there he was way ahead and going at a perfectly dreadful rate.

" 'Ho, ho!' cried the seven-league-boot men. 'You little upstart, you! What do you mean by going by us without a word?' For you see they didn't like it to see such a very little person treat them so coolly, and there he was way off ahead of them. 'We'll teach you better manners,' and off after him they raced."

"And did they catch him?" cried Van. "And what did they do to him?" asked Percy. Little Dick, who hadn't spoken but had been lost in thought, now got out of his chair and stumbled into the center of the group.

"Ha, ha, ha!" he screamed suddenly, as loud as he could.

"Goodness me, Dicky, how you scared me!" exclaimed Polly with a jump.

"He scared us all, I guess," said Ben.

"And you would better get back into that chair of yours," said Jasper, "if you don't want the house to come down on our heads after that noise."

Little Dick, thus adjured, plunged back as suddenly as he had come, and climbed into his chair.

"But step as long and as high as they could, the seven-league-boot men couldn't come up to the queer little man with the green umbrella, for just as soon as he flew out of one city over the church spires and the big houses they would just be coming in, and so all they could see of him would be the green umbrella flying along and a little twinkling thing, with tiny sticks of legs and arms, under it. And at last, besides being very angry they were very much puzzled. 'We've never had anything beat us before,' they called to each other as they stepped along.

"And all the while, don't you think, the queer little old

man was calling and screaming back at them, 'Oh, you dear big boot men,' for he didn't know anything about seven-league boots, 'do stop me, for I'm running away, and I can't stop myself.'

"And at last the seven-league-boot men stopped in surprise, unable to take another step they were so much astonished.

" 'Let's talk it over,' they said, 'and then when we've come to a conclusion what the matter is, why we'll start again after him.'

"So they all stopped on the tip of the nearest mountain and sat down and put their chins in their hands.

" 'It's something about that umbrella,' at last said one boot man, suddenly lifting his head.

" 'Sure enough,' cried another, slapping him on the back. "That's the brightest thing that has been said yet. Think some more.'

" 'I believe it's because it's green,' said another who wanted to be just as bright too.

" 'Sure enough,' said the boot man who had said so before. 'Now we must get him to throw away that dreadful green umbrella, for we can't be beaten you know.'

" 'We must get him to throw away that dreadful green umbrella,' repeated every one of the boot men. Then they all got up, and—"

"And did they get the queer little man to throw away the green umbrella?" cried little Davie impulsively. "Oh, I didn't mean to interrupt, Polly," he cried as soon as he thought.

"I know, Davie, you've been real good," said Polly, smiling approvingly at him. "Well, now you'll see. So off they all stepped with their dreadfully long steps after the queer little old man with the green umbrella, and pretty soon one of the boot men who was a little ahead called out, 'I spy him. He isn't more than seven miles off.' "

"Oh, my!" screamed Joel.

"And sure enough, there he was—running along—the green umbrella just flying through the air, and the little sticks of arms and legs under it twinkling in and out.

" 'Hurry! Hurry! Hurry now for your lives!' roared all the boot men at each other, and they raced as they had never in all their lives raced before. And at last when they were nearly ready to drop they came so near to the queer little man that they could hear him faintly squeal out, 'Oh, do stop me! I'm running away, and I can't stop.'

" 'Throw down that dreadful green umbrella,' roared all the boot men at him together.

" 'I can't,' squealed the queer little man, running on faster than ever. 'It won't let go of my neck,' for you must know, I forgot to tell you, that the crooked handle that used to hang on the golden peg in the woodshed, where Araminta Sophia hung it up, had hooked itself, after he got to running fast, around the neck of the queer little old man and there he was fast and tight."

"Oh, dear me!" exclaimed ever so many voices.

"Did it hurt him?" asked Phronsie piteously.

"Oh, no! I guess not, pet," answered Polly. "He was running so fast I don't believe he felt it much. Anyway, he couldn't get it off, try as hard as he would. And so he ran, worse than ever."

"Can't he *ever* stop?" asked little Dick suddenly, in great excitement.

"You'll see, Dicky," said Polly with a smile, while the others begged her not to stop but to hurry on. " 'Shut up that dreadful green umbrella, then,' screamed out one of the boot men with the first thing that came in his head. And in a minute, before they could take another step, *flap!* went the green umbrella; *snap!* went the green umbrella; and *stop!* the poor little legs and arms of the queer little man came to a standstill.

" 'How very queer!' he gasped. 'Why didn't you tell me that before?' he snapped out as the boot men all came up, for he was very cross by this time. 'Why didn't you think of it yourself instead of making us chase you all over the world?' they snapped back, for you see they were very cross too."

"Oh, Polly! Had they been all over the world?" cried Percy in astonishment.

"Pretty much," said Polly, "and you see they were very tired. And besides they didn't like it, for they never had been obliged to take such a chase before."

"I should like to ask," said Ben, "what this queer little man happened to be standing on when the green umbrella got shut up? You stopped him in the air, you know, Polly."

"Oh! I forgot to say," Polly answered briskly, with a little laugh, "that they happened to be just running over a very high mountain. So when the green umbrella got shut up, why, of course, all he had to do was to stand still on the top of it."

"Oh!" said Ben.

XXI

The Little Snowhouse

"Dear me, how we have all run!" exclaimed Polly, sitting down and wiping her hot face.

"And I beat, I beat!" whooped Joel excitedly. "I got to the big gate first of all."

"That's because I didn't hear Ben say 'three' in time to begin with you," said Percy, his face growing unpleasantly red, and wishing he hadn't run at all.

"Ho, ho!" screamed Van. "That's a good one. Just hear Percy. Well, I stubbed my toe, so I didn't beat."

"You've won the prize, Joe," said Jasper, coming up and drawing a long breath. "Well, that was a race, to be sure."

"You said you'd let the one who beat have a wish, and you'd do it if it was a possible thing," cried Joel with a crow of delight. "Well, I chose for Polly to tell us a story now," and he flung himself down on the grassy terrace by her side.

"Oh, Joel Pepper!" exclaimed Jasper in dismay, "we none of us thought you'd choose that because we knew you wanted so many things."

"Well, I do choose that," declared Joel obstinately, and shaking his stubby black hair, "and I don't want anything else. So begin, Polly, do," and he drummed impatiently against the green bank with his heels.

"Ben," said Jasper in despair, rushing up to that individual, "isn't there anything we can do to bring Joe to his senses? Polly's tired to death. Oh, why did we promise?"

"No," said Ben with a long face, "not when Joe makes up his mind. And we did promise. But I'll tell the story." And he drew a long breath and his face dropped longer yet.

"Ben's going to tell the story," announced Jasper, rushing back cheerily. "Now all sit down," as Phronsie pattered back along the winding road through the shrubbery, having run a race with herself quite contentedly. "Here, child," and he sat down on the grass and drew her into his lap.

"But I don't want Ben to tell the story," cried Joel coolly. "I want Polly, and you promised you'd give me my wish if 'twas a possible thing," he asserted in a loud and positive tone.

"Well, 'tisn't a possible thing. Polly's tired to death," said Jasper shortly. "Here, Ben, come along, and dash a story at this persistent chap."

"Polly isn't tired," contradicted Joel, looking in surprise at Polly's blooming cheeks. "She's never tired. And you've promised," he repeated in an injured tone.

"And I'm quite rested now," exclaimed Polly, tossing back the damp rings of hair away from her brow, "so I can tell it just as well. But what in the world shall it be about?" and she broke into a merry laugh.

"Don't try to think," said Ben, who threw himself on the

grass by her side. "Joe's a mean little beggar to ask it, Polly," he whispered in her ear.

But Polly tossed him a scrap of a whisper back again, and then she began. "Now, it's so hot today, and the middle of summer, it doesn't seem as if it ever had been winter with the snow on the ground. It will make us cool, with nice little creeps all down our backs, if I tell you about our little snow-house, and—"

Joel jumped to his feet with howls of delight. "Oh, Polly!" he screamed. "Do tell about it. That's the most splendid story of all!" Then he suddenly became very grave and stood quite still.

"Come along and sit down, then, Joel," said Polly, "and I'll begin." But Joel didn't move.

"Come along," cried Ben, quite out of sorts, "and get into your seat, and don't stand there like a stick." But still Joel stood very still. "I don't want any story," he blurted out suddenly.

"Don't want any story," repeated Percy and Van in surprise, while little Dick began to cry piteously and laid his head in Polly's lap.

"Polly doesn't want to tell it," began Joel in a gasp, and wishing very much that he had stayed at the big gate where he won the race.

"Oh, yes I do!" cried Polly brightly. "I want to tell it, Joey, I do truly, so sit down like a good boy, and I'll begin right off."

"Do you really?" asked Joel, edging up, with both black eyes fixed on her face.

"Yes, indeed. I'm all rested now," declared Polly. "And

if I don't tell that story I shall feel very badly indeed, Joey Pepper."

So Joel, feeling that it was quite right to be glad that the story was to be told since Polly had said that she should feel badly if she didn't tell it, gave another whoop of delight and scuttled back to crowd in next to Polly, while the others settled down in great satisfaction and Polly began in her cheeriest fashion.

"Well, you must know, boys, that we used to have just the best times in the Little Brown House the minute it began to be winter and the snow commenced to fall, and we could look out and see it all, and plan what we could do."

"And you could get your sleds out," burst in Van—"And go sleighing too," said Percy.

"Oh, we didn't have sleds!" said Polly quickly; "at least, only one that Ben made us."

"Didn't have sleds!" exclaimed the Whitney boys.

"I helped," said Joel sturdily, "and so did Dave."

"Well, I guess it wouldn't have been much of a sled unless Ben had made it," said Polly, looking up at Ben affectionately. "But you two boys did help, though," she made haste to add, as she saw their faces.

"And we couldn't go coasting only when we had all our work done," Polly went on, "because, you see, we were poor and that was play."

There was silence for the space of a moment, it being quite beyond the power of the Whitney boys to say anything. "But when Mamsie did let us go, oh, it was perfectly splendid!" and Polly's cheeks grew rosy red, and her eyes kindled in delight at the remembrance.

"Tell us, tell us," begged Percy and Van, coming out of their deep reflection.

"Well, maybe, some time," said Polly, "but now I'm going to tell you about our little snowhouse. You see, it had been awfully cold one winter," here Polly hurried on with all her speed, after a glance at Ben's face, "and we hadn't had much snow, because it was 'most too cold to snow, and we children had been hoping that we might have some. And every day Joel would come shouting in that he guessed it would snow before night, and—"

"And we had to fill the wood box and chop kindlings all the time, I remember," grumbled Joel, "and our fingers most froze, didn't they, Dave?"

"Maybe," said David, with a glance at Polly's face, and very much wishing that the question had not been asked.

"Never mind," said Ben. "Don't bother to tell any more about the cold, Polly, but get along to the story."

"And so I will," she said briskly, with another look at his face. "Well, and one day—oh, I remember it as well as could be, for Joel had said the same thing about the snow coming, over and over, and—"

"And it did come," interrupted Joel triumphantly, "so, there—"

"You mustn't tell before I get to it," said Polly.

"That's a fact," said Ben. "If Polly tells this story, she must be let alone. Now, Joe, don't you say another word."

Joel, at this, subsided and folded his chubby hands tightly together, and Polly went on. "Well, and pretty soon, do you know, down came the white flakes of snow, so soft and pretty and white, and Mamsie said we might stop our work for five minutes, and watch it from the window. We'd wanted it so, you know, for days and days.

"And then David and Joel began to scream how they were going to take the sled Ben had made, out that afternoon, as soon as the ground was covered, and have a fine time coasting. And then Mamsie told us to look around at the clock. And we did, and then our time was up, and we had to fly at our work again."

"Oh, dear me!" exclaimed the Whitney boys with one voice.

"Well, in the middle of the afternoon the snow was pretty deep. It had been falling just as thick and fast as could be, and Joel came stamping in from the woodshed where he had been cutting kindlings, and he pulled on his mittens and said, 'Now, Mamsie, may we?' and 'Come on, David' all at the same time."

"Just as he says two things together now," said Ben, bursting into a laugh, in which all joined at Joel's expense until he laughed too.

"But Mamsie shook her head. 'Not until I've gone into the Provision Room and seen how many potatoes, and how much Indian meal we have left, Joey,' she said. And then off she went, and Joel pounded his heels on the kitchen floor, and slapped his hands in the mittens together, and kept calling on David to hurry and be ready when Mamsie came back. Oh, I remember just as well as can be—just everything about that afternoon," and Polly came to a sudden stop, lost in thought.

"Polly Pepper! Polly Pepper!" cried Van, shaking her elbow. "Do tell us the story."

"And did she let Joel and David go coasting?" begged Percy, trying to conceal the eagerness he felt in the recital.

"You'll see," said Polly, waking out of her revery. "Well, at last Mamsie came back from the Provision Room, and the very first look that we had of her face we knew that Joel and David couldn't go."

"Oh, dear me!" exclaimed the Whitney children, horribly disappointed.

" 'Boys,' said Mamsie, 'there isn't very much Indian meal ahead, and the stock of potatoes is getting low. Now I could let you off this afternoon, but it's wiser not to live from hand to mouth so we must lay in another supply now.' And that's all she said, but she just looked."

"And I didn't want to go to the store after that old meal and those old potatoes," blurted out Joel suddenly, not looking at anyone.

"But you did go, Joel," cried Polly immediately. "Oh, yes he did, boys!" she repeated emphatically. "He went real good, and Mamsie was pleased."

Joel brightened up at that and brought down his gaze from the tip of one of the tallest trees on the opposite terrace, as he drew a sigh of relief.

" 'Yes,' said Mamsie, and I remember just exactly how she looked as she said it, 'it is always the right thing to get what will be needed, before it is needed.' And then the boys ran off and dragged the sled out of the woodshed, and away they ran off down the road pulling it after them."

"And couldn't they go coasting as soon as they got the potatoes?" demanded Percy.

"And the meal?" begged Van anxiously.

"Why, you see, Mr. Atkins, the man who kept the store, you know, had a great deal to do that afternoon, and it took so long to wait on all his customers that it was dark before the boys got home, and they had to fill the wood box for the next morning, and so Mamsie said they must wait until tomorrow."

"Oh!" exclaimed the two Whitneys.

"Well, we all went to bed early that night. Joel and David meant to get up as soon as it was light and go out and coast, they said. It was snowing beautifully when Mamsie looked out the last thing, and it was dreadfully deep, and Ben said he'd be sure to find time to give Phronsie a ride on the sled. And the first thing we knew it was morning, only we didn't know it was morning," said Polly, with a funny little laugh.

"What do you mean—that you didn't know it was morning?" asked Van.

"Oh, I mean—never mind, you'll see when I get to it," said Polly, who never liked to be pushed ahead of her story. "Well, the first thing I knew Mamsie was calling me, 'Polly,' in such a funny voice that I hopped right up into the middle of the big bed.

" 'Get on your clothes as quickly as possible and come out here,' said Mamsie. And I flew out of bed. Oh, how I wanted to just peep into the kitchen and see what was the matter, but I knew Mamsie wouldn't like it so I got dressed as fast as ever I could and ran out. There was Mamsie in the middle of the floor. 'Polly, child,' she said, 'we're snowed in!' "

There was a breathless silence for a minute, that nobody

seemed able to break. "Yes," said Polly, "and don't you think, there we were buried up in our Little Brown House."

"Oh, Polly!" cried Van in a horrified tone. "Didn't you ever get out?"

"Why, yes," said Polly, "of course, or else we wouldn't be here. Don't feel so, Van," as she saw his face. "It didn't hurt us any, you know, because we all got out in good time. And we had some fun while being shut up in our little snowhouse."

"Is that what you mean by the little snowhouse the story is about?" asked Percy, who was so bound up in the story he had lost sight of the opportunity to laugh at Van.

"Yes," said Polly gaily, "it was, and our Little Brown House was made into a little snowhouse; and now I'm going to tell you about it. Well, when Mamsie said that, I just put my arms around her, and she held me close for a minute, for, you see, we didn't know what to do. And then I said, 'I'm going to call Ben.'"

"But Polly didn't call us then," said Joel in an injured tone, "and Dave and I slept over till ever so late."

"And so did Phronsie," said Ben. "And I wish we could have kept you all in bed the rest of that day."

"But you couldn't," said Joel, bobbing his head, "and just as soon as we did wake up, we found out all about it."

"Well keep still now, Joe," said Ben, "and let Polly finish the story."

"It was just as dark," Polly was saying, "oh, you can't think how dreadfully dark it was till Mamsie lighted her candle, for when we tried to look out of the window, why we couldn't, because, you see, there was the white snow piled up against it tight. And we couldn't open the door."

"Why not?" asked little Dick.

"Because we'd go right into a big snowbank if we did, oh, ever and ever so much higher than our heads. And, besides, the snow would tumble in the house and then we couldn't shut the door again. So Mamsie told us not to touch it. Oh, dear, dear, it was perfectly dreadful!"

A shiver passed over the group that made the "nice little creeps" run down each back, as Polly began again, "Well, and there we were, shut up in our Little Brown House, and we didn't know when anyone would come to dig us out."

"Why didn't you run upstairs and look out?" cried Van, thrusting himself forward excitedly.

"Dear me, we did that the first thing," said Polly. "I mean, Ben did. He tried to look out of the window in the loft because, you know, we didn't have any upstairs, but a little place in the loft where the boys slept, and all he could see was the top of the snow where it had blown all up everywhere, and then he ran down and told Mamsie and me in the kitchen. Oh, you can't think how perfectly dreadful it was those first few minutes. We were so glad the children were fast asleep in their beds."

"Well, we weren't," grumbled Joel, who always felt defrauded out of every one of those dreadful minutes. "Dave and I wanted to be down in the kitchen with Mamsie and you."

"Why, you didn't know anything of it," said Ben with a little laugh.

"Well, we wanted to be there if we didn't," said Joel, not minding the laugh in which the others joined.

"And Mamsie said we were not to worry for God would take care of us," said Polly gravely. "And then she asked Him to do it, and to send some one to dig us out. And then she said—and I'll never forget it—'Now, children, we must set ourselves to think what we ought to do and go to work, because God doesn't help people who do not help themselves.' And then we all sat down to think up the best thing to do. And Ben said he thought we ought to tie something to a long stick, and run it out the window, and maybe—"

"No, that was Polly's idea," said Ben quickly. "She thought of it first."

"Oh, Ben! You surely said so," cried Polly, with rosy cheeks.

"Well, you spoke of it first, and so I said I'd do it," declared Ben positively. "It was Polly who thought it all out."

"Well, you got the red blanket, and tied it on the broom," said Polly, "so you did it, anyway."

"That's nothing," said Ben. "We all thought of the blanket because it was red and would show against the snow. And after that there was nothing we could do, so we all three sat down in the kitchen and looked at each other."

"Yes," said Polly, shaking her head very mournfully, "that was the hardest part of it all; there wasn't anything to do. Oh, dear me, it was perfectly dreadful! You can't think how dreadful it all was."

"And pretty soon Mamsie said, 'Now, children, we'll get breakfast the same as usual. Thank God that we have got a large supply of meal and potatoes in the Provision Room, so we shan't starve. Look at the clock, Polly, child.'

"And there, don't you think," said Polly, "the old clock

in the corner was ticking away the minutes as fast as it could, and it was half past eight, and we always used to get up at six o'clock—in winter, I mean."

"Six o'clock in winter!" cried Percy in amazement, who dearly loved his bed of a morning. "Oh, dear me! That's the middle of the night."

"Well, if you think that's early, what do you think of five o'clock," said Ben under his breath.

"And just think of Ben," Polly was saying, with a little pat on Ben's back. "He used to have all his chores done by six o'clock, because he had to go and help other people, and earn money."

Percy tumbled right over on the green bank, quite overcome by this, and lay there lost in thought.

"Yes, it was half past eight," said Polly impressively. "And when I looked at the clock I jumped up, glad of something to do, for I'd been twisting my hands together, trying not to cry," she confessed, drooping her brown head in a shame-faced way.

"But you didn't cry," declared Ben stoutly. "Polly didn't let a single tear come out of her eyes. She was just splendid all the time."

"No, I wasn't splendid," said Polly; but the color ran over her cheek again, and up to the little waves of hair on her brow as she smiled at Ben. "And when Mamsie told us to get breakfast, why Ben and I were glad enough to hop up and set to work. So he ran and kindled the fire, and pretty soon there it was blazing away, right merrily, because, you see, we had our new stove then. What we should have done with our old one, I'm sure I don't know," said Polly, holding up both hands.

"And I said it was lucky we had such a splendid lot of wood all cut in the woodshed," said Ben, "when I came back to fill up the wood box again, after I had made the fire. And Mamsie said 'Never say "lucky" again, Ben, but say "faithful work provides for the future."' I've thought of it ever since."

"'And that's the reason you've got plenty of wood now,' said Mamsie." Polly took up the story quickly. "And she said that Ben had been plucky instead of lucky, to stick to it when he wanted to rest. Well, then we heard an awful noise up in the loft."

"What was it?" cried Van, getting involuntarily nearer to Polly and Ben. "Was it bears?"

"Worse than bears," said Ben decidedly.

"Worse than bears?" Van was quite delighted but he drew still farther within the center of the group and cast a glance over his shoulder as if he expected something to jump from behind the trees.

"Yes," said Ben, nodding his head.

"Was it a snake?" asked little Dick, huddling up close to Polly to lay his head in her lap again.

"Worse than a snake," said Ben.

"Oh, dear, dear! What was it?" cried Van and Dick together, while Percy got up quickly, and pushed in between the others. "What was it?" he asked too.

"Those two boys," said Ben, pointing to Joel and Davie. "They made more noise than a dozen bears as soon as they woke up and found out how things were. I tell you, it was pretty lively then down in the kitchen."

"And we hadn't seen Ben run out the stick with the red blanket on," said Joel in a dudgeon, flinging himself flat on the grass to drum his heels on the greensward. "It was mean not to wake us up."

"Well, you saw it afterward," said Ben coolly. "And if you'd had your way, Joe, the old broom would have rattled down a dozen times, you wanted to shake it so hard."

"That was to make folks see it, and come and dig us out," said Joel, squinting up at the sky.

"Well, let Polly tell the story," said Jasper, who had been quiet all this time. "And then just think what Mamsie said to those two boys." Here Polly jumped up to her feet. "Oh, it was so splendid!" and her eyes kindled, and the color came and went in her cheeks. "She said, and these are just her words, 'Boys, you've maybe saved all our lives by giving up your play yesterday and getting that meal and those potatoes.' Just think of that," cried Polly again, clasping her hands. "Mamsie said that to *our* two boys. Oh, I'm so proud of them!" With that Polly ran back to the green bank and in a minute she had her two arms around Joel and David. And Jasper proposed three cheers, and Van led them off, Percy coming in in time for the end, as Phronsie gave a delighted little gurgle.

" 'Twasn't anything," said Joel, red and shining in his efforts to escape all praise. "Dave and I didn't do anything."

" 'Twas meal and potatoes," cried little Dick, stumbling up and down the path, and getting in everybody's way. And then they all laughed, and settled down for the end of the story.

"Well," said Polly with a long breath, and beginning again, "you can't think how glad we were to have work to do on that dreadful day. We washed every dish in the house, over and over, and cleaned and tidied up, and then when we hadn't any more work we sat round and told stories."

"Oh! Will you tell us some of those stories you told in the little snowhouse, Polly Pepper?" cried Van in a shout.

"Some time," said Polly.

"Go on, Polly," said Ben, "and tell about sitting around the stove."

"Oh, yes!" said Polly briskly. "You see, children, we couldn't burn our candles all day because Mamsie hadn't such a very great many. And so after Phronsie woke up, and our work was done up we sat around the stove and told stories in the dark."

"Oh! Oh!" exclaimed the Whitney boys.

"Yes, and then," said Ben, "Polly asked Mamsie if we might play blindman's buff. She said yes—and so we did."

"Yes, and we played puss in the corner, and all sorts of things we never had the time to play on other days, we played in our little snowhouse. Oh, we had a lovely time, after all!"

"And didn't anybody come to dig you out?" asked Percy, feeling as if the delights of such a frolic wouldn't pay him for being shut up in a little snowhouse; and he shivered as he spoke.

"No," said Polly, "at least not till the next day. And then all of a sudden some one screamed, 'Hallo, there!' and don't you think we heard Deacon Brown's voice through the snow. They'd dug quite a piece toward us, and they were shouting to let us know they were coming."

"And didn't you scream back, Polly Pepper? Didn't you?

Didn't you?" cried all the Whitneys together in intense excitement.

"I rather guess we did," said Ben, with shining eyes. "It's a wonder the roof of the Little Brown House didn't fly off with the noise we Peppers made."

XXII

Lucy Ann's Garden

"It was about the middle of the afternoon," said Polly, as the little group settled down in one corner of Mother Pepper's room, "when I told the others the story of Lucy Ann's Garden. I remember the time because we were all feeling pretty badly to be shut up in the little snowhouse; for we always ran outdoors every now and then, you know, even when we were working, and it seemed just like a prison, and then we didn't know when we would be dug out, and—"

"But you were dug out sometime, weren't you, Polly Pepper?" interrupted Van anxiously.

A shout greeted this question.

When they came out of the laugh, Polly said, "Yes, but it was two whole days, and every single hour seemed—oh, as long—you can't think! You see, everybody else was snowed in too, and great high drifts were piled along the roads so they couldn't get to us, and so all we could do was to wait. But, oh, dear me!" Polly had no further words at her command, and her hands fell idly to her lap.

"Well, go on." This time it was Percy who pulled her sleeve.

"So, I know all about the time when I began to tell about Lucy Ann's Garden," said Polly, beginning again. "I thought I'd make up a story about summer and flowers, and all the things we have when it is warm and sunny, so we could look forward to it all, and that's the reason I told them that."

"Tell us now," said Jasper. "Do, Polly."

So Polly began the story in earnest. "Lucy Ann's Garden wasn't a bit like any other garden in all the world; it was up on the tops of ever so many trees—"

"Oh, oh!" exclaimed the bunch of Whitneys in delight, Jasper adding his approval to the rest.

"This is a splendid story," declared Joel to Van, who was next, "you better believe."

"Hush!" said Van, edging away. "I can't hear Polly when you talk."

"You see, Lucy Ann's father had ever so many apple trees he was going to cut down, because they didn't have anything on them but shriveled up miserable little apples; and he got his big ax, and went out one day, and Lucy Ann saw him, and she ran after him. 'Father, father,' she cried, 'what are you going to do?' And then he told her.

"'Oh, dear me!' said Lucy Ann. And then she just sat down on the grass and cried, for she couldn't bear to have a tree cut down around her home, or a chicken killed, or anything changed."

"How could they ever have chicken pies, then?" asked Percy abruptly.

"Why they had to send Lucy Ann over to spend the day with her grandmother," said Polly, "and then they killed all the chickens they wanted to eat for a week. But Lucy Ann always cried quarts of tears when she came home and found out about it."

"Oh, Polly!" exclaimed Van. "Lucy Ann couldn't cry quarts of tears—no one could."

"Lucy Ann isn't like anybody else in the world," said Polly stoutly, "and I'm making up a girl who could cry quarts of tears, so she cried them every time she came home and found one of those chickens killed."

"Now, it's hard enough to have to tell stories by the dozen as Polly Pepper does, and be called to account for every word," said Jasper. "Polly has a right to say anything in her stories she has a mind to."

"And do make it quarts," begged Joel, glowering at Van. "Make it gallons, Polly."

"No," said Polly decidedly. "Lucy Ann cried quarts of tears. Well, so when she sat down on the grass and cried, her father fell into a tremble and he shook so the big ax in his hand went every way, for he couldn't hold it straight, and he looked at Lucy Ann, and he said, 'Daughter, I wish you would stop crying.'

" 'I can't,' said Lucy Ann, crying worse than ever, till her tears ran into the grass and off, a little stream trickling away like a tiny, wee river.

" 'Oh, dear me!' exclaimed her father in despair. 'This is something very dreadful.' Then he set his ax carefully up against the first tree he was going to cut off and he went to Lucy Ann. 'Daughter,' he said, 'if you'll stop crying this very minute by my watch, I'll give you this first tree I was going to cut down.' So Lucy Ann took her face up—for she was bending over to sob—and she wiped the tears that were coming out of her eyes away with her hand, and her father ran cheerfully back, and picked up his ax again. 'Now, that is good, my daughter,' he said in a gleeful voice, and he hurried to the next tree and raised the ax just like this." Here Polly swung an imaginary ax over her shoulder, " 'Now, then'—but he didn't bring it down, for Lucy Ann squealed right out, 'Oh, father, don't! Now I've got to cry some more,' and away she went to sobbing, just as much worse than at first as you could think; and the tears got bigger and rounder, and they raced through the grass so fast that they wet her feet till she began to sneeze like everything."

"Oh, dear me!" exclaimed little Dick in dismay.

"Well, Lucy Ann's father, when he saw that, set down the ax again and he pulled his hair in distress. I forgot to tell you that he always pulled his hair when he felt troubled about anything—"

"That was much better than to pull any one else's hair," observed Ben under his breath to Jasper.

"And he said, 'Oh, my daughter Lucy Ann, if you only won't cry any more, I'll give you all those trees this very minute, and you may do what you want to with them.' So Lucy Ann stopped sobbing and wiped her eyes again, and got up from the grass, and went around and around those trees. She went around twenty-seven times before she could decide what she would do with them. And at last she said, 'Father, I'll have a garden up on top of them.' "

"Oh, dear!" exclaimed Van.

"The minute Lucy Ann said she would have a garden up on top of the trees her father put his fingers in his mouth and made a perfectly awful whistle, and—"

"Oh, I know how he did it!" exclaimed Joel, springing to his feet. "Dave and I used to do it—this way," and he clapped his fingers to his mouth but Ben pounced on him.

"No, you don't, Joel Pepper," he cried.

"Oh, no, no, Joey!" exclaimed Polly too, in alarm. "Now be quiet, that's a good boy, for I'm going on with the story. Well, as soon as the whistle echoed all over the place there came running from every direction ever so many men, and every one had an ax on his shoulder; and as soon as they reached Lucy Ann's father and Lucy Ann, they stopped and leaned on the handles of their axes, and said, 'Did you call us, Master?'

" 'Stop talking,' roared Lucy Ann's father at them, for he wanted to be cross with somebody and he didn't want to scold his daugher. 'Do just as she tells you to,' and then he picked up his own ax, and ran off as fast as his feet would carry him into the house, and shut the door and locked it.

" 'Cut off all the tops of those trees,' commanded Lucy Ann, pointing to them, 'every single snip of a leaf.' "

"I thought she didn't want the trees cut down," cried Percy abruptly.

"Hush!" cried Van, delighted to catch Percy interrupting,

while Polly made haste to say, "Oh, this is different. It's only the tops she wanted cut off." And Ben said, "Wait and hear the rest of the story."

"And so the men with the axes did exactly as Lucy Ann told them, and pretty soon all the trees were snipped off even, and just alike.

" 'Now go and bring a board big enough to set on the tops of all those trees,' she commanded, 'and lay it on them, for I'm going to have a garden up there.' "

"Oh, oh, oh!" screamed the Whitneys delightedly.

"And in just ten minutes by Lucy Ann's little diamond watch in her belt, it—"

"Oh, Polly! Did Lucy Ann have a watch all made of diamonds?" asked Percy. "Ladies have them, but girls don't."

"Lucy Ann had one, anyway," said Polly in her most decisive fashion, "and hers was just one big diamond, with the minute hand and the hour hand set in the middle—"

"Oh!" gasped Ben, tumbling back in his seat.

"And in just ten minutes," repeated Polly, "by that little diamond watch stuck in her belt, the board was up on top of all those trees. And then she commanded the men to cover it all over with dirt, ever so deep, and after that she made them build some cunning little steps leading up to it —two pairs of steps, 'because I never mean to go down the same pair I come up,' she said to herself. And in just half an hour from the time she began to think about it, there was her garden all done. And her father peeped out of the window all the time, and he called her mother and all the people in the house, and everyone took a window and watched to see how the work went on."

"I should think they'd want to," said Ben with another gasp.

"And then Lucy Ann said, 'Now run away, just as fast as you can, every single one of you,' and she stamped her foot to make them run faster. So they picked up their axes and scampered off, and she was left alone. And then she walked around her garden twenty-seven times more, trying to think what she would plant in it."

"And what did she, Polly Pepper?" demanded Van eagerly. "What did she plant in it?"

"Wait and see," said Polly gaily. "Well, when she had got around the twenty-seventh time she sat down quite tired out, and then she clapped her hands, and over the grass came running a little girl not much bigger than she was. 'Go and bring the flower basket,' commanded Lucy Ann, 'and be quick, Betserilda.'"

"What did she tell her to bring the flower basket for?" asked little Dick, crowding into the center of the group.

"Why, because she wanted to use it," said Polly.

"And who was Betserilda?" asked Percy.

"Why, the girl she told to bring it," said Jasper. "Don't you understand?"

"Oh!" said Percy.

"You see, Betsy's name was really Betsy Amarilda," said Polly, "but that was too long for sometimes Lucy Ann was in quite a hurry, and so she always called her Betserilda."

"Oh!" said Percy again.

"So Betserilda ran with all her might, and came back dragging the flower basket after her; and then the two girls took hold of the handle and went off into the woods after flowers."

"Polly," cried Phronsie suddenly, "I very much wish we might go into the woods after flowers." She gave a long sigh and everyone turned to look at her.

"We can't," said Polly. "There aren't any woods in this big city," and she sighed too.

"But think what splendid grounds these are, and what monstrous trees," cried Ben hastily, and pointing to them, as Joel began to kick his heels and loudly wish he could run into the woods too. "Polly, what are you going to say next?" asked Ben, catching her eye.

"What? Oh, let me see!" cried Polly, bringing herself back from the delightful vision of a day in the woods. "Well, off they trudged, Lucy Ann and Betserilda, and they began to dig and—"

"What did they dig, Polly?" asked Phronsie, very much interested, and laying her little face on Polly's arm. "The little violets under the moss?"

"Yes," said Polly, "lots and lots of them, Phronsie."

"And the red berries?" Phronsie kept on, "and the long green stems, and the cunning little cups in the moss."

"Yes," said Polly, "they did; all those, Phronsie."

"Every single one, Polly?" asked Phronsie, a little flush stealing over her cheek.

"Every single one," declared Polly positively. "Lucy Ann dug them all up and Betserilda put them in the flower basket, and then they covered them with moss, and then they both took hold of the handle again; but they didn't start to go back until Lucy Ann had most politely invited all the birds and squirrels to come and visit her garden."

"And would they come, Polly?" cried Phronsie greatly excited.

"To be sure; yes, indeed," said Polly. "Every one of them said 'Thank you,' and every one of them said they would, and they'd bring all their friends."

"Oh, how nice!" cried Phronsie; and she sank back in great satisfaction.

"Well, when everything was at last ready in Lucy Ann's Garden, and Betserilda had brought the big water pot and watered it all over, and every little leaf was pulled and patted out, and nothing more was left to be done, Lucy Ann sat down a minute to think, and she put her head in her hands, like this." Down went Polly's brown head and everything was still a minute.

"Go on, Polly Pepper," begged Van, pulling her sleeve. "Don't think any more, but tell the rest of the story."

"Lucy Ann screamed out," said Polly, lifting her head so suddenly they all started, " 'I've got an idea!'

"Betserilda set down the watering pot and dropped a courtesy, for she wasn't allowed to speak, you know, unless told to."

"Why not, Polly?" asked Van, who wanted the last bit of information possible.

"Because she was kept to wait on Lucy Ann," said Polly, "and unless Lucy Ann told her to, she couldn't speak."

"Oh!" said Van.

" 'I'm going to give a party,' screamed Lucy Ann, jumping up and down, 'in my garden. Now speak, Betserilda, and say that is a most beautiful idea.'

" 'That is a most beautiful idea,' said Betserilda.

" 'I thought so,' said Lucy Ann. 'Now, do you run all through the wood and give my invitation to every bird and squirrel you see, and every snake and hoptoad, and every chipmunk and woodchuck, and tell them to come tonight as soon as the moon gets up. Hang up the watering pot on the first crotch of the tree you find going down, and run as fast as you can.' "

"Oh! Oh!" screamed the Whitney boys in glee.

"Didn't I tell you 'twas a prime story?" cried Joel, punching Van, who never could get so far away as to be beyond his fingers.

"Ow! Be still!" said Van, edging off again.

"So Betserilda did as she was bid, and hung up the watering pot on the first crotch of the tree she could find underneath Lucy Ann's Garden, and then away she ran on the tips of her toes into the wood again. And pretty soon every squirrel and bird and hoptoad and snake and chipmunk had his invitation, and—"

"You left out the woodchuck," said Ben. "Poor thing, do let him come to that wonderful party, Polly."

"Of course he came," cried Polly gaily, "we wouldn't let him be forgotten, and so—"

"Couldn't the poor dear sweet little brown worms come, Polly?" asked Phronsie, leaning anxiously forward.

"Dear me, yes," cried Polly, catching sight of Phronsie's face. "Of course those nice angleworms came. We wouldn't leave them out for all the world. Well, and in a minute or two every one of the people, I mean the wood creatures, were dressing up and combing their hair, and—"

"Oh, Polly Pepper!" exclaimed Percy in distress, "now I know this story can't be true because squirrels don't comb their hair, and birds, and—"

"How do you know?" cried Polly at him.

"Well, hoptoads don't, anyway," declared Percy obstinately.

"Well, my hoptoads do," said Polly. "I shall make every one of them comb their hair, and clean their clothes, and prink up to go to that party, so there, Percy Whitney!"

"And this is Polly Pepper's story," said Jasper. "Do keep still, Percy, or out you go from Mother Pepper's room."

"Oh, she can have them do it if she wants to," said Percy, shrinking back in alarm, with one eye on Jasper and another on Ben, and trying to keep himself as small as possible.

"And they couldn't hardly wait for the moon to come up, they were all so anxious to go," Polly ran on. "You see, none of them had ever been to a party before in all their lives."

"I just hate parties!" exploded Joel, having experienced several trials in that line since coming to live at Mr. King's, "and they were very silly to want to go."

"Now, what do you think Lucy Ann had thought out while Betserilda was away?" asked Polly suddenly.

No one of the children could possibly guess, so Polly dashed on. "Well, she had it come in a flash into her head, and off she ran and did it and got back all out of breath, running up one pair of steps to her garden, just as Betserilda came up the other pair.

" 'Betserilda,' she said, 'what do you suppose I've done? Speak.'

" 'I don't know,' said Betserilda.

" 'That's a good girl, because if you'd said you did know, you'd be a naughty girl, because it all came out of my head. I've engaged the band, and we're going to dance.' "

The Whitney boys clapped their hands and shouted approval.

"Betserilda said nothing, because, you know, she couldn't speak unless Lucy Ann told her she might. 'You may talk now,' said Lucy Ann, 'and say, "What a good idea." ' So Betserilda said at once, 'What a good idea.'

" 'Isn't it?' cried Lucy Ann, quite delighted."

"Was Lucy Ann really to have a band play? And where did she get it?" cried Percy and Van together.

"Yes, indeed," said Polly, "she was—a real true cricket band. She'd engaged every one of the black crickets, and she commanded them to stop chirping so as to save their music till evening. And every one said he would. And one of them said he'd bring some cousins that were visiting him, called fiddlers, and—' "

"Oh! there isn't any cricket called a fiddler," cried Van.

"There is a black bug down by the seaside with a fiddle up over his shoulder," said Polly. "I saw a picture of him in Parson Henderson's book before I told this story in the little snowhouse, so there, Van!"

"And don't you interrupt again," said Ben at him, "or out you must go. Now then, Polly, let's have the rest of that story."

"Where was I? Oh, yes. 'We're surely going to dance,' cried Lucy Ann, hopping on all her toes. 'Now run into the house, and get my pink gauze gown all ready, and my little silver shoes, and lay them on the bed, and then tell the cook to make five hundred little ice-creams and cakes and put each on a big green leaf when it's ready to bring up to the garden. Run for your life, Betserilda.'

"So Betserilda ran for her life down one pair of stairs and Lucy Ann hopped down the other pair, and the birds and the squirrels and the hoptoads and the snakes and all the rest of them kept combing their hair and prinking up, and peeking out of the wood, and saying to each other, 'Hasn't the sun gone down yet?' and, 'Isn't the moon ever coming up?' until at last it was time to go to the party.

"And everybody in Lucy Ann's house kept peeking out of all the windows. They didn't even stop for dinner but had the servants bring it to them, and they ate it sitting in the windows so they needn't miss anything. So when the moonlight really did come they were all ready to see every bit of the party too. Well, Lucy Ann in her pink gauze gown tripped away across the grass in her little silver slippers, and went up the stairs to her garden with Betserilda coming after. And when all the wood creatures saw her going up and knew that the party was actually to begin, they all started in fine shape; but they had to wait a bit, which was quite a pity, for the biggest squirrel and the long brown snake fell into a quarrel which should go first in the procession.

" 'Lucy Ann invited me first,' said the big squarrel, chattering so fast they could hardly hear the words.

" 'She likes me best,' said the long brown snake, lashing the pine needles on the ground with his tail.

"This made the big squirrel very angry and he cried in a

sharp voice, 'I'll bite you,' and he was just going to do it, when somebody, way back in the procession, cried out, 'You're mussing your hair, flying in such a rage.'

" 'To be sure,' said the big squirrel, putting up one paw to smooth his head carefully, 'let us not quarrel and bite till after the party. We will both go in together, that's the best way.'

" 'As you like,' said the long brown snake, who didn't want to fight. 'There is room enough for us both, as I am quite thin.' So they both led off, and soon they were all up in the garden and making splendid bows and curtsies to Lucy Ann. And as fast as each one made his bow or curtsy, she would say, if it pleased her, 'That's a good one—check it off, Betserilda,' and Betserilda would make a little mark in a big black book she had in her hand. And if it was very bad Lucy Ann would say it must be done over again. But at last they were ready to dance."

"Who danced with Lucy Ann?" asked Van, breaking in, but Jasper pulled him back and Polly went on.

"And the cricket band struck up, and then Lucy Ann stood upon a mushroom she had had brought up in the garden for a stool, so she looked very tall and big, and she said, 'Look at me,' and everybody looked at her with all his eyes. 'I am going to say something.'

" 'I'm not going to dance with any of you,' she said; 'for, you see, I cannot dance with all; I should be quite tired out, there are so many of you. But I must dance, so I am going to wait for my prince, for of course someone will come,' and she smoothed down her pink gauze gown in great content- ment, and fluttered her pink feather fan. 'Now begin. I shall wait for my prince,' and she hopped off from her mushroom stool and the cricket band struck up their liveliest tune. And while Lucy Ann sat down by a little clump of violets at the very end of her garden, every single one of the party folks began to dance.

"Now, there was in the wood one person who didn't happen to be invited to that party. Lucy Ann didn't know he was there, so she couldn't send him an invitation you see. And he had only arrived that day, being on his way to another place when he succeeded in running away from a cruel master. And when he saw the nice cool wood he thought he would stop awhile and get rested. And then he overheard the chatter about the party, though nobody saw him, and after that he made up his mind he would stay and see it all from an overhanging tree."

"I know what it was," piped Phronsie in a gleeful voice. "He was a—"

"Hush—hush!" cried Ben, springing forward, and "Don't tell, pet," said Polly as she rushed on.

"And when he heard Lucy Ann say that about her prince, and waiting for him to come and dance with her, he said to himself—

" 'Why shouldn't I be the prince?' and the next minute he was combing his hair and prinking up, and then he was ready."

"Oh! Oh!" screamed all those who hadn't heard the story in the little snowhouse; and Joel kept nudging Van and saying, "Didn't I tell you it was a prime one?"

"Well, it was getting pretty late now, you know, for the prince was so anxious to look nice he took a good deal of time to prink up. And Lucy Ann began to look sad, and she called Betserilda who had to stand perfectly still behind the clump of violets. 'I am really afraid I shall have to cry,' said Lucy Ann, 'for my prince doesn't come and I don't know what to do, for my tears will make it so wet in the garden that they will all get cold.' Just then up came the prince, his cap in his hand, along the stairway, and there was the sweetest, dearest little monkey you ever saw in a red coat, standing before her!" cried Polly, with a sudden flourish, and jumping to her feet.

XXIII

The China Mug

"OH, NO! I won't have them on," declared little Dick, shaking his head savagely till it seemed as if every one of the small bits of brown paper must fly off.

"Oh, Dicky!" exclaimed Polly in dismay. "You've bumped your head so falling downstairs."

"Haven't bumped my head," cried Dick, whirling around so that none of the children could investigate the big lumps on his head. "I wish they'd all tumble off," and he gave another vigorous shake that made the biggest piece of wet brown paper settle over his left eye.

"Very well," said Polly coolly, "we must go to Mrs. Whitney then and tell her that you are shaking off all the brown paper. I was going to tell you a story, but we can't have it now."

Little Dick plucked off the big bit of wet brown paper from his eye and looked at her. "I'll stick them on again," he said.

"Very well," said Polly once more. "I'll put them back, that's a good boy," and she proceeded to do so till Dicky was ornamented with the brown paper bits, all in the right places. " 'Now, says I,' as Grandma Bascom used to say, we'll have the story. I'm going to tell you about the China Mug."

"I'm glad of that," said Jasper, "because that was one of the stories we had on a baking day in the Little Brown House—do you remember, Polly?"

"As if we could ever forget," cried Polly happily. And thereupon ensued such a "Do you remember this?" and "Oh! You haven't forgotten that in the Little Brown House!" that the Whitney children fell into despair and began to implore that the story might begin at once.

"You're always talking of the good times in the Little Brown House," cried Van, who never could forgive Jasper for his good fortune in having been there.

"Can't help it," said Jasper, showing signs of rushing off again in reminiscence; so Polly hastened to say, "We really ought not to talk any more about it, but get on with the story. Well, you know, the China Mug was *our* China Mug, and it stood on the left corner of the shelf in the kitchen of the Little Brown House."

"Is it a true story?" clamored Van.

"Oh, you mustn't ask me!" cried Polly gaily, who wasn't going to be called from the land of fancy just then by any question.

"Don't interrupt, any of you," said Jasper, "or I'll ask Polly not to tell about the China Mug; you would better keep still, for it's a fine story, I can tell you."

So Van doubled himself up in a ball on the corner of the big sofa and subsided into quiet, and Polly began once more.

"Yes, the China Mug was really and truly our China Mug on the left corner of the shelf in the kitchen of the Little Brown House. It was a very old mug, oh, I don't know how many years old, two or three hundred, I guess, for you see it was our father's mug when he was a little boy, and his father had it when he was a little boy, and—"

"Did they all drink their milk from it?" broke in little Dick, forgetting all about the indignity of having his head plastered up with bits of wet brown paper. "All those little boys, Polly?"

"Yes, I suppose so," said Polly, "for you see they were all called Samuel, and every Samuel in the family had this mug, so—"

"I wish I could be Samuel and have a mug that was in the Little Brown House," said Dick reflectively.

"Well, it had a funny twisted handle," said Polly, hurrying on, "and oh, the loveliest lady with a pink sash, and long, floating hair, and she had a basket of roses on one arm, and she was picking up her gown and curtsying just like this." Polly jumped to her feet, and executed a most remarkable curtsy.

"Was she standing on the handle?" asked Percy, who had a fancy for all minute details.

"Oh, dear me, no!" said Polly, laughing merrily; and she nearly fell on her nose, as she was just finishing the curtsy. "She couldn't stand on the handle. She was on the front of the China Mug, to be sure; and there was a most beautiful little man, and he had a cocked hat under his arm, and he was bowing to her as she curtsied."

"Tell how the beautiful little man bowed," begged the children. So Polly, who had hopped into her seat, had to jump up again and show them just exactly how the beautiful little man with the cocked hat under his arm bowed to the lovely lady with a pink sash on, and a basket of roses hanging on her arm. Then she hurried back, quite tired out, to her place.

"He had on a blue coat, and his hair was all white, and—"

"Oh, Polly! Was he so very old?" cried Van from his sofa corner.

"Dear me, no!" said Polly again. "He was young and most beautiful, but his hair was powdered, just as the man's is in the big picture in the drawing room. And it was tied up in the back with a bow of ribbon just like that one too, and he had buckles on his knees, and on his shoes, just the very same. Well, he kept bowing and bowing all the time, and the lovely lady with the pink sash on, and the basket of roses hanging on her arm, kept curtsying to him all the time, and they had been doing that for two or three hundred years."

"Oh, Polly Pepper!" exclaimed Percy quite shocked. "How could they bow and curtsy for two hundred years?"

"Well, they did," said Polly, hurrying on, "and—"

"If you interrupt again, out you go," from Jasper.

"And at last one night when we were all abed—Mamsie and Phronsie and I in the bedroom, and the three boys in the loft—and all of us fast asleep, suddenly the beautiful little man exclaimed, 'I am quite tired out bowing to you!'

'And I am quite, quite exhausted curtsying to you all the time,' declared the lovely lady.

" 'And I shall stop bowing, and turn my back on you,' said the beautiful little man.

" 'And I shall not curtsy again, but I shall turn my back on you,' said the lovely lady.

" 'And I shall walk away,' said the beautiful little man.

" 'And I shall walk away from you,' declared the lovely lady.

"And so they both whirled around, and walked away as fast as ever they could from each other; and when they got to the funny twisted handle on the back of the mug, the lovely lady went under it, but the beautiful little man hopped over it briskly, and on they both hurried. And the first thing either of them knew, there they were on the front of the mug staring into each other's faces as they went by. And so around and around the mug they walked, and they never spoke when they went past each other except to say, 'I shall not bow to you,' and 'I shall not curtsy to you,' and then away they went again. Oh, it was too dreadful to think of!

"And at last they had been going on so, around and around, oh, two million times, I guess, and the lovely lady's poor little feet had become so tired out that she could hardly step on them, and she sobbed out to herself—she had just passed the beautiful little man on the front of the mug, so he couldn't see her—'I know I shall drop down and die, if I keep on like this,' so she gave a great jump and she flew clear over the edge of the mug and hopped down inside."

"Oh, oh!" screamed little Dick in a transport.

"And when the beautiful little man came stepping

around to the front of the mug the next time, lo and behold, there was no lovely lady with a basket of roses hanging on her arm, to say, 'I won't curtsy to you.'

" 'How glad I am that that tiresome creature has gone!' he exclaimed, as he skipped off around the mug. And he said it the next time, and—"

"I don't think he was nice at all," observed little Dick, bobbing his head so decidedly that some of the brown paper concluded to fly off at once.

"And he said it the next time," ran on Polly, "and the next. But when he came around again, he rubbed his eyes and tried to stop, but his feet wouldn't let him so on he had to go."

"Oh, dear!" said Percy and Van. "Couldn't he really stop, Polly?"

"No," said Polly, "he couldn't really, but around the mug he must keep going. And the time after, when he came to the front once more, it was all he could do to keep from bursting into tears. And at last he screamed right out, 'Oh, dear, lovely lady! Where have you gone?' "

"Why, she was in the mug," said Van, tumbling off from the sofa corner in a great state of excitement. "Do tell him that, Polly," coming up to her chair.

"Keep still," said Ben, holding up a warning finger.

"But he couldn't stop, for you see his feet wouldn't let him," said Polly, "and he began to cry dreadfully big tears all over his fine blue coat and his cocked hat. And every time before he reached the front of the mug he watched between his sobs to see if she had got back, and when he found that she hadn't he screamed worse than ever, 'Oh, dear, sweet, lovely lady! Where have you gone?' "

"I don't think she was nice," said Percy. "She might have said something."

"And there she was all huddled up in the bottom of the mug," said Polly, "crying so hard she could scarcely breathe, and she tried to call back to him 'Oh, dear, beautiful little man! Do come and help me out,' but her voice didn't reach anywhere for it was such a wee, little squeal. So on he had to go around and around, and she kept on shaking and trembling down in the very bottom of the mug."

The excitement among the Whitney boys was intense, the little bunch of Peppers and Jasper preserving a smiling content, knowing well what was to become of the lovely lady and the beautiful little man, since Polly had told it more than once in the Little Brown House.

"Do hurry, and tell them," whispered Ben in her ear, so Polly laughed and hastened on.

" 'I'll help you,' suddenly said a voice close by on the shelf. The lovely lady bobbing away in the very bottom of the mug and the beautiful little man crying his eyes out as he walked around and around the China Mug stopped weeping and screaming to listen with all their ears.

" 'I am Sir Bowwow,' declared the voice, which came out, you must know, of Phronsie's crockery dog that a lady in the center of Badgertown gave her, when she was a baby, to cut her teeth on. Phronsie used to put his head in her mouth, and bite hard, and that made her teeth come through quicker. Well, he was brown and ugly and one ear

was gone because she had dropped him a good many times.
Oh, and two or three of his toes were broken off, but he was
a great help now in this dreadful trouble that had overtaken
the lovely lady and the beautiful little man, because he had
a good head to think out things.

"I am so glad Phronsie didn't bite it off," said Van with a
sigh of relief.

"Well, go on," said Percy briefly.

"Sir Bowwow cleared his throat; then he asked sharply,
'Are you sure you won't ever say such dreadful things as
I heard from you, ever again, in all this world?'

" 'Oh, quite, quite sure!' said the lovely lady, heaving a
long sigh. 'If you will only get me out of this dismal place,
Sir Bowwow, I will be just as good as I can be.'

" 'And if you will only bring back that lovely lady I will
be just as good as I can be,' said the beautiful little man.
'Sir Bowwow, I promise you.' And they couldn't hear each
other, only what the brown crockery dog said; and he asked
again, 'Are you sure you won't turn your backs on each
other, but you will bow and curtsy as prettily as you always
used to?'

"And they both promised him most solemnly that they
would do that very thing, if he would only help them now
out of this dreadful, dreadful trouble. So the brown crockery
dog jumped up to the top of the funny, twisted handle of
the China Mug and sat there and scratched his head very
gravely, and thought and thought, while the beautiful little
man walked twice around the China Mug. 'The very thing!'
at last exclaimed Sir Bowwow. 'Now, then, hurry, lovely
lady,' and he put one of his paws over the top of the mug

and then peeped over. 'Can't you reach up?' he asked.

"But the lovely lady down in the bottom of the China Mug, although she stood on all her tiptoes couldn't so much as touch the end of his paw. 'I shall die here,' she said, in a faint voice, huddling down in a miserable, little heap, and beginning to weep again.

" 'Nonsense!' cried Sir Bowwow, although he was terribly afraid that she would. 'I'll think again.' So he scratched his head once more and thought, while the beautiful little man walked twice around the China Mug. 'This time I have it!' declared the brown crockery dog, and he put his paw over the edge of the mug. 'Twine the roses in the basket on your arm into a vine, and throw up one end over my paw, and I will pull you up.'

"And the lovely lady stopped crying and began to laugh, all the while she set to work busily making a vine out of the roses in the basket hanging on her arm. And she twisted the thorns and leaves all in and out so nicely, that before long she had a streaming garland. She threw up one end of it over the paw of Sir Bowwow, just as he had told her to do, and in a minute there she was standing on the edge of the China Mug, up by the funny twisted handle.

" 'That's fine!' cried Sir Bowwow, so greatly pleased that he wanted to bark, but he didn't dare for fear of scaring the beautiful little man who was now approaching the funny twisted handle. 'Hurry and hop down, oh lovely lady, and run to your place, for here he comes!'

"So the lovely lady hopped down, and hurried with all her might to her old place on the front of the China Mug, crowding her rose garland into the basket hanging on her arm as she went along. And she had just got there, and was picking up her gown to make a little curtsy when the beautiful little man came up and stood quite still.

" 'I will make you a bow all the rest of my life,' he said, bowing away as fast as he could.

" 'And I will curtsy to you as long as I live,' she said, dropping him a most beautiful one. And so as there was nothing else for him to do, Sir Bowwow ran to his end of the shelf and stood up as stiff as ever. And that's the way we found them all the next morning when we got up and went into the kitchen," said Polly.

XXIV

Brown Betty

MRS. WHITNEY sat in her room, her soft hair floating over her dressing gown, with little Dick in her arms, just as he had run wailing with his story of distress.

"My throat isn't sore," he screamed between his tears, "and I want to go out with the other boys."

Polly, running along the hall, with a new book that Jasper had loaned her tucked under her arm, a happy half hour dancing before her eyes, heard him, and stopped suddenly; then she turned back and put her brown head in the doorway.

"Oh, dear!" and she came close to Mrs. Whitney's chair.

"I'm not sick—and I want to go out with the boys," roared Dick, worse than ever. "I want to go out—I want to go out."

"I suppose that's just what Brown Betty cried," said Polly, saying the first thing that popped into her head of all the stories she used to tell in the Little Brown House.

"Eh?" Little Dick lifted his head from the nest where he had burrowed under his mother's soft hair, and regarded her closely through his tears.

Polly knelt down by Mrs. Whitney's side and turned her back on Jasper's new book, where she laid it on the floor. "You don't know how Brown Betty wanted to get out," she said, "but she couldn't do it, not a bit of it."

"Why not?" demanded Dick suddenly, edging along on his mother's lap to look into Polly's eyes. "Why couldn't she get out, Polly?"

"Why, because she fell in," said Polly, shaking her brown head sadly, "and there was no one to help her out, no matter how much she cried. So she made up her mind not to cry at all."

"Didn't she cry a teenty, wee bit?" asked little Dick, trying to wipe away the drops on his cheeks with his chubby hand.

"Not a single bit of a tear," said Polly decidedly. "What was the use? It wouldn't help her to get out. You see, it was just this way. She was hurrying down the garden path, just as fast as her feet would carry her, and she had a big bundle in her mouth—"

"In her mouth?" repeated little Dick in astonishment and, slipping from his mother's lap, he cuddled on the floor beside Polly and folded his small hands.

"Yes, in her mouth," said Polly merrily. "Oh! Didn't I tell you? Brown Betty was a dear little bug, just as brown as could be, and the bundle in her mouth was a piece of a dead fly she was taking home for her children's dinner."

"Oh!" said Dick. "Tell me, Polly."

Mrs. Whitney slipped out of her chair to finish her dressing, first pausing to pat Polly's brown hair.

"So you see poor Brown Betty couldn't look very well where she was going, for the piece of a dead fly stuck out in front of her eyes so far that the first thing she knew, down she went—down, down, down—and she never stopped till she stood in the midst of hundreds and hundreds of black creatures."

"Oh, Polly!" exclaimed little Dick in dismay.

"Yes," said Polly, "and there she was, and she couldn't speak for a minute for she had come so far and so fast that it was impossible for her to catch her breath, so the black creatures ran around and around her in great glee, and every one of them said: 'How very nice and fat you are. Now we'll eat you up.' "

"Oh, Polly!" cried little Dick again, and snuggling up closer. "Didn't she cry then?"

"No," said Polly, "she didn't, because you see it wouldn't have done any good—she'd got to think up things, how to get out, and all that, you know, so there wasn't any time to cry. And she spoke up just as soon as she could catch her breath, 'Oh, what a wonderful place is this!' and she rolled her little bits of eyes all around, and the ants said—"

"Oh! Were the hundreds of black creatures ants?" asked little Dick.

"Yes, indeed. Oh, didn't I tell you?" cried Polly, all in one breath. "They were dear little black ants, and the deep, deep place that Brown Betty tumbled into when she was carrying home the piece of a dead fly was their house. And when she said, 'Oh, what a wonderful place is this!' they were all very much pleased, and they ran around and around her faster than ever, all talking together, and they said, 'She seems to be very wise—it's a pity to eat her just now. We will wait and let her tell us things first.'

"And Brown Betty heard them say that as they were all running around and around her; for you see when she made up her mind not to cry, she thought she would better keep her ears open as well as her eyes, and find out some way to escape."

"What's escape?" interrupted little Dick.

"Oh, to get out so they wouldn't eat her up!" said Polly. "Well, and so when she heard them say that, why, Brown Betty thought of something else that would give her more time to think up things, how to get away. And she said, 'Oh! if I might only see some of the splendid places you've got in your house, I should be so happy,' for you see she had heard how the ants build great, long halls and rooms, and ever so many nooks and crannies. And the big ant that made them all mind everything she said heard her say it, because Brown Betty called it out as loud as she could; and so the big ant spoke up and ordered a company of a hundred ants to get into line."

"Oh, Polly, a hundred ants!" cried little Dick with an absorbed face.

"Yes, indeed, that's nothing," said Polly, "sometimes they had a thousand march off somewhere, wherever the big Queen Ant would tell them to go. Well, these hundred ran right around Brown Betty and got her in the middle.

" 'Now, go and show her the long corridor,' said the big Mother Ant."

"You said she was the Queen Ant," corrected Dick.

"Yes, so she was, and the Mother Ant too," said Polly, "but I like that best, so I'm going to call her so. Well—"

"Polly," said little Dick hastily, "I very much wish you'd call her Captain Ant."

"Well, I will," said Polly, bursting into a merry laugh that made Mrs. Whitney smile too, a smile that went right down into Polly's heart and made her forget all about Jasper's new book lying there on the floor. "Now she's Captain Ant. We mustn't forget that, Dicky."

"We mustn't forget that," repeated Dick in great satisfaction. "Now go on, Polly, do."

"So the company of a hundred ants went off just as Captain Ant had told them to show Brown Betty the long corridor."

"What's a long cor—what is that word, Polly?"

"Corridor. Oh, that's a great long hall, ever and ever so long," said Polly, "and it was broad and splendid, and the walls were as smooth as a board, and the top was just as smooth too, and out of it ran different rooms, and nooks, and crannies, and funny little places. So when Brown Betty heard Captain Ant command them to show her the long corridor she began to set her busy little head to thinking that perhaps she might steal away from them and hide somewhere in one of these queer little spots."

"And did she?" cried little Dick eagerly.

"Oh, I can't tell you now!" said Polly. "Wait and see. Well, off they went down the long corridor with the smooth dirt walls, and—"

"You said it was board," corrected little Dick.

"Oh, no, Dicky!" said Polly. "I said it was as smooth as a board, but they were all made of dirt—dirt walls; and everything was all polished off by the ants till it was straight and high and splendid. Well, off they went.

" 'What a perfectly remarkable place,' cried Brown Betty, rolling up her little bits of eyes at everything as they marched her along in the middle, which pleased them very much, so they let her drop behind the procession once in a while to admire something or other."

"Oh! Now she is going to run away, I know," said Dick in great excitement.

"Oh, she can't get away yet!" said Polly. "You wait and see, Dicky. Just then, while she was hanging back from the rest of the company—for they were all talking together as they ran around and around and saying how extremely wise she was and what a pity it was that they had got to eat her up after they had shown her all about—she heard a little noise. You see, she was peering into a little cranny."

"What's a cranny?" asked Dick abruptly.

"Oh, a little hideaway place in the wall," said Polly. "Well, she was peering in there, and wondering if she could slip in when the hundred ants weren't looking, when she heard this little noise."

"What was it?" asked Dick, getting as close to Polly as he could.

"You'll see. And then as she peered in, she saw another brown bug, just like herself only bigger, chained to the side of the wall so she couldn't get away."

"Oh, dear me!" exclaimed Dick. "How big was the chain?"

"Oh, it wasn't big at all," said Polly. "How could it be, to fasten up that wee brown bug? It was all made of the hairs of the black spiders dropped in the garden, where the ant house was; and the ants had twisted them together, and made chains to tie up their prisoners with."

"Oh!" said Dicky, drawing a long breath. "And was she tied up tight?"

"Oh, just as tight," said Polly. "The chain went all around her leg and over her neck, and there she was sobbing away as if her heart would break."

"What made her cry?" asked Dick. "Why didn't she think up things, how to get away, just like your brown bug, Polly?" and he drew himself up with the determination to be like Brown Betty.

"Well, you see she didn't," said Polly. "That's just the difference. So there she was chained to the wall of that cranny.

" 'They're waiting till I get fat enough,' said this poor creature to Brown Betty, 'then they'll eat me. I heard them say so.'

"Now, Brown Betty couldn't act as if she heard anything you know, for all those hundred ants would pounce on them both and cut their heads off, maybe, so she said, 'Hush, and I'll try to save you.' Then she hurried off to the company. 'Now show me something more wonderful yet,' she said.

" 'We'll show her the Hall of Justice,' said the ants one to another."

"What is that, Polly?" asked little Dick.

"Oh, you'll see! The ants are going to tell Brown Betty all about it; then you'll know. Well, so off they went, and by this time they thought so much of Brown Betty's wisdom, for they were all talking of it together, that they got very careless about keeping her in the middle, but they let her wander at the end of the procession, and stop when she wanted to admire anything very much."

"Oh, now I know that she is going to run away!" exclaimed little Dick, striking his hands together in great delight.

"And at last there they stood in the middle of the great Hall of Justice. Brown Betty just blinked her eyes, she was so afraid she should cry, when the ants all screamed out together, 'We try our prisoners here before we eat them up.' But she pretended she didn't care, and she said, 'What's that big chair up there?' pointing to the end of the long room.

" 'That is not a chair,' said the ants all together. 'That is the throne.'

"What's a throne?' asked Brown Betty, to gain time to think out things by keeping them talking. Besides, she was trembling so with fright that her poor little knees knocked together and she had to say something or she would have dropped in a dead faint.

" 'Oh—oh—so wise a creature not to know what a throne is!' exclaimed all the ants together in astonishment, and they ran around and around worse than ever, till poor Brown Betty's head spun to see them go, they made her so giddy.

" 'It's where the Queen Ant sits to—' "

"You said you'd call her Captain Ant," broke in Dick.

"Oh, yes, so I did! Well, Captain Ant," corrected Polly.

" 'Well, it's where the Captain sits,' said the ants all together, still running around and around, 'to try the prisoners.'

" 'Oh!' said Brown Betty, her poor knees knocking together worse than ever. Then she managed to pick up courage to ask the first thing that came into her head. 'How does she try them?'

"One of the hundred ants ran out from the company and close up to Brown Betty. 'She is so wise,' he said to himself, 'I want to show her that I am wise too.' So he hurried up to her side. 'Do you see that sword hanging up there?' he whispered, and the other ninety-nine ants were all talking together and running about so they didn't hear him.

" 'Where?' asked Brown Betty, peering up above the throne. 'I see nothing.'

" 'Of course,' said the ant who wanted to show how wise he was, and he laughed softly, he was so pleased that he could tell her something new. 'You can't see it till I tell you where it is, so I am wiser than you. Well, when the Queen has that in her hand she can do anything she pleases—it all comes to pass. It hangs just back of the throne, at the top. Now, don't you think I am wise?'

"Brown Betty's heart gave a great jump. 'Oh, sir!' she cried, 'what a wonderful creature you are!' which so delighted the ant that he ran around and around her sixty times without stopping, talking to himself all the while: 'She says I'm a wonderful creature.'

"All this time Brown Betty was thinking how she could get up into that throne, and presently she said as loud as she could, 'One of the most wonderful places that ever I was in is this very spot. But I must sit on that throne before I can say it is *the* most wonderful place,' she added boldly, while her poor knees shook and knocked so together she thought she should die.

" 'She must say it is *the* most wonderful place she was ever in,' declared the company of ants in consternation, 'else Captain Ant will have our heads off when we carry her back,' and they ran around and around her worse than ever, saying this over all the time.

"At last they all stopped and swarmed around her, keeping her in the middle. 'Will you say "This is *the* most wonderful place I was ever in," if we let you get up in the throne?' they cried at her.

" 'I will,' promised Brown Betty as quick as a flash. So they opened their ranks and before she could think twice, there she was up in the throne and looking down into their faces. But how to get hold of the sword, she didn't know."

"Oh, Polly, do let her get that sword!" cried little Dick in great distress. "Please show her how. Please hurry, Polly, and show her how quick."

"And there she was, looking down into their faces, and she knew she must hurry and say the words she had promised, and then get down; and she was at her wits' end to know what to do."

"Please hurry, and show her how quick," begged little Dick, his knees knocking together.

" 'What a wonderful top to that throne!' cried Brown Betty. 'I must see that first.' And as quickly as she said the words up she ran with all speed to the very tip of the throne spread over her head. The wise ant who had told her of the sword, just then screamed out, 'Hold her back!' but it was too late. Brown Betty's little bits of eyes were keen and sharp. There was the sword, hanging before her, and in a second it was in her mouth, and she was waving it over the hundred ants.

" 'Stop where you are!' she screamed at them, 'or I'll cut your heads off!' and not a single ant moved."

"She killed them all, she killed them!" piped Dicky in the most joyful tone, and springing to his feet he danced all over the dressing room, singing, "Brown Betty killed them all!"

"Oh, no, she didn't!" said Polly, as soon as she could make herself heard.

"She didn't kill them!" exclaimed little Dick, coming to a dead stop in amazement.

"Oh, no! of course not," said Polly. "Brown Betty wouldn't do such a cruel thing if she could get away and help the other brown bug off without hurting them. She just slipped down from the throne, waving her sword at them and telling them she would cut their heads off if they stirred. But they couldn't, you know. Then she slammed the door of the Hall of Justice tight to, and locked them all in."

"That was worse," said Dicky, coming up quite close to her.

"Oh, some of the other ants would come by and by, to look for them," said Polly comfortingly, "and let them out. So down the long corridor she ran with the Captain's sword in her mouth, till she reached the cranny where the other brown bug was tied.

" 'Stop crying!' she commanded, and with one flash of the sword she snipped the chain everywhere it was fastened.

'Now come on,' and she dragged the prisoner out. And away they went, Brown Betty waving the sword high, for she didn't know when she would meet any ants and she must be ready to keep them off.

" 'You've been here longer than I,' she cried to the other brown bug. 'Don't you know some way out?'

" 'Let me stop and think,' begged the other brown bug. 'You hurry me so I can't think of anything.' So Brown Betty pulled her into a little cubbyhole they were racing by in the corridor, while she stood on guard, still waving the Captain's sword.

" 'I will give you till I can count ten,' she said. 'One—two—three—four—five—six—seven—eight—' "

"Oh, dear!" groaned little Dick.

" 'Nine—ten—'

" 'Straight ahead! Turn to your right!' screamed the other brown bug, and out into the long corridor they stepped once more and ran like lightning. And then, after awhile, 'Turn!' she said. 'I heard them say that they had built a secret way.' And there was a little narrow slit of a way down which they turned; and they turned, and they turned, till finally after they had got through turning, all of a sudden out it came into the green grass, and, don't you think, right around the door, only they didn't see it, it was so covered with a clump of leaves, were six little, wee, tiny brown bugs, all crying and screaming and rubbing their eyes for their mammy, and there she was right in their midst."

"Oh, Polly! Was it Brown Betty's home she got to?" screamed little Dick, throwing his arms around her, his cheeks aflame.

"Yes," said Polly, "it truly was; and Brown Betty would never have found it at all if she hadn't gone back to save the other brown bug."

"And what did she do with the Captain's sword?" at last asked Dicky, coming out of his entrancement.

"I don't know," said Polly, "but here come the boys, Dicky."

XXV

The Silly Little Brook

"PLEASE, Polly," entreated Phronsie, pulling Polly's gown gently.

"Oh, pet! There isn't time," said Polly hastily, "to tell you a story now. Why, Mamsie will call us in a quarter of an hour."

"Just the Silly Little Brook," pleaded Phronsie, folding her hands.

"Why, you've heard that fifty thousand times," said Polly. "Oh—oh! Don't ask for that." She gave a long yawn and flew back to the table. "Where is that pink embroidery silk Auntie gave me? Now I'll try that new stitch."

"Here 'tis," said Phronsie, getting down on the floor and spying it where it had trailed off on the tablecloth, and she quickly brought it up in her hand.

"Oh, that's good!" exclaimed Polly in great satisfaction, with one eye on the French mantel clock. "Now, if I had to hunt for that tiresome pink silk, the whole quarter of an hour would be gone, and I must try this rosebud to show to Auntie Whitney." She seized her embroidery work, huddling up silks and thimble and all, and ran to ensconce herself in a cosy corner of the libary sofa, humming softly to herself the last piece of music Monsieur had given to her.

"I might have a *piece* of the Silly Little Brook," said Phronsie, standing quite still by the table.

"What is it?" cried Polly, coming out from the trills and runs, to stare at her. "Oh, that story! I forgot all about it, Phronsie. Yes, indeed, you shall have it." And a remorseful wave made her cheek rosy red. "I'm a selfish little pig, Phronsie. Come over, and I'll tell it right away."

"You're not a little pig," said Phronsie, hurrying over to the sofa to tuck herself away in a blissful frame of mind close to Polly, "and I am so glad you are going to tell it, and please begin right off, Polly," all in one breath.

"Yes, indeed, I will," said Polly with a sorry little twinge for the minutes lost. "Well, you know the Silly Little Brook was not our Cherry Brook," she began, well knowing that fact must usher in the story.

"It was not our Cherry Brook," repeated Phronsie distinctly, and smoothing down her white apron, "because our Cherry Brook was a nice brook and didn't do silly things."

"That's so," assented Polly, wondering if she was making her rosebud pink enough. "Well, one day, quite early in the morning when the sun was peeping over the top of a high mountain—"

"Tell how he peeped over, please, Polly," begged Phronsie, who dearly loved to have Polly act out her stories.

So Polly laid down her rosebud, thimble, and all in

Phronsie's lap and got up and told it over again, to Phronsie's intense satisfaction. Then she hopped back to her embroidery work.

"And at the same time the Silly Little Brook awoke, and opened its eyes to the sun and the world. 'Oh! how do you do?' said the Sun, laughing as the Silly Little Brook blinked its eyes at him.

" 'Who are you?' asked the Silly Little Brook. 'I never saw you before.'

" 'Of course not,' said the Sun, laughing worse than ever, 'because you have never been awake before. Come, now, it is time for you to get to work. You've been a long time asleep. Look back of you.'

"The Silly Little Brook did just as the Sun told her, and looked back of her. 'I don't see anything,' she said, 'except a black hole in the ground.'

" 'Of course you don't,' said the Sun, 'because that's all there is to see. You've just come out of that hole, where you've been asleep all your life. Now look ahead!'

"The Sun said this so loud and stared at her face so long that the Silly Little Brook began to feel quite uncomfortable, so she winked and blinked and said nothing.

" 'Look ahead,' commanded the Sun sharply. 'Oh, you silly, stupid, little thing!' And this time she obeyed, and there was a tiny, wee, little stream of clear, white water trickling away like a thread down the mountain."

"It was the Silly Little Broook," cried Phronsie, clapping her hands in glee just as if she hadn't heard the story time and again.

"Yes," said Polly, bobbing her head and setting in quick

stitches, "so it was. 'Now hurry up!' said the Sun—by this time he was very fierce for his face had been getting rounder and bigger every minute—'and set to work, for you have a great deal to do. Be a useful little brook and don't stop on your way, and I shall be glad that you woke up. Good day!' And the Silly Little Brook felt her feet give way before her, and in a minute she was slipping and sliding down, down, the mountainside.

" 'I'm not going to be sent down in this fashion,' she grumbled as soon as she could catch her breath, while she rested a bit in a hollow. 'I shall choose my way, and what I'll do. And I'm not going to work all the time either, and that cross old Sun needn't think he can command me to do it. I'm going to play as much as I want to.' With that she rested in the hollow all that day, and the next, and the next."

Phronsie shook her yellow head mournfully, as one who knows a sorrowful tale too well.

"The first day," said Polly, hurrying on, "the birds came to see the Silly Little Brook, and they sang sweet songs over her head, and they told her pretty stories, and they dipped their beaks in her clear little pool of water in the hollow. And the Silly Little Brook said to herself, 'Oh, what a lovely time this is! How good it was for me that I didn't mind what the cross old Sun said to me when he told me not to stop. Forsooth! I shall stop here as long as I want to.' "

"What does for—what is it, Polly—mean?" asked Phronsie who always asked this question at this particular stage of the story.

"Oh, it doesn't mean anything!" said Polly carelessly.

"Then, why did she say it?" persisted Phronsie.

"Oh, because it sounded nice!" said Polly, twitching her pink silk thread out to replace it with a green one to begin on the calyx. "People have to say things sometimes that don't mean anything—in a story."

"Do they?" said Phronsie with wondering eyes.

"Well, she did anyway," said Polly, "so she said 'Forsooth!' and tossed her head, and immediately she felt very big and grand. And the next day the birds came, and everything was lovely, and the Silly Little Brook went to sleep at night and dreamed of all sorts of beautiful things. But the day after she looked up, and saw to her astonishment a flock of birds that was whirring along over the tip of the mountainside, pause when they got to her, and look down. Then they whispered together and presently off they flew, chattering, 'Oh, no—no; we'll not stop there!'

"What to make of it the Silly Little Brook did not know. She only tossed her head, and grew angrier and angrier, and said she didn't care. But she went to sleep sobbing as hard as she could that night, and her pillow, a clump of moss, was wet with tears."

Phronsie moved uneasily, but said not a word.

"At last, as morning broke, the Silly Little Brook heard a voice close to her ear say, 'Oh, dear Brook, wake up! I have something to say to you,' and there was Robin Redbreast."

"I am so glad he has come, Polly," ejaculated Phronsie in relief.

"The Silly Little Brook at that opened her eyes. 'What is it?' she asked sadly.

" 'Don't you know why the birds are flying over your head

to seek other streams, without so much as giving you a gentle word—and no one remains to tell you the truth but me?' asked Robin.

" 'No, I don't!' said the Silly Little Brook. 'Tell me, Robin.'

" 'Look for yourself,' said Robin Redbreast.

"So the Silly Little Brook turned her eyes to look at herself in the little hollow where she had rested, and lo and behold, instead of the clear, white water with the shade just like the violets in our woods at Badgertown, you know, Phronsie," and Polly's hands with their work dropped to her lap, "why—"

"Yes, yes, I know," said Phronsie with a small sigh, hearing which, Polly picked up her work again and hurried on.

"Why, there was a dark, dirty pool of water with a little green scum coming all over the top of it.

" 'Oh, Horrors!' screamed the Silly Little Brook. 'Why, where have I gone? That isn't my little Brook.'

" 'Yes it is,' said Robin, shaking his head sadly; 'you're turned into this hateful thing because you stayed still. Oh dear Brook! Why didn't you obey the good Sun, and go on?'

" 'I will now,' said the Silly Little Brook, bursting into a torrent of tears, and she tried to start. But her feet were all tangled up in a mess of leaves and green things that weren't nice, and she couldn't stir a step."

Phronsie here moved uneasily again, but waited for Polly to go on.

" 'I'll help you,' said Robin Redbreast quickly, and, jumping down, he picked patiently all the sticks and leaves he could in his bill and carried them out of the way of the Silly Little Brook when she should once more start to run down the mountainside."

"He was a nice Robin Redbreast, Polly, and I like him," Phronsie exclaimed joyfully.

"So he was, pet," Polly made haste to answer. "Well, but as fast as he picked off the leaves and sticks out of the way of the Silly Little Brook, ever so many others would come blowing down on her from the trees and choke up the path again. So at last poor Robin Redbreast had to sit down quite tired out, and declare he could do no more."

"Please hurry and tell it, Polly," begged Phronsie, pulling her sleeve, for Polly dearly loved to stop a bit in the most impressive spots.

"Well, and then the Silly Little Brook began to sob and to scream louder than ever; and the sticks and leaves flew around her thick and fast, for it was a very windy day; and the birds flew over her head, never so much as giving her a glance; and it was very dreadful indeed," said Polly, holding up her embroidery at arm's length to see if the calyx was beginning to look exactly as if the rosebud were just picked from the garden.

"Please hurry," begged Phronsie, pulling her sleeve again.

"So I will," said Polly; "I think that is just as near right as I can get it, although it doesn't look like a real rose," she sighed, "but you must let me stop once in a while, child, for the story sounds better."

"But I want the Silly Little Brook to stop crying and get out," said Phronsie in gentle haste.

"Well, so I will let her out, you'll see," promised Polly,

hurrying on to set in more green stitches, determined, since she couldn't make it like a real rose from Grandpapa's garden, she would have it as good a one as possible.

" 'I shall die here,' mourned the Silly Little Brook, and the wind in the trees sobbed over her, 'She will die there,' until Robin Redbreast let his head droop on his pretty red bosom."

"Please hurry, Polly," said Phronsie pleadingly, and there were tears in the brown eyes.

"But suddenly up jumped Robin," cried Polly, casting aside her embroidery on the sofa, and suiting the action to the word she sprang to her feet and waved her arms. "And he trilled out loud and clear, while he flapped his wings, 'Stop your crying, dear Brook. I will go and bring some help,' for he had heard what the Silly Little Brook had not been able to hear, as she was weeping so hard—the notes way up in the sky of some little birds that he knew."

"Polly!" exclaimed Phronsie, in great excitement, and slipping from the sofa to plant herself in front of Polly—still waving her arms, and crying, "Stop your crying, dear Brook, I will go and bring some help"—"I love that Robin Redbreast, I do."

"Well, we must get back to the sofa and finish this story, or Mamsie'll call us before we're ready," laughed Polly, her arms tumbling to her sides; and she picked up Phronsie and in a minute there they were in the cosy corner once more.

"So off he flew posthaste," hurried on Polly, picking up her needle once more to set quick stitches, "and oh, as soon as you could think, back he came with a whole troop of Robin Redbreasts who were on a journey together, and there were so many of them that they picked out every stick and leaf before the new ones had a chance to choke up the way. And pretty soon, 'Start now!' they said, and the Silly Little Brook put out her feet and away she went slipping and sliding and trickling and running like a mad little thing down the mountainside."

Phronsie clapped her hands and shouted in glee.

" 'Don't stop again,' screamed every one of those Robin Redbreasts after her, 'but go on—and on—and on.' "

"Pol—*ly!*" called Mamsie over the stairs—and "Phron—*sie!* It's time to go downtown to buy your shoes."

XXVI

Down in the Orchard

"It was such a comfort to have an Orchard," said Polly, clasping her hands in delight at the remembrance. "You can't think. And we used to have such fun out there when the work was done up—"

"How many trees were there?" asked Percy, with an eye for details.

"Oh, there weren't any *trees!*" said Polly quickly. "There was just one, but we played there were ever and ever so many, so we called it an Orchard."

"Oh, dear me!" exclaimed Percy and Van together.

"It was an apple tree," said Joel, "and there weren't any apples on it either, only we used to play there were."

"Oh, Joel!" exclaimed Polly. "Have you forgotten? Don't you remember one year that we got some?"

"Mean old things," declared Joel, "and so hard, they'd almost break your teeth!"

"Well, you and Dave managed to eat them," said Ben, laughing.

293

"Because we couldn't get any others," said Joel, "and they were only about a dozen of them, I guess."

"That was better than nothing," said Polly. "Well, you see we did have apples on the tree sometimes, so we could call it an Orchard; and when we had our work done, we could go out there and play. And Phronsie could always take Seraphina and stay there ever so long, because it was just a little way back of the kitchen door. So you see we thought a great deal indeed of our Orchard."

"Tell us what you used to do out in your Orchard," begged Van abruptly; "every single thing."

"Oh, dear me!" said Polly, drawing a long breath at the delightful remembrances. "I can't tell you all the things we used to do there any more than I can about all the good times we had in the dear old kitchen."

"There's no use in asking the Peppers to tell all the good times they had in the Little Brown House," declared Jasper, with kindling eyes, "because, you see, they just can't do it. I know, because I've been there."

"Jappy always feels so smart because he's been at the Little Brown House," exclaimed Van enviously.

"Well, why shouldn't I?" retorted Jasper gaily. "It's something to feel smart over, I can tell you, to go to the Little Brown House."

"I wish we could ever go there," said Percy wishfully.

"Well, if you want to hear Polly tell of what we did down in our Orchard, you would better stop talking, and let her begin," advised Ben.

"I think so too," laughed Jasper. "I'm as bad as the rest. But when it comes to talking about the Little Brown House, why I just forget and pitch in. Now do go on, Polly; we beg your pardon," and he shook his head at the other boys.

"Yes, we do beg your pardon," Percy and Van made haste to say, seeing that Jasper had said it first.

"All right," said Polly. "Then, I'll begin straight off to tell you of one nice time we had down in our Orchard. You see, Mamsie was off at the minister's house helping to make over the parlor carpet, and we really hadn't any work to do. And, for a wonder, Ben was home because there was no wood for him to chop anywhere; and it was a long, hot summer afternoon. First, we thought we'd go off to the woods, and—"

"And why didn't you?" broke in Van, with wide eyes for the indifference to the charms of the woods.

"Hush!" said Jasper, holding up his hand.

Percy was just going to say, "I should think you'd have gone to the woods, and dug up moss and flowers and cunning little roots." But hearing Jasper's "Hush!" he ducked involuntarily, very glad he hadn't spoken.

"Oh, Phronsie wasn't very well," said Polly. "That is, she hadn't been, and we knew Mamsie wouldn't want her to walk so far. And besides, it was just as much fun to play in our Orchard. So we all decided to go there. Well, off we started—"

"Why I thought you said it was just a little way back of the kitchen door," said Percy surprised out of himself.

"So it was," answered Polly, "but we played it was ever so far off, and we walked around and around the Little Brown House, all but Phronsie. She sat on the back steps till we were ready to go into the Orchard; then she got down, and we all went in together," said Polly, with a grand flourish as if escorting her auditors into enchanted space, big beyond description. "Well, and don't you think there was the greatest surprise when we got there!"

"Oh, tell us!" begged all the Whitney boys impatiently.

"Why, Ben had run off—after we had talked over whether we would go to the woods or not, and we didn't think we ought to, for Mamsie wouldn't like to have Phronsie walk so far—and he had brought back some flowers and some moss, and ever so many things."

"That's nice," said Percy in a satisfied way.

"And there they were on the little stone table," said Polly.

"Oh, did you have a stone table in your Orchard?" asked Van.

"Yes, I've seen it ever so many times," said Jasper. Then he pulled himself up laughing, "Beg pardon, Polly."

"Ho! Ho! You're talking," cried Van at him.

"Can't help it," said Jasper recklessly, "when you begin to ask about the good times in the Little Brown House, I must talk."

"You see," said Polly to the Whitney boys, "we had to have a table for our tea parties and ever so many other things, and so Ben chose a big stone in a field—it was Deacon Brown's meadow, and he—"

"You said it was a field, Polly Pepper," interrupted Percy in his most literal way.

"Well, it was just about the same thing," said Polly, laughing.

"Never mind him, Polly," said Jasper; and "You never will get this story if you keep stopping her all the time," from Ben. So Polly hurried on. "And Deacon Brown was just as glad as he could be, of course, to have that big stone carried off from his meadow."

"Why?" asked Van. "I should think all the Brown children would have wanted it to play on."

"Oh, there are such oceans of stones in Badgertown," cried Polly, lifting her hands.

"Oh, Polly!" exclaimed Ben. *"Oceans* of stones?"

"Well, I mean such a very, very, great many," said Polly, with the color flooding her face, "you can't think, boys, and they bother the farmers dreadfully when they want to cut their grass. The poor cows have such hard work to get their noses in between them—the stones, I mean—in order to get anything to eat."

"The farmers almost have to whittle off the cows' noses for them to get a bite," said Ben.

"And Joel and David would pick rocks for the farmers sometimes," said Polly, "but that was nice, because—"

"Mean old work," said Joel, stretching himself, "picking rocks. Didn't our backs ache, Dave?"

Little David twisted uneasily in his chair, unwilling to say how very unpleasant he had found the task of picking rocks and wishing that the question had not been asked.

"Well," said Polly brightly, "it was nice when the boys brought home the fresh vegetables that the farmers would give them for picking those rocks. You ought to have seen Mamsie's face then!"

Joel straightened up at that and forgot all about his aching back, and little David was very glad he hadn't been obliged to say anything. "So now you see," ran on Polly, "how very glad Deacon Brown was to give Ben the big stone for our orchard table. So Ben tugged and tugged and—"

"And we helped, Dave and I did," shouted Joel. "Didn't we, Ben?"

"Yes, indeed," said Ben heartily, "you did, both of you. I don't believe I could ever have brought the great thing down to the Orchard without you." Thereupon Joel felt very big and tall, and little David sat up as high in his chair as possible.

"Oh, it was a perfectly splendid table!" exclaimed Polly. "You can't think how fine it was when it was all set up under our apple tree. It was most flat on top, and it was as high as this, and as big as this," and she put out her hands and began to measure it all off briskly.

"Ho—that isn't near big enough!" cried Joel, springing to her side. " 'Twas as big as this," and he executed the most remarkable series of curves, spreading his arms to the infinite discomfort of everyone in his neighborhood.

"See here," called Ben at him, amidst the general laugh at Joel's table, "if you go on knocking off all our heads in this fashion we'll put you out this second—yes, sir! The idea of such a stone as that. Why, it would have taken a pair of horses and a cart to bring it, let alone our digging it up. Oh, Joe!"

"I don't care," said Joel sturdily, "it was as big as that, anyway," bring his arms in with a sudden swoop.

"Well, now, Joe," said Jasper, "if you don't keep quiet we shan't get any further in this story than that table," which had the effect of sending Joel into his seat as quickly as he had jumped off. And Polly began again before he had a chance to speak. "And there on the top of the table was a big bunch of flowers. We had a teacup that Mamsie had given us because it was cracked and the handle was gone, and Ben had put some of the flowers he brought from the woods into it; but the rest he made up into little bunches and laid one on every little stone seat, for I forgot to tell you, the boys had brought five little stones, one for each of us, so we could always have our chairs ready for us, you know."

"Oh, dear me," sighed little Dick, quite overcome with longing. "How I do wish we could have little stone seats!"

"And a stone table," added Van enviously.

"And a whole Orchard," finished Percy, "just like the Peppers."

Meantime Polly was hurrying on. "Well, when we saw all those lovely things that Ben had done—Phronsie spied them first—we just danced around him and we held our hands together tight so he couldn't get out of the ring, and we all curtsied and bowed, and thanked him as much as we could."

"I should think you did," said Ben, laughing.

"Then we made him take the best seat in honor of it all," went on Polly.

"And Polly made a speech of thanks," said Joel. "It was prime. And Ben said 'Much obliged for the speech.'"

"And then we set about giving our play," said Polly quickly.

"Our what?" asked the Whitneys.

"Why, our play," said Polly. "Didn't you know that was what we were going to do that hot afternoon, when we decided to go out in the Orchard? Well, I must tell you. We were going to act a little play."

"Oh—oh—how fine!" exclaimed Percy and Van, while Ben cried, "It was Polly's play; she thought it all out."

"Well, they helped to act it," said Polly, "and that was best—"

"Do go on," begged the Whitney boys, and this time Jasper said, too, "Do go on, Polly."

"Well, the play was The Little White Rabbit and Mr. Fox."

"Oh! Oh!" exclaimed the Whitneys, while Jasper smiled approval. "Yes, Phronsie was to be the White Rabbit, you see. We'd got an old white bedspread Mamsie let us take for our plays, and we tied up two ends so they stuck up high, and those made the ears. And when she was in it, and the paws all puckered up, she looked very nice, and—"

"And I was the White Rabbit, Jasper," said Phronsie gravely, turning to him.

"I know, pet," he said, smiling at her. "So you were, to be sure," as Polly hurried on.

"Well, Ben was Mr. Fox, and he did look so funny," cried Polly, bursting into a laugh in which Joel and David joined in the remembrance. "You see he had a big piece of an old fur rug that the minister's wife gave him one day to carry away, because the moths had got into it and she didn't want it any longer. And it made just a splendid bear, or a wolf, or a lion, only this time it was a fox—"

"Oh, that old fur rug was fine!" exploded Joel with sparkling eyes, breaking in. "And one time we"—but Ben pulling him down, Polly was allowed to go on.

"Well, the first thing in the play," said Polly briskly, "the Little White Rabbit is fast asleep under the tree, and old Mr. Fox comes stealing up behind her and says very softly, 'My dear Miss Rabbit,' and she opens her eyes and wakes up.

" 'Oh!' she says. 'Is that you, Mr. Fox?' and he says, 'Yes, and won't you come home with me and see my little teenty wee foxes?' "

"Oh! Were there little foxes, Polly Pepper?" cried the Whitney boys delightedly.

"Yes, indeed, there were," said Polly quickly. "There were two little foxes in a hole a little way off. They were Joel and David, you know. They were spectators with me while Little White Rabbit was asleep and Mr. Fox was waking her up. Then when he invited her to go and see his little foxes, why, the boys scampered off and got into their hole."

"Where was the hole, Polly?" asked Percy.

"Oh, we had scooped a place under the bank where the grass grew high," said Polly, "and it made a splendid cave whenever we wanted wild beasts. Only today it was the house of the teenty wee little foxes. Well, so then Little White Rabbit said she would go with Mr. Fox and see his little foxes, and he gave her his hand and off he led her."

"Oh, Polly! The Little White Rabbit didn't really go with Mr. Fox, did she?" exclaimed little Dick in horror.

"Oh, yes, she did, Dicky!" said Polly. Then seeing his face, she made haste to add, "But it was Ben, you know, so she wasn't afraid."

"Oh, yes, it was Ben," repeated little Dick, hugging himself in relief.

"Well, and so off they went to the hole where the teenty wee little foxes were," said Polly, "and the Little White Rabbit put her paw in Mr. Fox's paw, and when they got there, Mr. Fox says, 'Now just step down into my hole where the teenty wee little foxes are, because you can see them so very much better.'"

"And did she, Polly? Did she?" interrupted little Dick anxiously.

"Yes," said Polly, "but the teenty little wee foxes were Joel and David, you know, so they couldn't hurt the Little White Rabbit."

"Oh, yes! They were Joel and David," said little Dick, drawing a relieved sigh.

"Well, when Phronsie—I mean the Little White Rabbit —had stepped down into the hole, up jumps the two teenty little foxes and they ran; and they ran past her, and past Mr. Fox as quickly as they could, so as to be audience, you know, because I was the man with the big gun to go out and shoot Mr. Fox, and it was time for him to do it. So Joel and David, I mean the two teenty little wee foxes, sat down on their stone seats and the man with the big gun picked it up and he ran and he ran to the hole, and just as Mr. Fox was going to eat up the Little White Rabbit, he put his gun up to his shoulder, and *Bang!* it went, and over tumbled Mr. Fox, and Little White Rabbit was safe!"

It was impossible to describe the excitement that now possessed the entire group, and it was some minutes before anybody could be heard. Then Joel cried, "Polly, tell the rest—tell the rest!"

"Oh, yes!" cried Polly with shining eyes. "The best was what came after. What do you think we found when we all raced back—you know I had hold of the Little White Rabbit's paw, and Mr. Fox was scampering after?"

"Why, I thought you said when the man's big gun went *Bang!* Mr. Fox tumbled over dead," cried Percy.

"Oh, yes, so he did," said Polly coolly, "but he had to jump up, you know, and come and be audience, because then the little foxes were going to try to get the Little White Rabbit; and you see he had to take their place and look on, or there wouldn't be any spectators."

"Oh!" said the Whitney boys.

"Yes. Well, we were all three running along, Mr. Fox just behind, when Joel and David, I mean the little teenty wee foxes, came racing over the grass. 'Oh, Polly Pepper!' they screamed, 'Come—come!' and then they turned and flew back. I can tell you we all ran then!"

"What was it? Oh, what was it?" screamed Percy and Van and little Dick together.

"Why, there on the stone lay—what do you think?—a big orange, and a bag of peanuts!"

"Oh, dear me!" cried all the Whitney boys, tumbling backward in dreadful disappointment. "Is that all?" gasped Percy.

"All?" repeated Polly. "Why, you can't think how perfectly splendid it was to see that big orange, as yellow as gold, and that magnificent bag of peanuts standing there on that stone table. Why, it seemed as if they must have dropped right down from the little puffy white clouds sailing above our heads, for we couldn't imagine where they came from. And we never thought of finishing up our play, but the Little White Rabbit hopped out of her white skin, and Mr. Fox tumbled out of his old fur rug, and it took us all the rest of the afternoon to cut and divide that splendid, big, yellow orange, and to count out those magnificent peanuts, and to give them all around, except the time it took to eat them."

"That was best!" exclaimed Joel, smacking his lips.

"And we saved some for Mamsie," said little Davie, "didn't we, Polly?"

"Why, of course," said Polly. "We all saved the best for her."

"And Polly kept saying, 'I do wish we knew where they came from,' every minute or so," said Ben.

"But we didn't tell, did we, Dave?" said Joel, chuckling at the remembrance.

"No," said little David, "but I wanted to when Polly kept trying to find out."

"And did you know?" cried Van, turning on him.

"Of course we did," said Joel, puffing with importance. "We knew every single bit of it all because we were sitting on our stone chairs and we saw it all. Only Polly thought because we didn't tell, that they'd been put there before— while we were all at Mr. Fox's hole. But we could keep a secret, couldn't we, Dave?"

"Yes," said little Davie slowly.

"It never entered our heads that you could keep still if you knew it, Joe," said Ben.

"Well, who did put them there?" demanded Van, bursting with impatience.

"Why, our good, dearest, and loveliest Dr. Fisher," said Polly with glowing cheeks. "Papa Fisher—only he wasn't Papa Fisher, then, he was just Dr. Fisher. Why, here he comes now!"